D1006265

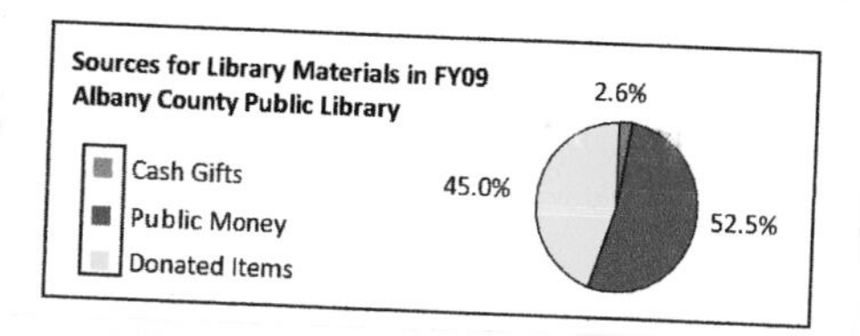
Sources for Library Materials in FY09
Albany County Public Library
Cash Gifts
Public Money
Donated Items
2.6%
45.0%
52.5%

THE LAST WORDS OF

Will Wolfkin

STEVEN KNIGHT

THE LAST WORDS OF *Will Wolfkin*

WALDEN POND PRESS
An Imprint of HarperCollins*Publishers*

Walden Pond Press is an imprint of HarperCollins Publishers.
Walden Pond Press and the skipping stone logo are trademarks and registered trademarks of Walden Media, LLC.

The Last Words of Will Wolfkin

For information address HarperCollins Children's Books, a division of HarperCollins Publishers, 10 East 53rd Street, New York, NY 10022.
www.harpercollinschildrens.com

Library of Congress Cataloging-in-Publication Data
Knight, Steven, date
The last words of Will Wolfkin / Steven Knight. — 1st ed.
p. cm.
Summary: Fourteen-year-old Toby, paralyzed since birth and raised in a convent, suddenly finds himself capable of movement and speech when his longtime companion, a cat, takes him on a magical and mysterious journey to Iceland.
ISBN 978-0-06-170413-0 (trade bdg.)
[1. Adventure and adventurers—Fiction. 2. Magic—Fiction. 3. Human-animal relationships—Fiction. 4. Identity—Fiction. 5. Paralysis—Fiction. 6. Cats—Fiction. 7. Iceland—Fiction.] I. Title.
PZ7.K7413Las 2010 2009035008
[Fic]—dc22 CIP
AC

Typography by Amy Ryan
10 11 12 13 14 LP/RRDB 10 9 8 7 6 5 4 3 2 1
❖
First Edition

For my children

THE LAST WORDS OF
Will Wolfkin

PART ONE

Dreams

1

My name is Toby Walsgrove, and before I begin to tell you my story, I should give you a short explanation of who I am.

I was born at the Royal Free Hospital in Hampstead, London, England, fourteen and a half years ago. I was named by the nurses there. Apparently one of the nurses had a cat called Toby, and when I was first born, my ears were slightly pointy like her cat's ears, so they named me Toby. But it's okay. I'm not in the least bit bitter. I like cats. A cat saved my life once, but I will tell you about that later.

I was named by the nurses because my mother ran away a few hours after she had given birth to me. I don't know anything about her; I was just told that she wasn't very well and was in no position to be able to look after me. You see, almost the moment I emerged into this world, it was obvious that I wasn't a normal boy. Most babies wriggle and squirm and clench their little fists as if they were furious at being taken from the nice warm embrace of the womb. But when I was born, I didn't move a muscle.

I was totally paralyzed.

I won't go into boring detail about my condition, but I was diagnosed as being born with practically *nothing* working. The medical name for my condition is static encephalopathy, which to me means "nothing works." (Why do doctors suddenly start talking in Greek when it comes to giving you the crucial information? Imagine if car mechanics did that. When they got to the part where they tell you exactly what's wrong with your car, they'd suddenly start to speak in Mohican.) Anyway, even if they had a name for what I had, they had no idea how to cure it.

So there you are. That's life, all that guff. Life is mostly an "oh well" here and an "oh dear" there anyway.

It's funny. If you're born a certain way, you don't really understand how it is to be any other way. Until this story began, I had only ever known total powerlessness. I was like a frosty window that passersby could peer through. Inside . . . just dark furniture, a pale glow of something . . . maybe a computer screen with its screen saver on.

I could hear but not speak, be touched but not touch. But I could think.

For my first fourteen years I was just a thought process out of control. All the strength and energy that should have gone into my muscles went instead into my imagination. And I was an athlete of the imagination. I would fly to Mars, become a privet hedge, twist on a pinhead, invent a city . . . glow in the dark like a glowworm. Anything. Anything to kill the time.

I "lived" (note the quotation marks) in a Carmelite convent that was hidden behind a high wall on a busy road in East Finchley, London. It was like a sort of very cheap castle, or a dark but well-meaning prison. The whole place smelled of damp, bacon fat, and especially cabbage. There were stone corridors, cheap lampshades, and bright bulbs that the nuns bought in bulk to combat the narrowness of the windows. I sat every day beside a window with my head held in place by a metal brace, and I peppered the windowpanes with my thoughts. I'm surprised the window didn't smash.

I was cared for by nuns, a word that makes them sound all the same, but they weren't. Mostly they were kind, but their hearts sometimes failed in the compassion department. They wore the real nun outfits, long black robes made of some heavy material that smelled of cupboards and sometimes (Hail Mary!) cigarette smoke. There was Sister Cremer, who was older than the moon, Sister Bagshott ("who has *seen* an angel but never talks about it"), Sister Ubo, who had a voice like a cattle prod, and most important of all . . . Sister Mary.

Oh, how I loved Sister Mary. She was my daily carer, her gentle hands wiping my milk from my mouth, her soft little waist pushed against my knee as she hummed that little tune I've never heard anywhere else. Perhaps she wrote that tune herself. She was like a small finch with little round glasses.

Once she pushed open a window in summer and pointed out a tree that was rustling in the breeze. "Toby, will you look at that? The sun on the underside of the leaves. Isn't it like a fire?"

"Yes!" I wanted to yell. "That's exactly what it looks like! Just like fire! And Sister Mary, when the moon's half full, it looks like an old grandfather eating a lemon, and . . . and . . . and . . ."

But of course I couldn't yell any of these things. I couldn't make a sound of any kind. It was a one-way conversation, so I just had to trust Sister Mary to say the things I was thinking. And as the years passed, most of the time, she did.

Sister Mary was in charge of my education, which mostly involved her letting me watch TV and also reading to me from books she got from the local library. No one else cared what I learned, so Sister Mary just made it up as she went along. We started with nursery rhymes when I was two years old and then went on to story books, then history books, poetry, and science books. I liked the smell of the books when she opened them, especially the really old science books that no one else had opened for years. My sense of smell was almost as strong as my imagination. Sister Mary soon realized I liked the smell of mildewed paper and began to haul huge, dusty old textbooks from the rarely visited advanced science section just so I could smell the pages as she read softly to me from the text.

This eventually led to me taking a mild interest in physics, which in turn led Sister Mary to tell me about Stephen Hawking. She said that Stephen Hawking was a man who was stuck in a chair just like me, and yet he was the cleverest human being in the entire world with no question. She could tell I was impressed, and after that she read me at least one paragraph from his books on physics every day, even though they didn't smell particularly interesting because they were so new. I didn't understand the details and yet I sort of absorbed the general idea of what he was saying. Stephen Hawking said that time was bent and the universe curved and nothing was really real or solid, which meant that absolutely *anything* was possible. When you are stuck in a chair, you can take great comfort from that.

There was also a convent cat, a scatty black thing called Shipley, who often managed to sneak into my room when no one was around. Over the years I became certain that I had some kind of psychic connection with the sly little feline, and as a result he became my best friend. I always knew he was coming to visit a few minutes before he came into the room, and when he licked my hand with his rough tongue, I felt he was leaving messages on my skin for me to read (very odd things can seem normal if they have been that way since you were born). The messages would sometimes be practical warnings, such as "Sister Ubo is looking for mess to be angry about" and I would shrink a little. A few minutes later I would inevitably hear Sister Ubo's sandals slapping on the stone tiles outside, the way they did when she was on the warpath. Other times the messages he left were meant to make me laugh . . . like the time he said he'd looked up Father Reece's robe and seen that he had legs like a pink flamingo's. Sometimes he just licked the words "It's okay, it's okay" over and over again when I was feeling that life wasn't okay at all.

In summer he kept the flies away from my face with his tail; in winter he kept me warm by snuggling in my lap, purring and vibrating in that electrical way cats have. I wanted more than all the world to stroke him, but I think he understood that I couldn't, and maybe even was glad of it.

Sometimes I was sure I could make my thoughts enter his head. I used to give commands like "jump," "scratch," "purr," and on occasion it seemed to work. When he angled his head and stared at me with those oak-leaf-green eyes, it was as if a gentle beam of light were being shone into my head to scare away the darkness. I wondered about my having had pointy ears when I was born. Perhaps I had been born part cat, and maybe that explained the connection with Shipley.

Often Shipley would accompany me in my dreams and turn into a ferocious saber-toothed tiger when I was in danger. Other times we would march together side by side into battle and talk to each other like comrades. I could never quite remember how he was able to talk to me in my dreams if he was just a cat, but I had learned not to question my dreams too much. Dreams were the only *real* excitement I ever got.

The finest moment of the year was when the swallows returned to the nest tucked behind the drainpipe outside the convent kitchen. Then I knew the warm weather was returning (my room was quite drafty). There were two swallows, and I named them Look and Leave. Sister Mary told me that they'd been all the way to Africa, and I wished that I had been born a swallow instead of a human. This, of course, was back in the days when I still believed I was completely human.

By chance it was on the very day that Look and Leave arrived from Africa that this story begins. It begins with Sister Mary bursting into my room holding a letter in her hand and with a look of utter astonishment on her face.

"Toby!" she said, the envelope trembling in her hands, "there's a letter. And it's addressed to *you*!"

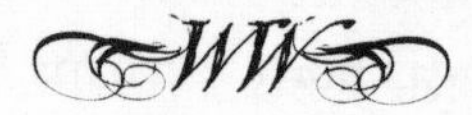

As far as I knew I had not a single relative in the world, at least not one who cared to acknowledge me. And the only friend I had was Sister Mary, who even now was tearing open the envelope, mumbling logical explanations to herself.

"Probably junk mail . . . mix-up . . . inoculations . . . some official thing from the hospital . . . handwritten address, though. . . ."

She stopped opening and turned the envelope around to show me. "And look at the postmark! It's all the way from Iceland. . . ."

"Just open the damn thing!" I yelled silently, and Sister Mary sort of heard me.

Infuriatingly she sat down and began to read the letter without reading it out loud. Her eyes began to widen with astonishment. I wanted to grab a vase and clunk her over the head with it. She gasped a little, shook her head like a dog shaking off a puddle, then read it again. Finally she put her hand to her breast.

"Toby!" she said in a sharp voice, "it's from a doctor." She stopped and took my hand. "He says he has some kind of . . ." She let go of my hand and took a quick breath. "He says he wants to try some new sort of . . ."

She stopped talking and I could see her mind was racing. She suddenly folded the letter in half and got to her feet. "I'll have to speak to Mother Superior," she said, and with that she hurried out.

Sister Mary could be like that. Sometimes, to tease me, when she was reading stories to me she would deliberately stop right at the crucial moment and close the book, leaving me to stew all night long. She said it was good exercise for my imagination. But this was different, and I could tell from the look on her face that it was serious.

It was a full two hours before Sister Mary came back into the room, and the moment she opened the door, I just knew something wasn't right. I knew Sister Mary as well as she knew herself, and it wasn't possible for her to conceal anything from me. She came in all calm and smiling, a bowl of white protein goo in her hand, as if this were just another feeding time. She also had her white tea towel hooked under her plastic belt, and she sat down beside me with a soft little "So . . ."

She tried to spoon the goo into my mouth, but she could tell from the look on my face that I would refuse to swallow. Only Sister Mary could read my expressions, and she *knew* I was aching to know more about the letter. Finally she put the bowl aside and wiped the spoon as if making sure it was clean were the most important thing in the whole world.

"I suppose you want to know what was in it," she said at last.

"Just a bit," cried my silent voice.

Sister Mary turned to glance at the door, something she always did before she told me something she shouldn't.

"Mother Superior said I should zip my lips. But I suppose the cat's a bit out of the bag in a sense, and so maybe I should just unzip the bag the rest of the way. . . ."

When she was nervous, Sister Mary could talk nonsense in a very convincing way.

"You see, Toby, basically some crank of a so-called doctor—in Iceland, of all places—said he'd heard of you and your condition and thought he might be able to help you."

Sister Mary studied my face and read it like a book.

"There, you see," she said softly. "Exactly as Mother Superior said. False hope is a dangerous thing."

She placed her palms on her knees, something she did when she wanted to make a pronouncement she hoped would be taken as the last word on something.

"Well, we just spent two hours looking up this so-called doctor on the internet. I'm afraid he didn't appear. The so-called institute he said he worked at didn't exist either. We even phoned a nice man in Iceland who worked at an institute similar to our own, and he said he'd never heard of the doctor . . . or his so-called cure."

Sister Mary detonated the word *cure* in a controlled explosion and assessed the damage immediately by peering at my face, checking for the tiniest changes, which only she could see.

"So anyway, we think it's some kind of scam. Someone trying to take advantage of poor unfortunates with conditions like yours for personal financial gain."

Her palms stayed on her knees and she blinked quickly.

"So there," she said. "A cruel hoax. Excitement over. I'll keep the envelope and the stamp for you if you want."

Sister Mary looked at my face again and read my mind in an instant. She tried to speak dismissively, like someone sweeping away crumbs. "No, Toby, there's absolutely no point writing back to him. He's obviously a very unscrupulous man. Who knows what damage he might do?"

Sister Mary followed my fixed gaze through the windowpane.

"Oh look," she said, "the swallows are back from Africa."

She dared to glance at my face just once and saw the silent, wild protest behind my eyes. Unusually, she didn't do me the courtesy of addressing it. Instead she picked up the bowl of goo and headed for the door. A few moments later, Shipley hurried into the room, leaped into my lap, and began to lick my hand very gently.

Look and Leave raised a brood of three little chicks. I watched their fluffy gray heads poking out of the nest as their exhausted parents ferried flies and worms to them from the vegetable garden. I also watched as one of the little ones was booted out of the nest by the others and saw him fall to the ground, where he lay motionless on the gravel for some time before Shipley came and tidied him away.

For most of that summer I wanted some kind of celestial Shipley to come and tidy me away too. I'd had enough. This whole being-alive thing was a waste of time. The business with the letter had had a profound effect on my spirits, just as Mother Superior had predicted. Despair you can cope with, but a glimmer of hope, no matter how faint, can be torturous. Even Sister Mary could no longer console me. Our games of psychic chess ended in bad-tempered silence. She could read the hopelessness in my eyes, and by the time the swallow chicks were fledged, she was running out of ideas.

Finally she tried putting on a production of the *Sister Mary Theater of Mystery and Imagination*. She put on these productions only on special occasions, like Christmas Day, my birthday, or whenever Mother Superior went back to Poland for a holiday. Sister Mary would always take me outside into the garden for the performance, and when I was little, I used to get so excited as my chair bumped over the threshold of the back door that I swear I almost found enough voice to yell out.

Once we were outside, Sister Mary would reach into her pockets and take out two glove puppets that had been through one too many spin cycles inside the convent washing machine. There was a sort of teddy bear thing that had only one ear for her left hand, and something that looked like a skunk or a badger for her right hand. The basic premise for these little plays was that the one-eared bear was Sister Mary and the badger was me. She would prepare the story in advance, and the two of us would go on some adventure to places with names Sister Mary found funny, like Medicine Hat in Canada, or Walla Walla in Australia, or some tiny village in Africa called Hope Eternal. I think she got the names from visiting sisters who came to the convent.

In all the stories, Sister Mary and I would come across some baddie who wasn't really that bad at all. It was usually a highwayman or a pirate or a sad old king. But unlike my adventures on the moon with Shipley, these adventures were always peaceful, because at the crucial moment, Sister Mary and I would always find a way to talk the baddie out of being so bad. In my own adventures, baddies just got zapped and that was that.

I knew it was a last throw of the dice when Sister Mary sat down in a hard-backed chair in the vegetable garden before my blank face and produced her two battered glove puppets. She did it like a Western gunslinger producing his revolvers. I almost felt sorry for the two bits of fur, since they were being given such an impossible task. She began to tell a tale that involved an evil doctor who lived in a cave in faraway Iceland and who used to steal money from poor children who happened to pass by his cave or walk over his bridge or something. I really wasn't listening very hard. I think in the end we managed to talk him out of it, and he went back to being a proper doctor.

Sweet Sister Mary ended the production with a song she'd written, as she always did, and as she sang it, my eyes wandered up to the nest where Look and Leave were peering down at us, almost as if they were listening to the song too. I really did *want* to be made better by the story and the song, but some big boulder inside refused to budge. I realized that I was now way too old for the *Sister Mary Theater of Mystery and Imagination*. That thought made me even sadder.

Sister Mary finished her song and peered at me hopefully, with the glove puppets held at either side of her face. The moment lasted a long time. Of course my facial expression didn't change, but Sister Mary knew me well enough to know that her theater of last resort had failed to work its magic. She took the glove puppets off her hands in silence and stuffed them back into her pockets, and I think she knew she would never wear them again. Then she bumped me back into the darkness of my room without another word. All her ammunition was spent.

But it was on that very night . . . at around midnight . . . that my world exploded.

It was a full moon. I remember because I was having a halfhearted imaginary battle with a brigade of indescribably weird monsters on the surface of it, and Shipley was helping me. The battle was going badly, and I was preparing to flee to one of the craters that make up the eyes of the man in the moon.

Then the door to my room opened softly. You have to understand, the door to my room never opened at this time of night. Sister Mary would be asleep. Sister Ubo always entered the room like a herd of startled giraffes. But this was someone with a soft footstep . . . a small stride, a heavy breath. . . .

Of course I couldn't turn my head to see who this intruder was, so I had to paint a picture from the sounds, something I was very good at. Three little steps, a catching of breath, a clearing of the throat, the smell of rain and cold air coming in with the intruder. My eyes widened and filled with moonlight.

Suddenly I felt the hairs on the back of my neck stand on end. Hairs that I hadn't ever felt do anything at all until that moment!

The soft footsteps came closer, and I felt a breath on my

neck. Then I felt a hand on my shoulder . . . a small hand, gentle and cool. I could feel the fingers squeezing and felt a strange icicle of pain forming on my spine.

Then the throat was cleared again and I heard a voice. "Toby Walsgrove," it said, and in those two words I heard a boy's voice with a strange accent and a sense of triumph, as if whoever had said it had been waiting to say my name like this for hundreds of years.

"Who are you?" I asked, and I swear it took me at least five seconds to realize that I had actually spoken those words out loud.

2

He stepped from the darkness into the moonlight, and I could see that the boy was about sixteen years old, skinny and dressed in tight black clothes with a black, two-cornered hat pulled down tight on his head. When he removed his hat to reveal himself, an extraordinary shock of black hair exploded in all directions. As it settled I noticed a pair of piercing green eyes that looked down at me with great urgency.

"Hurry, Toby," the boy whispered. "We must get out of here before the moon has set."

The boy ruffled his hair with his free hand and scratched his ear quickly with the back of his wrist. Then those remarkable green eyes began to dart around the room in pursuit of a moth.

"But who *are* you?" I asked again, and hiccuped with surprise at the sound of my own voice.

"Who I am is not important, Toby Walsgrove," the boy said with a very serious expression, but still following the moth with his eyes. "We two warriors must get into the moon and swim for it. That's it. Questions at sunrise."

I felt his bony fingers as they squeezed my hand. He abandoned the moth and looked at my astonishment. He read my question as easily as Sister Mary would have.

"My grandfather wrote you a letter," he whispered, "but when he got no reply, he decided it was time to"—he squeezed my hand sharply—"pull you *up* and *out* of this easy, sad little life once and for all."

Then, as if it were the most natural thing in the world, I felt my own fingers slowly beginning to squeeze his hand just as he was squeezing mine.

I shrieked. A silly little gasp of shock. My bizarre visitor smiled.

"Toby, I'm so happy that this moment has finally come that I want to dance. Why don't you dance with me?"

By now I was squeezing his hand with all my might, as if I were hanging from a cliff and his hand were the only thing preventing me from falling. After a moment, the visitor peeled away my fingers and jutted his chin. He placed his palm on my neck where the pulse of my heart was beating through my flesh.

"Sit up, Toby," he said softly.

A cloud passed before the moon. An owl hooted. And then a warm surge of something like thick milk passed through my body. It wasn't a sharp feeling, or electrical or even unfamiliar . . . it was a wave of some sort.

The next thing I knew, I was sitting up straight in my chair.

"Ouch," I said out loud, as my head twisted inside the metal brace that had held it in place for fourteen long years.

"Here," said the visitor, "let me help you."

He unscrewed the clamps on each side of my head with the expertise of a nun. He pulled the metal supports free.

It would be impossible to describe that feeling of cool air suddenly hitting the sweaty skin behind my ears. It was an explosion. In the cool draft of air my head was swept free. And then it was taken away on a cool current like a coconut in a raging river.

"Don't let it go," the visitor said, but my head flopped down onto my chest. He used his long thin fingers to raise my head and then very carefully removed his hand, balancing my head on my neck with delicate precision.

"Just concentrate on keeping the old dream box stuck on the spine like a melon on a spear," he said, and I was too busy being startled to notice that he said things in a very odd way.

I felt a dull ache in my neck and back. I stared at the visitor with eyes wide. Then, after a moment, a terrible tug inside . . . a bursting feeling . . . and my head dropped onto my chest again.

"Stop doubting," the boy said. "Take deep breaths and suck in the moonlight."

My visitor began to rub my arms briskly to warm them up. Then he lifted my chin with his forefinger once again. This time my head settled slowly into position.

"There," he said. "Just let the sticky stuff set."

Our faces were now close. His eyes were staring into mine, and something about the green light that shone from them was familiar. His breath vibrated in his throat like a gentle purr. I gasped with shock.

"You're Shipley the cat," I said, and the shock of being able to speak was nothing the shock of knowing for certain that I was right.

"I always, *always* hated that name," the boy said. "From now on please call me Egil. It is a hugely more appropriate name for a warrior. Now, Toby, about that dance . . ."

He took my hand and began to pull, as if I might simply spring out of my chair and dance a pirouette. I resisted and stayed put purely in the name of reason.

"Wait, wait, wait," I said. "Cats don't just suddenly turn

into boys. Shipley, how come you're a boy? This isn't even a dream. I know it's not a dream because I can smell cabbage . . . and I never smell cabbage in dreams. . . ."

As I continued, my visitor lazily lifted his wrist and checked an imaginary watch to tell me I was wasting time with questions.

". . . And how come I can suddenly talk and move for no reason? It doesn't make sense. Shipley, what on earth is going on?"

Shipley the cat and Egil the boy were perfectly blended into one curious creature that stood before me in the moonlight with an arched back. When I ran out of questions, he let my hand go, but my arm didn't flop onto my lap as it would have done just a few minutes before. Instead, my hand clenched into a fist and I stared at it, remembering that just holding up my arm in the air was a small miracle.

"Firstly, as I have told you, my name is not Shipley; it is Egil," he said. "And as for what on earth is going on, the answer comes with sunrise. We must use the half-truth of moonlight to get ourselves to the boat."

"What *boat?*"

He smiled and stared into my eyes. "Instead of asking questions," he said, "just enjoy the taste of words on your tongue. You can speak! Isn't that just a tickle! Say your name out loud, Toby Walsgrove. Introduce yourself to the world."

I was silent for a moment. Then, without thinking, I did as I was instructed.

"My name is Toby Walsgrove," I said softly. "My name is Toby Walsgrove," I said again . . . and then again and again, and my voice grew louder and louder.

For so long my thoughts had been whizzing around silently inside my head like bubbles, and now they were being set free. I was taking the top off a bottle of fizzy cola that had been shaken up for fourteen years.

Soon my voice was so loud that Egil became alarmed, and to shut me up he twisted the skin on my arm with both hands, the way you would if you were wringing out a wet cloth, and it hurt.

"Ouch," I said, and pulled my arm away.

"*Ouch* is a good word, isn't it?" Egil said. "That's twice you've said it now. 'Ouch' is better than silence. Now, Toby, I need you to stand up quickly."

I stared at him. My legs had never supported the weight of a robin. He saw my look of uncertainty and didn't care for it.

"Forgive me, Toby—I don't mean to rush you, but we really do have to be out of here before first light."

"Where are we going?"

"To see my grandfather," he said, "Doctor Felman."

"The doctor from Iceland," I guessed.

"Humans call it Iceland."

"What do you mean, 'humans'?"

Egil glanced out of the window at the moon.

"The boat won't wait for us. If we're not on it, Grandpa will kill me."

Egil suddenly yanked my arm and pulled me forward. I thought I was going to fall onto my face, but some invisible lever in my head jerked into life, and my leg shot forward to break my fall. I was actually standing on my own two feet for the first time in my life.

Egil studied my body with narrowed eyes and nodded his head. I wanted to say something, but no words would come . . . because there were no words to describe this feeling. All I knew was my eyes were balancing somewhere on top of a rickety scaffold, and the scaffold was made from bits of me. I could feel the pieces all held together by feelings and bones, and I was pretty sure I could use the feelings to move the bones. It was another miracle, and I almost sat down again to contemplate the event.

"You'll do," Egil said at last. "Now let's walk."

Every child knows you don't go wandering off with strangers. Not in the middle of the night. Not to set off for God knows where and who knows why. But you must understand that at this time all my attention was being taken up by the utterly bizarre and outlandish business of walking.

Imagine trying to maneuver a badly constructed scarecrow made out of reeds, broomsticks, wet cloth, and old shoes down a narrow chute greased with pig fat. Imagine that in the dark. And all the time I was yelping with a mixture of terror and frantic delight while Egil held my hand and urged me to be quiet.

I began to giggle and flopped my feet forward, one after the other. I'd seen people walking many times, and I'd always thought it looked terribly easy. I was delighted to discover that it wasn't. Almost instantly my balance deserted me, and I rolled over through three hundred and sixty degrees.

Egil the boy was as playful as Shipley the cat, and he put his bony hand over his mouth to stifle a laugh. We were just outside the door to my room, and the long corridor stretched away toward a moonlit window. If we turned left at the window and continued on past the statue of Saint Bernadette, we would be on our way to the big double doors that led to the reception area and then . . . out into the world.

As Egil hoisted me back onto my feet, it seemed like a terribly long journey. And what was worse, I had no idea if I actually wanted to make it. Things had happened so fast that reason was having trouble keeping up. Egil began to whisper to me that I simply had to put one foot in front of the other and soon I would be free.

"Free to do what?" I gasped as I stumbled against the door to the broom cupboard.

"To do *everything*," he said, "instead of doing *nothing*."

I turned to Egil and his green eyes comforted me. Shipley and I had been on many adventures together, and we had always come out victorious. Why should this one be any different?

Walking gradually became easier, and I found myself making progress toward the moonlit window. However, I couldn't overcome the fear that at any moment I would topple forward and land on my face. I held on to Egil's arm, but he kept assuring me that I didn't need his support. When we reached the window, Egil instructed me to stop for a moment and soak up some of the moonlight.

"What good will that do?" I asked.

"Moonlight makes things soft, even for humans," Egil said as if it were the most obvious thing in the world. "When the moon is full, things can shift more easily. Now take some breaths of moonlight, and let's press on."

I had no idea what he was talking about, but as I leaned against the window frame and sucked in some air, I felt my body growing stronger with each breath. Egil seemed to be pleased with my progress.

"The power is *in* you like invisible lungs," he said, and he patted my chest. "We shall have mighty adventures."

Mention of adventures brought back uncertainty.

Waiting at the window allowed reason to catch us up.

"What adventures? I asked. "And if your grandfather is a doctor as you say, why are we sneaking out like this?"

Outside, the church clock began to ring three A.M. Egil took a deep breath and struggled to find the words. When he spoke, all the youthfulness had left his voice and he sounded almost afraid.

"Toby Walsgrove, you have inherited a great fortune," he said. "As well as being a doctor, my grandfather is also the executor of a will, and he told me that I must get you to a certain place at a certain time in order that you be present for the reading of that will."

At that moment we heard the slapping of Sister Ubo's slippers on the stone floor of a distant corridor. Three A.M. was the time for the first morning prayers. The sound of the footsteps alarmed Egil, and instead of explaining any further, he put his hand on my shoulder and peered deeply into my eyes.

"Toby, if you decide you really don't want to come with me, I will take my power from your body right now. They will put you back into your chair, and you will stay there for the rest of your life and never again move a single muscle. If instead you choose to come with me, you will run and dance and fight and fall and struggle and live a thousand lifetimes."

The footsteps died away, but more would soon follow. I

thought about the goo, the boredom, and the swallows who always deserted me in autumn. I spent a moment thinking about sweet Sister Mary. Even my love for her couldn't compete with the sudden joy of standing upright on my own two feet.

"Toby? It is time to make your choice," Egil whispered.

3

Once we got outside into the cold night air, I stamped my feet and twirled around in the moonlight and bashed against walls and fell sideways into hedges, as unstable as a newborn deer. I was wearing cotton pajamas and a dressing gown with zigzags and stars, but for the moment I didn't feel the cold. Egil watched my performance with a hoot of laughter that sounded almost exactly like the hoot of an owl. I rolled along the side of a car and set off the alarm.

"Toby, I know it's boring, but you really must apply yourself to putting one foot in front of the other," he said, hurrying me away. "When you're a cat you can run across cars with an arrogant twirl of the old tail, but with two legs it's just a case of tedious left, right, left, right until you're there."

I was hanging off a lamppost to steady myself.

"Shipley . . . I mean Egil . . . explain to me exactly *how* you changed from a cat into a boy." I was staring up at the yellow lamp, a little drunk on all these miracles.

"Please, Toby, we must hurry."

"I don't think I can untangle my leg. . . ."

Egil hopped around the lamppost and unhitched my foot. I stumbled forward.

"Shifting from cat to boy is rather easy," he said. "Just a little hop across the pond, really."

"But *why* did you do it?"

"Because the time has come," he said.

"*What* time has come?"

"The time of your life, Toby," Egil said with a hiss. Then he pushed me hard in the back. I thought I was going to fall flat on my face, but instead my legs moved quickly to break my fall. The next thing I knew, my legs were trotting along all by themselves, and Egil was trotting beside me. Once I had momentum, moving forward became easier.

"I have been a cat for seven years," Egil said, "and my job was to prepare your mind for what lies ahead. That's why I took you up to the moon for all those adventures. I have been teaching you the noble arts of the warrior. Now my job is to get your body ready too."

"Egil, I think I am actually running."

"Fun, isn't it?" He grinned. "Race you."

Egil suddenly put on a burst of speed and soon was ten yards ahead of me.

"Wait," I said rather meekly. "My nose hurts when I breathe too fast."

"Last one to the pavilion is a chicken," he called out.

"What pavilion?" I shouted, but Egil had already begun to race ahead. I realized right then and there that I had a very strong competitive streak now that I had a body to compete with, so I decided to try to catch him up. At first my heels fell heavily on the road, but then I discovered that my toes were much springier, and soon I was actually sprinting. A car drove past and I glimpsed the driver, but he didn't even glance in my direction.

At the next bend in the road there was a white wooden fence, and beyond it a cricket pitch with a rotten old cricket pavilion behind a rotten old scoreboard. I stopped to rest against the fence and get my breath. An iron gate behind me began to creak in the wind. I turned and saw a path choked with nettles that led past the cricket pitch. The moonlight shone down the path, and I saw the shadow of something I thought was a large animal with a hump on its back. Then as it got closer I saw it was Egil, carrying a sack.

"Seriously, the little devils get so arrogant," he said, dropping the sack at my feet. The sack was made from some heavy, shiny material and was bound with red ribbon. "There was a rat behind the pavilion, and because I am no longer Shipley the mighty hunter, he just laughed at me."

Egil's eyes suddenly darted at the darkness. "There he goes! Little pompous devil." Egil was about to leap forward onto all fours, but he stopped himself. "Seven years is a long time to be a champion ratter," he said softly. "Leaves its mark, you know?"

He looked up at me with his remarkable green eyes, and once again reason caught me up. I remembered that it was seven years since Shipley the cat had wandered into the convent as a stray and been adopted by the nuns.

"Are you saying you came to the convent just to find *me?*" I asked.

"But of course. Grandpa sent me. You have been in my care ever since."

I closed my eyes tight and spoke through gritted teeth. "Egil, if I think rationally about what is happening, my legs go weak."

"So don't think," he said. "I have some clothes for you here"—he buried his head in the sack—"that will keep you warm and also keep you from asking too many questions."

Egil pulled a thick fur coat from inside the sack, and then a pair of trousers made from some slick, furry material that shone as if it were drenched in animal fat. Both the coat and the trousers looked far too big for me, but before I could speak, Egil spoke up with a smile.

"They're magic clothes," he said. "They change size to fit whoever wears them."

A cloud passed before the moon. Egil angled his head a little, the way cats do when something interests them.

"What have you got against the word *magic?*" he said.

Egil had read my thoughts. If he started to talk about "magic" clothes or "magic" anything, I would start to think that this was all just another dream, and I didn't want it to be a dream. I wanted it to be real—even though I had been out of my chair for less than an hour, I already wanted to run and race and feel the cold air in my nose more than anything in the world.

Egil spoke softly. "If you don't like the word *magic,* I will use the proper word for it. These are *Fellish* clothes. And to make you walk and talk, I have used Fellish power. Does a different word make you feel better?"

"No, because I don't know what *Fellish* means."

Egil studied me with what looked like pity mixed with a little amusement. "Grandpa is very strict," he said. "He made me promise I wouldn't try to explain any of the important things until we get to Iceland."

"But Iceland is . . . miles and miles away," I said at last, not *really* sure where Iceland was. I had a vague idea that it was up at the top of the world somewhere. Egil didn't hear me. He had spotted a bat flying across the moon, and his head twitched to follow its flight into the trees.

"Did you know that bats taste almost exactly the same as leather sandals?" he said. Then his darting eyes glimpsed the moon, and he quickly pushed the fur coat into my hands.

"Once we get to Iceland, you can ask Grandpa all the questions you want," he said. "But for now, look . . . the moon is almost set. Please, put the clothes on, and let us be on our way."

I looked back up the winding road that led to the convent. It was a silver river of moonlight, apart from the litter and parked cars. I had been down this road in my chair many times with Sister Mary at my back, singing her songs and trying to make it all seem so jolly. In truth, every time she had taken me out into the world, I had ached with the desire to just once leap to my feet and run for it.

Now it was really happening, and I decided asking sensible questions might make sensible things happen—and that was the last thing I needed.

I pulled on the trousers over my pajamas and they contracted to fit me, just as Egil had said they would. The coat also seemed to shrink as I put my arms into it, and I felt the musty warmth of animal fur all around me. Something about the way the fur moved as I crooked my arm made me feel that the coat was alive.

"You look like a very smart, large rodent," Egil said. Then to my astonishment he reached into his pocket and produced a set of car keys. They were ordinary, everyday car keys. He turned and skipped toward an ancient-looking rusted two-seater car that had its nose pushed deep into the hawthorn hedge beside us. His green eyes sparkled as he beckoned me to follow him.

"This is the car I drove to get here seven years ago, before I turned myself into a cat," he said, "but I just *know* she'll start the first time."

I hesitated. There were lots of questions, but I came up with the silliest question first. "Are you actually *old enough* to drive?" I asked.

"Ah well, let me see now," he said, putting a finger to the dimple in his chin. "Next birthday I will be . . . five hundred and seven. I think that's old enough, don't you?"

My mouth fell open. Egil opened the passenger door, and it creaked like a coffin lid. He urged me to climb inside. After a moment I took my seat, and Egil put the key in the ignition.

"Now let's burn up some road," Egil said, and before the engine fired I heard the rattle of mad excitement in his throat, the kind I used to hear from Shipley when he was about to do something fast and improbable that would end with something spilled or the wrong way up.

I have no idea whether it was some magical power Egil used or simply a very old car on its last day of glory. We drove through the wet deserted streets of London at a hundred miles an hour with Egil constantly brushing back his hair and purring and occasionally scratching his ear with his shoulder.

I wasn't used to being in vehicles. I'd been in the convent bus, of course, but its driver drove at a reasonable speed and obeyed the rules and knew the difference between red, green, and yellow. Egil didn't care for colors. I think I read somewhere that cats are color-blind. This one was insane and color-blind. Nor did he care for the presence of other cars. He simply leaned on the horn if he saw an obstacle and licked his lips, or hissed if they dared to hoot back.

When we drove through the Smithfield meat market, Egil saw a rat racing across the road and instinctively chased it . . . in the car. We hit a row of plastic bins and narrowly avoided a lamppost before rattling down an alley of uneven cobbles. When the alley narrowed, we stopped dead at the entrance to some kind of drinking club, where a man and a woman, who before had been kissing, turned to us with looks of astonishment.

"Sorry," Egil said as he shifted gear to reverse back onto the road. "Partly my fault, but the *arrogance* of these creatures just running around everywhere. Still, no harm done."

And we were off again.

After we had left the built-up part of London, we drove into the dark quilted lanes of the countryside, where the stars and moon were visible. By now I had worked out how to use the manual window winder, and I rolled the window down. I felt the air rushing into my face and for the first time realized how fast we were traveling. Close by, the hedges were blurred by speed, and the rushing wind took my breath. I could smell the rich deep odor of plowed fields and wet grass and stagnant ditches. My especially keen sense of smell made each gulp of rushing air intoxicating.

Egil was now occasionally licking the steering wheel as he stared out through the windshield to follow the winding road. He didn't bother with headlights. He explained that he'd been a cat for so long that he had retained some of his ability to see in the dark.

The fur coat and trousers I'd been given were more than warm; they were *company*. I knew they were alive around me, and it became hard to keep from falling asleep. I tried to keep my eyes open as Egil drove us across the dark fields of England, but the warm concern of the fur and the oilskin made my eyes droop. I tucked my head into the fur collar and let it support the weight of my head. Then, without thinking, I settled back into the exact position I'd been in for fourteen years . . . arms curled up like herons' necks, legs twisted slightly to keep them together, head leaning to the left.

The soft hum of the car washed away my thoughts.

I was woken by Egil, who put his hand on my neck in the same way he had when he'd first come into my room. I felt the same icicle down my spine, and then I jolted in my seat.

"We are at the dock," he said. "The captain is waiting to push off."

It was still dark. I could hear metal clanking against metal in the rhythm of tame harbor waves. On the horizon the sky was just showing streaks of orange and blood red. The light hurt my eyes. As I got out of the car, the cold morning air made me shiver, and once again I was shocked to feel anything at all.

"What you see before you is a gangplank," Egil said. "Very unforgiving to the experimental walker. Remember left, right, left, right. I doubt you know how to swim."

Egil chuckled, and I could sense that being at the harbor and near to the boat was a huge relief to him. He led me aboard a small fishing boat, with a steel mast and a large reel of rope and nets at the stern.

The moment we stepped on board, Egil stopped dead still and peered at the skipper, who was half in and half out of the cabin, checking a shirt pocket for something. Egil nodded toward him, then put his finger to his lips. The skipper peered at Egil for a moment and nodded back gently.

We waited while the skipper located a small wooden pipe in the pocket of his shirt, which he filled with tobacco. He was no more than two yards from where we were standing, and the light from his match illuminated our faces. I guessed the skipper was using the casual lighting of a match to check us out. He seemed satisfied with what he saw, and once the pipe was lit, he went back into the orange light of the cabin and busied himself with some papers.

"Why doesn't he speak to us?" I whispered. Egil began to lead me carefully over ropes and nets toward the stern.

"He is from western Iceland," Egil said. "An old human family that has had dealings with Fels for many generations. We Fels have agreements with certain humans."

"And you are a . . . Fel?" I said.

He blinked at me and smiled. "Of course. Only Fels can make Fellish things happen."

Before I could ask another question, Egil lifted a tarpaulin that was tied to some barrels on the back of the boat. He gestured for me to crawl underneath. A few seconds later, he joined me.

The engine of the boat coughed into life. I could feel the deck vibrating beneath me, then the motion of the boat as it reversed from its mooring. I heard the heavy tread of sea boots on the deck and frantic clanking around the mast as ropes and pulleys played in the wind. There was also the intoxicating smell of sea air and gas, of tar and rotten fish, even the whiff of tobacco smoke lacing the stiff breeze.

Ever since I had been born, I had been cocooned mostly in a cloud of *inside* smells. Cabbage, disinfectant, mice, breath. But these ocean smells were vast and wild, and they caused a vibration inside my head that was exciting. Without thinking, I got to my feet to gulp more air but bumped my head on the barrel above us. Egil told me to sit down and stay silent and held my hand to keep me in place. An hour later it was daylight, and Egil lifted the tarpaulin so that we could look back over the stern of the boat to watch the churning wake.

We were already out of sight of land.

4

All day the sea was calm, but that night a storm blew up. There was no moon and no stars. There was no horizon and no land, and the waves crashed over our tarpaulin shelter. With drenched salty hands Egil and I clung to the parts of the boat that were nailed and riveted down. My fur coat grew thicker and warmer as the wind blew more strongly, and I could feel a mysterious life vibrating inside it.

When the storm worsened, Egil listened intently to the moaning of the wind through the rigging, softly imitating the eerie wailing sound. After a while the soft sounds he made sounded like words in some strange language. He seemed to be trying to understand the words he was repeating, like someone listening to important instructions down a bad telephone line.

Finally Egil buttoned his thin black jacket and said he should go and help the skipper. "We Fels are fine sailors," he said as he prepared to pull back the tarpaulin. "I can direct the captain through the soft parts of the wind."

When Egil turned to leave, I took hold of his arm. "Will you at least tell me what Fels are?" I said.

Egil peered out at the raging storm, then glanced back at me. "My grandfather said I must not."

Another wave fizzed over the deck.

"But Egil, I'm scared," I said. "I've never been in a storm before. I've never even been on a boat before."

A sudden spray smoothed Egil's hair to his head. With wet hair he looked even more like Shipley the cat than before, and that helped comfort me. He blew a drop of seawater from his nose.

"You mustn't be scared, Toby. A storm can't hurt you. Fels can ride storms like humans ride ponies."

"But I'm not a Fel—I'm a person," I said. The boat rolled violently, and we were both thrown against the tarpaulin. Egil's eyes never left mine. When the boat righted itself he spoke softly.

"Toby, all I can tell you is that you are not what you think yourself to be." With that he hurried out of the shelter of the tarpaulin and out into the raging storm.

Once I was alone, I began to hum the tune that Egil had been singing in imitation of the storm, and it made me feel better. I decided there and then that even if the boat should sink and I drowned that night, this adventure would still have been worth it. To have walked, talked, climbed, and sailed in this beautiful world, even if only for a day and a night, was preferable to a whole lifetime sitting motionless in my chair.

When I opened my eyes, I sat up like a jackknife and bumped my head on the barrel again. The sun was shining. The sea was flat calm, beautiful and amenable as if its quarrel with our boat the night before had never happened.

I peeked up over the tarpaulin and saw the crew laughing and smoking and drinking tea around the cabin. There were three men apart from the skipper. I could sense their relief as the engine chugged contentedly beneath their feet and the sea parted for the prow with hardly a splash. The skipper drained his cup, then tossed the dregs overboard. As he did, I thought he caught sight of me, though he didn't acknowledge me.

Egil was nowhere to be seen.

I heard a cry and turned to see a large herring gull making a gentle landing on the edge of the boat. I imagined the smell of the bacon had attracted him too. He folded his wings and blinked at me with his yellow-rimmed eyes. Then he angled his head to say hello. I remembered my silent conversations with my swallows, Look and Leave.

"Hello, Mr. Seagull," I said, just to hear the sound of my own voice and check it was still working. The seagull retched out a loud scream. As he did, there was a flash of black fur and claws and a hissing sound I knew very well.

The gull had been leaped upon by Shipley the cat, the familiar black scatty creature who had always been my best friend. I guessed that in the night Egil had changed himself back into a cat, though I had no idea why.

"Shipley!" I cried instinctively. "Leave the poor bird alone."

The "poor bird" was having none of Egil's nonsense. He shrieked and flapped and then began pecking at Shipley's face. The gull was so vicious that I feared Egil might come out of the dispute minus an eye. I turned to see if the crewmen were looking, but they had begun to go about their business with the nets. I shuffled forward on my knees and tried to shoo the gull away, but he already had a beak full of scruff fur, and Egil was arching his back in pain.

The fight had its own momentum, and the cat and the gull bit and clawed their way around the back of the barrels where I had been hiding. When they were out of view, I could hear only the shrieking of the bird and the vicious hissing of Egil.

Then the sounds of combat became deeper. Instead of shrieking, the gull was now grunting. Instead of hissing, the cat began to curse.

Suddenly, from behind the barrels, Egil's head emerged. Not Egil the cat but Egil the boy with the wild black hair and the green eyes. He was pushing against the barrels with his shoulder, something pinning him down.

"Run, Toby!" Egil yelled.

Then Egil's adversary came out from the cover of the barrels, and I saw that he had been transformed too. He was no longer a herring gull but a full-grown man, taller than Egil and squared off around the shoulders. His eyes were sharp and ringed with yellow, and his nose was hooked like a beak. His white hair was swept back off his face, and his skin darkened toward his shoulders. He was wearing a robe of fur and feathers, and even in the gentle wind it billowed around him. I saw a sword flash as he let out a mighty shriek.

He took a swipe at Egil with the weapon, which had a gold blade and three emeralds on the handle. The jewels caught the sun as he slashed at Egil's neck. Egil managed to yank a barrel from its position to stop the blow as he rolled across the deck.

Then the creature caught sight of me and stopped to gather his breath. He smiled and spoke in a low voice. "Pretender," he growled. "You will never reach Langjoskull."

He fired the strange new word at me like a bullet. Then he hopped onto the barrels and drew back his sword. My coat swirled around my chest, and the fur began to harden as the sword came crashing down toward me. I raised my arm to block the blow—and to my surprise, the fur on my sleeve was suddenly as tough as chain mail. The creature hopped down onto the deck, and his eyes darted around, looking for a chink in my armor. He tried for my chest, but Egil managed to use his strength to grab the creature and for a few seconds held him tight against the barrels.

Egil again yelled at me to run.

"Run where?" I yelled back.

At that moment a black-backed gull with a vivid yellow beak flew directly at my face. My coat took control, and with the sleeve powering my arm, I managed to swipe it away and slam it onto the deck, breaking its neck. But then a dozen more gulls appeared from nowhere, a mob of them, all as angry as last night's storm, pecking and clawing my exposed face and hands. I could see that Egil was being mobbed by them too, and he began to hiss and claw at them like a cat.

Finally Egil ran to where I was flailing my arms against the gulls. He shoved me toward the edge of the boat, and I saw blood flowing down the side of his face where he had been pecked. Then there was a glint of sunlight as the golden sword flew toward my face. My coat snarled around my throat, and I felt my arm parry the blow once again.

"Jump for it!" I heard Egil yell.

"I can't swim!" I managed to cry back.

"Twenty-four hours ago you couldn't walk!" he yelled. "*Jump!*"

The edge of the deck was at my heels, and I wouldn't have been able to keep my feet for much longer anyway. I saw Egil falling backward toward the foaming white water around the prow. The gulls were pulling my coat apart to give my attacker some unprotected flesh to aim at.

Egil was right. I had no choice. I let my weight take me over the edge and into the unknown.

5

At first it felt like stepping into a raging fire. Then the ice-cold numbness knotted my toes and fingers and pulled the knots tight. Even in summer, the sea this far north is just a degree away from being ice, and I felt my head being squeezed in a vise. I thought the roof of my mouth would cave in or my teeth shatter like glass.

Pain was new to me. Imagine if you had lived in total silence all your life, then were suddenly dropped into the middle of a raging orchestra. The cold felt like crashing cymbals and booming drums and screeching violins.

Then my ears popped and I realized I was free of the foaming wake of the boat. On the surface the waves were gentle. The gulls were circling overhead. After a few moments I felt a strange warmth rising from my legs and then penetrating my chest, where breath had been hard to find during the initial shock of hitting the water. My coat was now slicked down, like the skin of a seal, and no water penetrated it. My trousers were milky white beneath the rippling surface, and I could feel the enchanted material begin to expand around my joints, allowing me to tread water. I pulled my hands inside my sleeves to get protection, and somehow my trousers were now flapping around my feet like flippers, keeping out the worst of the cold.

Then I felt a hand grab my ankle, and I was pulled under the surface.

The sudden cold had made me forget that I couldn't swim. But now I was being dragged to my death by an invisible force, and the instinctive panic made me thrash my arms and legs in a kind of frantic dog paddle. The ocean below was a universe of dark blue and black, the kind of depth that makes you sick and dizzy, but as I looked down, I also saw a face looking up at me.

It was Egil, and it was his hand that was pulling me down. His cheeks were puffed out; his black hair was floating around like wild seaweed.

I kicked at him as hard as I could, but he held me like an iron anchor. He held me in place until the tiny breath I'd gulped down before he grabbed me began to run out. The panic subsided, and a strange calm overcame me. I saw my own arm begin to float up past my face, and the darkness of the ocean began to seep inside my head. I was sure that I was about to die.

Then there was sunlight and blue sky and a wave that slapped me in the face as I sucked in air, precious air, along with foam and spray. I saw a gull floating a few yards above my head, scanning the wave tops, looking left and right. When I had filled my chest I felt the hand pull me under again, and this time I realized that Egil was trying to keep me hidden from the gulls. I ducked my head and began to count the seconds. When at last I could hold my breath no longer, I exhaled a trail of bubbles and Egil let me go.

Egil and I hid beneath the waves in this way for almost half an hour. Each time I lasted longer and longer beneath the waves, and soon the feeling of being in the ocean was actually quite pleasant. The boat, of course, didn't delay its journey for us, but the gulls continued to circle overhead, shrieking and swooping. Finally the current had made us drift about a mile away from where the gulls were looking, and Egil allowed me to break the surface a bit longer.

"Toby, you have a kick like a bloody postman. Ouch," he said, sweeping back his long black hair.

"You said *ouch* is a good word," I said, and he splashed water in my face.

"What happened?" I asked through the spray. "Who was that man?"

"He was not a man," Egil said, scanning the skies. "He was a Fel. The worst kind."

"But why did he try to kill me?"

Egil ducked under the waves for a moment and then reemerged behind me. I turned to him.

"We must swim for land," he said.

I took his arm to keep myself afloat.

"He called me a pretender," I said. "What am I pretending? And where is Langjoskull?"

Egil narrowed his eyes at the sound of the word.

"Grandpa said my job is to keep you alive till we reach him. That is what I will do." He gestured with his chin at the thin line of unevenness on the horizon. "So let's swim."

"I've already told you, Egil, I *can't* swim."

"Then what are you doing now?" Egil asked.

The moment he asked the question, I began to sink and splutter. Egil grabbed my hand and then began to swim on his back, rippling his body from shoulders to feet in smooth hypnotic movements like a dolphin or a seal, dragging me along behind him.

I decided to concentrate on not drowning. As we began to make progress toward the land, my fur coat rippled in time with Egil's movements. I had no choice but to join in the dance because my clothes were dancing around me.

Soon I was able to let go of Egil's hand and almost keep pace with him, my head ducking beneath the waves with each forward propulsion.

To begin with, the salt water stung my eyes, but after a while I worked out a way of blinking the water away, and I felt my eyelids growing larger and thicker to suit the purpose. By the time low hills and rocky outcrops of the land became visible, I wanted this journey to continue forever. Swimming through the sparkling ocean like this, with the sun on my head and the air so clean and alive, was the most brilliant way to spend a day.

I felt as if I were going directly from feeling nothing in the chair to feeling everything all at once. I was so busy enjoying these new feelings that Egil was getting ahead of me.

I dived under the water and reemerged, just to feel the fizz of bubbles and foam around my body. I wanted to dive deep and explore the seabed. Swimming was now as natural to me as breathing. We swam for another hour, and in that time I forgot all about our destination. The sudden crunch of rock on the top of my head was a horrible shock. It was almost as shocking as that first moment when I fell into the ocean. There was something very dull and deathly about the firmness of the rocks, and some part of me wanted to turn back to the moving, living, breathing organism of the sea.

My hands felt hard stone and I tried to stand up. For a

moment it felt as if my legs were glued together, and it took a supreme effort to separate them. I saw Egil staring at me as I dragged myself through the shallow water, and he was shaking his head in wonder. It was only then that I looked down at the place where my legs were supposed to be and saw instead the slick fat tail of a walrus.

The sight was so shocking that my hands slipped from under me and my head flopped under the water. Each hour was bringing new shocks. After a few seconds I felt a warm hand on my neck, and my eyes flickered open. I was lifted from under the waves by Egil, who was now on his feet. When I looked down at my legs again, I saw that they were human legs once more. I imagined that the magic power inside my clothes had caused them to transform.

Egil was weaving some green seaweed into his hair for decoration and smiling down at me.

"Well, well, Toby," he said. "Grandpa *will* be pleased with you."

6

"Is Toby a name you like, or would you prefer to change it to something more . . . *inspiring?*" Egil asked as he led me up the slope of the shale beach. "Now that you are with us, you can call yourself anything you want."

The seaweed in his hair looked like a soggy crown. I remembered the story of the nurse's cat that gave me my name.

"What's wrong with Toby?" I said.

"It's like Shipley. Not a real name. Names have a certain *smell.* Shipley smells like stale bread on an unwashed plate. Toby smells like the inside of a wooden box with old newspapers in it and a candle."

I was rather proud of my own sense of smell, but I

couldn't say I had ever detected the smell of my own name. Egil had a way of saying things that made you stop walking without realizing you'd stopped.

"I have no idea what you're talking about, Egil, but my name is Toby and it's staying that way," I said.

Egil scanned the horizon.

"Prince . . . Toby . . . Prince Toby . . . Mmmmm . . . ," he said thoughtfully, as if the word *prince* were a new suit that "Toby" was being measured for. He obviously didn't think it fitted.

"What do you mean, 'prince'?" I asked, but before Egil could answer, he leaped into the air and clawed at some invisible thing. "Get away from me! Yik! Air knot!" he shrieked. Then he wrinkled his nose and hissed.

"What on earth is an air knot?" I said.

"Sometimes when people get confused, the air near them gets a sort of knot in it. Only cats can sense them. Horrible things. They feel like string around your middle. I *hate* things around my middle."

I stared at him as he looked all around suspiciously for air knots. Then he suddenly leaped up onto a tooth of black rock with the grace of a cat. My magical coat was already dry and protecting me from the cold sea breeze. The wind and the waves and the mournful cries of a curlew made the beach feel lonely. It felt like a place where you would sit and cry. Egil jumped down from the rock.

"What are you looking for?"

"Grandpa said he would meet us here," Egil said, and he set off, crunching along the beach. "I don't understand where he could have got to."

We startled a flock of puffins. They looked like tiny, fat waiters, all with the same unruly tuft of hair. The moment Egil saw them take flight, he raced after them and made a vain attempt to grab one with his hands. The birds easily avoided him and he shook his head, his hands on his hips.

"Must stop doing that," he said in a low voice. Then he set off again. After a few more paces he stopped dead and peered along the shoreline. His face became grave.

"Ah. Bad, bad, bad," he whispered.

He began to walk carefully on the black shale, exactly like a cat stalking a bird. Even though his feet were on wet gravel, he made no noise. I walked beside him and saw a snag of black seaweed ahead of us, wrapped around a piece of driftwood.

Egil stared at it intently.

"What's wrong?" I said. He turned to me with a look of puzzlement. Those luminous green eyes seemed to search my soul.

"I see you are not quite entirely with us yet," he said. "Let me help you."

Egil put his frozen hands over my eyes for a few seconds,

and I felt the hard skin of his palms against my soft eyelids. Then I heard some kind of loud crack out at sea. When Egil moved his hands, he said, "Now look again."

I blinked away a spray of foam and turned to look at the snagged seaweed. A wave rolled back and I froze in horror. It wasn't a clump of seaweed at all. It was a body. It had a face. And it was staring directly at us with dead, water-logged eyes.

"What is it?" I shrieked.

Egil stepped into the waves, and even though the thing was obviously dead, he didn't drop his guard. He whispered soft words to himself under his breath and kept me back a few inches with his outstretched arm. Finally we were close enough to see the body clearly.

The dead creature seemed to be only partly human. It was three feet tall with two feet of black hair growing from its head and chin. The hair looked like seaweed. Its face was gnarled and old, the color of stained pine wood, and its short arms waved gently at us with every movement of the sea. The only thing stopping the ocean from washing the body away was a gold-handled sword that had been stuck through its leather tunic and pushed deep into the shale and sand beneath.

The creature was pinned to the edge of Iceland like a message on a bulletin board. And Egil seemed to understand the message very well.

"Grandpa has been here with a pumping heart," Egil said, still staring at the creature as if at any moment it might pull the sword out and set upon us. "He smells angry on these rocks here."

"Your grandpa did that?" I said with disbelief.

Egil nodded gently. "He is quite the old flying slipper when he wants to be," Egil said. "This little assassin must have been sent to the surface to watch for our arrival."

A wave caught me and foamed around my ankles. I didn't like the way the dead thing seemed to be nodding its head in agreement with what Egil was saying.

"Sent by who?" I asked.

Egil was too deep in thought to remember he wasn't supposed to answer my questions.

"Helva Gullkin," he said in a soft voice, then turned sharply to me. "Stop tricking me."

"Who is Helva Gullkin?"

"No one."

"No one with a team of assassins."

Egil grabbed the hilt of the sword and yanked it out of the sand with both hands. He washed the blade in the next wave and held it up to the light.

"You're going to need this," Egil said.

"But why would someone I've never even heard of want to kill *me*?" I said. "All I've ever done all my life is look out of the window."

Egil pushed the sword into my hand, and I felt its great weight against my wrist bone. I had to use both hands to hold it above the waves.

"Grandpa must have gone on to Langjoskull, so we will meet him there."

"And this Langjoskull is the one place my enemies don't want me to reach," I said flatly.

Egil looked at me with pity. The dead creature waved its lifeless arms at us in a gesture of farewell and was sucked down the beach by the next retreating wave. Within a few seconds the body was rolling on the breakers like flotsam . . . and once again it looked like seaweed.

I'd allowed the sword to droop under its own weight, and Egil lifted it before the next breaker caught it and broke it out of my hands. Seawater dripped from the golden hilt and shaft.

"The scabbard is behind those rocks," Egil said. "Tie it to your belt and be ready to use it. I'm afraid from now on things are going to get a bit serious."

Egil ruffled his shocking black hair and forced a grin. I imagine he only did it to make me feel better. He then turned to stalk slowly up the steeply sloped beach, looking all around anxiously but coughing like a cat with a fur ball.

Beyond the salt marsh the Icelandic plain was eerily flat. There was very little vegetation apart from moss and tufts of scrub grass. Everywhere there were large boulders that had been dumped by departing glaciers. It looked like shrapnel from some battle between giants with slingshots.

As we walked we disturbed lots of ptarmigans, snow-white birds with a call like an alarm clock, that would appear suddenly from behind tufts of marsh grass. I could see that Egil was having great trouble stopping himself from tearing into the heather after them, and he very determinedly hummed under his breath.

One time a ptarmigan huddled down by a boulder and seemed to taunt us. Egil's hands clawed up in front of his face, and he let out a desperate gasp. "Seven long years," he hissed, and I laughed out loud.

"It's all right for you," he said, pushing his hands under his armpits; "you've never shifted. You have no idea what it's like. I am curling constantly, Toby, a tail that just isn't there. Can you imagine that? And instead of whiskers I have . . . *ideas.*"

I laughed and he seemed to like that.

"Am I becoming less ridiculous yet?" he asked. "Grandpa said it would take five days before the catness began to disappear."

"No, you are still very ridiculous," I replied. "And anyway, what exactly do you mean, 'shifted'?"

Egil was about to answer, then looked a little annoyed that I had almost tricked him into an answer. He turned sharply and walked on.

Here and there small Iceland horses grazed, their unkempt manes tangled with salt, their coats uncombed by any human hand. When we walked by, they raised their heads and blinked at us, their eyes full of blackflies and suspicion.

Soon the flies were unbearable. The moment we left the sea wind behind, the flies mobbed me and seemed to do it in a deliberately antagonizing way. They went for my eyes, my nostrils, and my ears, and I swiped at them and slapped my own face so hard that Egil was shaking with laughter. Of course, the flies didn't bother him. He said the Fels and the flies had made a peace treaty two thousand years ago.

Suddenly I got so angry with them that I pulled the sword from its scabbard. I don't know why I did this, because I had never owned a sword before today and certainly never held one, but it now seemed to be the most natural thing in the world to do. There was a sinew between my anger and the sword itself. And the moment the sword was free, something remarkable happened.

The blackflies, which before had been buzzing around me so fast that they were hardly visible, were now floating gracefully in front of my eyes in slow motion. I could make out the shape of their wings as they flapped and follow the arc of their flight, which I could now see made a series of interconnected circular patterns. Their movement was quite hypnotic, but at the same time they were moving so slowly that they would be easy to swat. I began to use the tip of the sword to good effect. Two, then three, then four of the slow-moving flies went into elegant tailspins at the touch of the sword before falling slowly to the ground.

Blackflies can be quite beautiful if you have the time.

The sight of my sword at work was so astounding that I hardly noticed the odd rumbling sound coming from my left. I turned to see Egil, who had a look of frozen horror on his face. He was almost completely still apart from his hand, which was moving painfully slowly toward my own hand as my sword continued to work on the flies. When his cold fingers finally touched the handle of the sword, the slow-motion dance of the flies suddenly stopped, and the world went back to its normal, frantic self.

The flies were buzzing fast again, and Egil was beside himself.

"Toby, you must not! You must not!" he yelled, wriggling inside his skin.

"Must not what?"

Egil grabbed my hand and forced me to put the sword back into its scabbard.

"Grandpa's sword is made from planets! From orbits!

From moons! You mustn't use it on flies! You must use it on great things! Of great weight! In hot places. Filling in big spaces!"

Egil clenched his fists and growled in a cloud of frozen breath. "Flies, Toby? Flies?" He suddenly began to laugh.

"So why did everything slow down?" I asked.

Egil angled his head like a cat and fixed me with that green-eyed stare. "When you wear a Fellish sword, it becomes an extension of your desires," he said as if I were an idiot, which I suppose I was. "When the flies were attacking you, you must have wished somewhere inside that they would slow down so that you could swat them. The wish traveled down your arm into your sword. The trick, of course, is making sure that your wish is the right one. And then you have to be able to take advantage of your wish coming true. In that sense, I suppose, you did rather well."

We stared into each other's eyes for a long time. I used to do this with Shipley, and Shipley always yawned and looked away first. Egil didn't.

"My sword can slow down time?" I said.

"It can slow down your enemies. Just for a little while. Meddling with time is for grown-ups."

I looked down at the golden handle at my hip and felt the weight of the metal on my belt. I tried to remember some of the things Stephen Hawking said about time being bent. I didn't remember him saying anything about swords and flies.

I could see by the way Egil was looking at me that through his silliness he was rather worried.

There is no place on earth like the roof of a glacier. You can feel the shape of it with your feet, but you have no sense of gradient or steepness. If the sky is white, as it almost always is from reflected snow light, then there is whiteness in every direction. Also, you can sense the depth of ice beneath you with some organ in your throat and ears. You stamp the ice and feel the vibration going down and down and down, mile after mile, all the way to the grit of solid ground.

Except in Iceland the ground is never solid. Iceland is a very old blister on a crack in the earth's crust, and there are a thousand holes and fissures that ooze with the hot insides of the planet. The water in Iceland is far too busy to be just water and is mostly either ice or steam. Thick sheets of ice sit on the island like weights to stop it flying up into the sky with the next volcanic eruption. The full power of the earth is just beneath the leather soles of your shoes.

Few people walk on the glaciers. They are hard to reach in the toughest vehicle, and apart from the odd Ski-Doo track, their surfaces remain unmarked by humans. And none who walk there know what is *really* beneath their feet.

We crunched and labored across the thick snow in a summer blizzard. My magical sword had shrunk to the size of a dagger, and I hardly felt its presence. The crystal sunlight made the snow beneath us sparkle. The air was so cold that it was drilling holes in my head, but it was also exhilarating and I wanted to stop and play. This was my first real experience of snow, and for all I knew, it might be my last.

Egil was busy studying the landscape, setting his eyes against the distant mountains, making calculations. Then he saw a small dip in the snowy surface a few yards to the left. He walked to it and then began to walk toward the sun, counting out his steps as he walked. When he stopped walking, he turned right and walked a few more paces.

As far as I could see, he was simply counting out paces on an endless expanse. Perhaps he had taken leave of his senses. However, at a certain point he took out his two-cornered hat from his pocket and dropped it on the snow to mark the place. Then he walked back toward me.

"We are almost at the gates of Langjoskull," he said.

"I don't see any gates."

"The gates are beneath the snow, but I can smell the air that comes from beneath them. And before we enter, there is one thing I really *must* explain for your own safety."

He sat down on the snow and I sat in front of him. My coat thickened at the back to make a warm seat that was also dry. My sword had a way of being unobtrusive, always adjusting itself to suit my needs. Egil began anxiously shaping the snow into mounds.

"The fact is, Toby," he said, "as you have probably gathered, not everyone is completely overjoyed that you are coming."

"Yes, I pretty much got the gist of that," I said.

"So when we go below, it is absolutely essential that your identity remain hidden. You must do exactly as I say and do nothing to draw attention to yourself."

I felt that ever since we had jumped from the boat, Egil and I had been playing a guessing game and now the game had to stop. I could see from the anxious way that Egil pawed the snow that my life was genuinely in danger.

"Exactly how many people down there want to kill me?" I asked flatly.

"There are no people down there," Egil said unhelpfully, "just Fels."

"Egil, you know what I mean."

"There is only one Fel who really wants your neck. . . ."

"Helva Gullkin," I said.

Egil nibbled a fistful of snow nervously, then looked away from me. "But the problem is that Helva Gullkin is actually . . . unofficially . . . *temporarily* . . ."

He hesitated as if the end of the sentence were the edge of a cliff. He covered his eyes with his hand and fell silent.

"Actually, unofficially, temporarily *what?*" I said.

"He is unjustly and *very* temporarily . . . the sort of . . . king."

Egil peeped out through the lattice of his fingers.

"The king?" I gulped.

"The 'sort of' king," Egil said.

"But he is in charge?"

"Only of the government, the police, and the army. The gull you met on the boat was one of his senior detectives."

I remembered the terrifying creature I'd met and imagined hundreds or even thousands more like him. Egil nervously extended his fingers like claws several times, scratching at the air knots that I was undoubtedly creating.

"So when we are below, you must pretend to be just another Fel. At least until the time comes," Egil said.

"What time?" I asked, a little desperately.

"The time when you are to be . . . announced."

"And what time is that?"

"Look at my hair, Toby. Do I look like the sort of person who knows important things?"

I looked at his hair and saw that the ends of his scattered mane were beginning to freeze white and hard. Bits of seaweed were tangled up in it and had frozen into amazing shapes. Egil glanced at me, and because he was also Shipley the cat, he knew I was being deliberately defiant.

"Why didn't you tell me this before?" I asked.

Egil got to his feet and looked all around at the endless expanse of frozen snow.

"Because Grandpa told me to wait until you were a hundred miles from the nearest human town, surrounded by snow and ice," he said, and all the silliness was gone from his voice. "He told me to wait until you had no choice."

I felt as if someone had kicked me hard in the ribs. Egil turned to me, and I could see the genuine remorse in his big green eyes.

"Sorry," he said, "but you will see soon that we have brought you here for a reason, Toby. There is a bigger purpose."

"Which of course you can't possibly explain," I said, and Egil lowered his head, saying nothing.

I remembered my warm chair in the convent. I thought about Sister Mary and her glove puppets and even longed for a taste of the warm white goo she used to feed me. A single tear began to run down my cheek but froze halfway down.

Then a ripple ran through Egil's body, and he leaped into the air. A wild grin appeared on his face. He grabbed my hand and pulled me to my feet.

"But Toby, oh, Toby, what wonders are in store for you!" he yelped. He began to drag me across the snow, and I fixed my feet in position, so I was actually sliding like a statue.

"There is magic and gold and hot springs and music and . . . meat! Reindeer meat!"

"I don't care! You tricked me! You said there was some great fortune waiting for me! I want to go home!"

"No, you don't, Toby," Egil said firmly, and his face looked more serious than I had ever seen it. "I know you don't because I have been inside your head many times and we are the best of friends."

"Some friend you are!"

"I am your *only* friend!" he yelled.

The cold wind blew between us, and I saw that he wished he hadn't said that. I thought about Sister Mary and turned my back on him. She was my friend too, and *she* would never trick me. He came to me and spoke softly. "This is your destiny, Toby. Believe me. It is the Jerlamar that brought you here."

"What is the Jerlamar?" I asked. "It's okay, don't bother, I don't expect an answer."

Egil let go of my hand and got down on his knees.

"The Jerlamar is the power that flows inside the earth," he said softly. "It is the power that kept you from losing your mind in the chair. The power that made your legs work. It is very close here. It is the source of all Fellish wonders."

Egil looked down at the snow and laid his hands on the crusty surface like someone stroking a living creature.

"You haven't really lived until you've felt it, Toby. That is the fortune you have come to inherit. Come with me and you will experience it for yourself. Please pretend you have a choice, and pretend you're choosing to come with me as a friend."

He looked at me for a moment longer, then turned to walk to the spot where he'd dropped his hat. He began to sweep the snow away with his arm. I watched him work, deliberately not helping. I felt another hot tear in my eye but this time cursed it away. What good was crying? I had made my decision in that darkened doorway, and now I had to stick with it.

Egil had cleared a patch of snow and, to my astonishment, revealed a set of gates. They were six feet square, ornately decorated with images of wolves and bears that appeared to be hammered out of solid gold. I stood back in astonishment as jewels in the eyes of the animals glistened in the snow light. Some were rubies and some were emeralds. Egil grabbed one of the golden handles and started to pull. Slowly the gate began to budge.

"Help me, Toby," Egil said softly, and at last I grabbed the handle with him and pulled with all my might. As the gate opened, a great waft of air hit us both in the face. It smelled of roast meat and smoke, a little of sweat and straw, and a little of cattle and goats. Under all this frozen silence, here was the breath of life. Suddenly the descent was irresistible.

A staircase carved from ice led down into the darkness. But there was also a scattering of lights, and the warm air carried the sound of distant music.

7

A staircase made of ice may not sound practical, and if you are human, it isn't. I took more than one tumble, and a nervous Egil hissed at me to be more careful. Egil's toes gripped the ice almost as if he still had claws. Our way was lit by small candles, no more than wicks floating in dishes, filled with what Egil told me was walrus fat. The small flames shed huge shadows on the ice walls of the staircase, but between their pools of light there was total darkness.

The music from below became louder, and soon the sound was thickened by voices. It sounded like some kind of market, with vendors calling out their wares. I could also hear horses' hooves on hard stone. It was impossible to look down without losing my footing, so I concentrated on putting one foot in front of the other on the ice.

On a small ice landing we crossed paths with two Fels who were buttoning their white furs, ready to climb out onto the glacier. They carried bows and arrows and small leather traps for hunting. When they saw Egil, they raised their hats and grunted a greeting, which he returned. I felt my fur collar growing around my face, responding to my anxiety. The crossing on the landing passed off without incident, but as the Fel hunters walked by, I noticed how small they were, and how lined and cracked their faces were, like saddle leather.

Just like leprechauns or elves, I thought. Egil was pulling a fur hat from inside his coat.

"Wear this," he said. "You're a boy, so with your height you'll pass as a Fel grown-up. If anyone asks, say you're seven hundred and eighty-five years old and from the other side. Everybody's from one side or the other, so if you just say you're from the other side, they'll leave you alone."

"How many sides are there?" I whispered.

"Just two. The light side and the dark side. They don't always get on. In fact . . ."

Egil suddenly spotted a bat hanging peacefully above one of the walrus-fat candles. He instinctively swiped it with his clawed hand and brought it to his mouth, ready to gobble it. I grabbed his hand to stop him, but he couldn't bring himself to let it go. Instead he pretended to examine the bat with great curiosity.

"Where was I?" he said distantly. The bat fluttered in his hand and Egil stared at it transfixed, licking his lips.

"You were telling me about the light side and the dark side," I said.

"Ah, *yes* . . . you see, the light we get down here comes through the ice roof. The snow covering on one side of the glacier is thinner than the other, and the ice is clearer. . . ." While the poor creature's fate was in the balance, Egil apparently forgot Doctor Felman's instructions about explanations and he spoke dreamily. "So one side of our world is light and the other side is . . . dark."

Egil angled his head. "All that walking has made me so, so . . . hungry." He suddenly opened his mouth wide and was about to take a bite out of the bat. I decided it was not something I could bear to see.

"They taste like leather sandals!" I yelled quickly. With that, Egil came to his senses, turned to me, and then let the bat go with a fluttering of dark wings.

"Well *remembered,* Tobes," he said before dusting his hands and setting off down the ice staircase once more.

As we descended, the staircase became less steep and the ice gave way to stone. We arrived at a balcony that looked down over this strange new world. To Egil's dismay, I couldn't help but stop and stare in wonder.

"Close mouth, bury head in hat, don't look like mad rabbit," he instructed through clenched teeth.

A whole city was laid out before me. The light came down in shafts from the roof of the glacier, and when I looked up I saw high above there were vast windows of ice that had only a thin layer of snow, allowing the daylight through. These gigantic shafts of sunlight were refracted by the ice and given a sparkling yellow tinge. As a result the world below looked to be vividly alive, the colors brighter and sharper than anything I had seen in the surface world.

I could see open country, bathed in yellow light; at one end of the city it stretched as far as the eye could see. Egil told me this was the east. There were forests and sunlit mountains and above them a giant peak that shimmered in a blue light that seemed to come from inside the mountain itself. To the south of the city I could see a huge castle that appeared to have grown like a living organism from the side of another mountain.

To the west, where the surface snow was much thicker, there was an eerie half darkness that stretched all the way to a shimmering horizon.

There was nothing electric that I could see, but there were seams of flowing red-hot and white-hot volcanic lava that gave off heat and a warm light. The streets were laid out around the volcanic flows, and the houses and shops followed their paths. The buildings were made from slate-colored bricks, stacked and constructed in a vast variety of shapes and designs. All the way across the city, great plumes of steam rose up from hot springs, and every few minutes towering geysers exploded steam and water a hundred and fifty feet into the air so that at any one time, two or three geysers were erupting and depositing a fine shower of water onto the stone rooftops.

"Pretty incredible, isn't it," Egil said with a hint of pride. "I found the human world pretty old bread after this. Smelled like something that's been in a bag for a long time. Our world smells of . . . hot shoe leather. Runaway *adventure,* don't you think?"

I did think.

Egil tugged my arm and made me continue down the last flight of steps, which I realized were carved from volcanic rock. As I got closer to street level, I saw Fels of all shapes and sizes going about their business, most of them trotting rather than walking, some riding Iceland ponies or riding in two-wheeled carts pulled by the same breed, tough, stocky, and mostly black. There was a market taking place, and hanging above the stalls I saw reindeer and seal carcasses, as well as unplucked puffins, cormorants, and other wild birds. Musicians played instruments that looked like tiny toy violins but made a loud droning sound that was hypnotically melodic. Passersby dropped gold coins into the musicians' rough wool blankets.

It wasn't until I actually stepped into the street that I saw just how much gold there was in Langjoskull. Door handles, brackets on market stalls, window handles, the hubs of cart wheels, even the nails that held everything in place—all were made from gold.

A cart came racing around a bend, and Egil had to pull me out of its path. He drew out his wild shock of black hair with clawed hands.

"Will you try to look *normal,*" he whispered.

I pushed my head into my fur collar and shoved my hands into my pockets before setting off at Egil's side. The market stallholders were swapping meat and bushels of seaweed for shining gold coins that were stacked up in huge towers on the stall covers. Behind the stalls, workshops were working at full capacity. I saw a cobbler, a candlemaker, a blacksmith, and a goldsmith. The smiths worked at forges that were fashioned around mounds of white-hot lava. They cooled their metal in buckets filled with shards of ice. The smell of the volcanic fire mixed with the sweet burned smell of roasting meat made the air itself feel like pungent dark cloth around my face.

Suddenly I heard someone yelling behind me, and then Egil whispered urgently in my ear. "Toby, run for it."

Egil raced past me and ducked down a dark alley. I turned around to see a big-bellied stallholder who was selling roast meat reaching for a meat cleaver and setting off in our direction.

"Toby, run!!" Egil cried again from down the alley. I ran as fast as I could after Egil and had to leap over a lava flow to join him in a darkened doorway. He had a big lump of reindeer meat in his hand, and he was staring at it in a kind of daze.

"What happened?" I said, catching my breath.

"I don't have any Fel currency," he said, staring breathlessly at the steaming piece of meat. "So I stole it."

The stallholder waddled by with his cleaver in his hand. We both froze until he had disappeared.

"I thought we were trying not to draw attention to ourselves," I said.

"Couldn't resist you, could I, little darling," he said softly to the piece of meat, and took a big bite. Almost the second he'd taken the bite, he sighed. "Oh, damn."

"What?"

"That special moment when you take your first bite of roasted reindeer after seven long years is one of the finest moments in your life," he said, then sighed again. "And now it's already over."

A tear appeared in his eye and he took his next bite with a mournful expression. We took turns taking bites of the meat. As someone who had never eaten meat before, I wanted to point out that this was an even bigger moment for me than it was for him. And I had to admit it did taste delicious. However, Egil looked so theatrically sad that I decided not to spoil his moment. When the meat was all gone, he began to lick his fingers, then his hands, then his forearms.

"Egil," I said at last, "you're acting like a cat." He stopped licking.

When we stepped back into the street, I saw the crowd scatter as a Fel in a dark green uniform hurtled down the street on a jet-black cart pulled by six snapping wolves.

"Police," Egil whispered darkly, and my coat purred around my throat to keep me calm. Egil raised his collar and kept walking. "If they look you in the eye . . . turn and yawn, turn and yawn."

The police rode past us, and we disappeared into the crowds. It was hard not to stop and stare at everything. Some of the Fel looked human, but others were smaller and hairier; Egil said these were Vela, a tribe who were cousins of the Fel. Apparently the Fel looked down on the Vela. There was another group of beings on the streets too. Creatures with bony foreheads and chins like bricks stomped through the crowds, most of them carrying heavy burdens on their shoulders. They stood a foot taller than an average Fel, and their hands were bigger.

Egil saw me staring at one of them and hissed at me. "Do you want to get your back broken?" he said.

"What are they?"

"They are Thrulls," Egil said.

"Are they the same as Fels?"

Egil thought for a moment. "I'm sure Grandpa won't mind if I tell you," he said in a whisper. "It is only history, and history can do no harm."

He waited for a particularly large Thrull to pass.

"The Thrull are a separate race related to the Fel who have always lived under the ice. The Fel have lived here for only a short while. Just three thousand years or so. The Thrull have been here forever. They have no magic powers, but they are strong and make good warriors. When we first moved to Langjoskull, they lived with us as brothers and sisters. But since Helva Gullkin seized the throne, they are forced to work as slaves."

Another large Thrull almost trampled me, and I ducked into a doorway. He was carrying a golden bucket full of glowing red-hot volcanic rocks. The heat didn't seem to bother him as the bucket pressed against his cheek. I noticed that he wore golden chains around his ankles and that his ankles were bleeding.

The constant drizzle that fell from the exploding geysers gave the air a pleasing freshness, even though the earth beneath our feet was splitting like an overstuffed sack with oozing lava. The constant haze of fresh water meant that tufts of grass grew in the unlikeliest places, including in the eaves of the houses and in the joints of drainpipes. The sprouting grass made the whole city appear to be a living organism, breathing in and out with the explosions of the geysers.

"So does everyone here change into cats and birds when it pleases them?" I asked.

"No," Egil said sadly, "not anymore."

His face darkened. He began to walk quickly along the crusted edge of a lava flow like a tightrope walker with his arms outstretched, even though there was plenty of pavement to walk on. I had to trot to keep up with him.

"What do you mean, 'not anymore'?" I asked.

"Toby, I realize you're tricking me into telling you things," Egil said, his arms still outstretched. "But we are almost at Grandpa's house, so you might as well wait."

Suddenly another detachment of policemen raced by in the opposite direction from the first, and this time their carriage was pulled by wolverines. As they bucked over a lava rock, a body was tossed from the back of the flat board and landed with a thud on the hard ground. I couldn't tell if the poor creature was alive or dead, and Egil put his hand over my eyes to stop me from staring.

"For now we pretend we just don't see," Egil said.

We walked across a golden bridge, and a carriage made entirely of gold rattled by, encrusted with rubies and emeralds. It was carrying straw. Beneath the bridge a river of bubbling lava flowed. How strange this new world was.

"It's actually all very beautiful here," I said under my breath to Egil, and he grunted.

"Actually reserve your judgment," he said.

We detoured so Egil could show me the university, which was milk white and built from pumice, with two geyser fountains that had been dyed blue and red. There was an armory with no windows, and a government administration building surrounded by a high fence, its grounds patrolled by wolves and uniformed Thrulls. I saw a school that appeared to be deserted and at the end of a long street, well away from the nearest shaft of sunlight, a giant fortress made from shining black obsidian.

"The prison," Egil said softly as we turned the corner. "It is full." He shivered and his shoulders arched.

Just then a detachment of Fel soldiers galloped into view, all wearing black uniforms and wearing towering pyramid-shaped helmets. Their horses were all white and larger than the average Icelandic pony. Three of the horses were bleeding from the lashes of their riders' whips.

As we continued to walk, the sunlight began to disappear. I had noticed that two hundred feet above our heads the ice roof sparkled in the sunlight. But as we walked on, the ice became less clear and the snow was thicker on top of it. On this side of the city, the gloom was lifted only by the red-hot lava flows. The light from the lava was orange or red, the mood was darker, the looks more suspicious. Even in the half-light I could see that the buildings were little more than crumbling hovels, belching a coarser kind of smoke from the fissures between the walls.

Here the Thrulls outnumbered the Fels, and the Fels who did live here were of the smaller, Vellish type. A ripple moved up my coat, as if muscles inside it were being flexed in readiness for a fight.

"This, I take it, is the dark side," I said.

"Bats and rats think it's heaven, of course."

Suddenly we were confronted by a green uniform with golden epaulets. A policeman had stepped into our path from the shadows.

"Where are you going?" the policeman asked.

"We are students," Egil said instantly, and he pulled out his mad hair into even wilder tufts with his bony fingers. "Our class just finished."

"Why are you walking into the dark side?"

"I work for the Helva Gullkin's Order of Mercy," Egil said. "Volunteer work. I help to feed the poor. I chase mice, then back they come into my teeth. Run, run, run, then scratch and turn, bite fast just there on the white fur that is softer."

The policeman looked puzzled. In his anxiety Egil was slipping back into being a cat. *Please don't talk when you're nervous, Egil,* I thought. Then the policeman turned his attention from Egil to me. I smiled.

"And what do you study?" the policeman asked me.

"Officer, exactly what is this about?" Egil asked.

"We are looking for humans," the policeman said, and he stared deep into my eyes, which had widened a little behind my collar. "We've been told there are two of them under the ice." He pulled my collar down from my eyes. "I asked you a question."

"I study history," I said, though I have no idea why. Perhaps because Egil had just said that history could do no one any harm.

The policeman rocked a little on his feet and smiled. "In that case, name the last three kings of Langjoskull."

A geyser erupted somewhere over the policeman's shoulder, but his fixed stare didn't shift from me. Egil wasn't breathing.

"Well?" the policeman said. I could see he was beginning to smell a rat, and he peered at Egil. Egil straightened his jacket with a tug.

"Okay, officer, we're students, but we're not very good," he said. "In fact, we're rubbish. Especially him. He spends all his time lying with curled-up knees, dreaming in the sun where the steam smells of slugs."

I couldn't tell if my coat was urging me to run or fight. When Egil ran out of nonsense, I could hear his throat rattling the way Shipley's throat rattled when he saw a bird through the window. The policeman reached down to his belt, where a short sword hung in a leather scabbard. At that moment someone tapped the policeman on the shoulder, and he turned around.

"Excuse me, I believe there is some sort of altercation taking place over by the saltwater well," said the stranger. "Thrulls attacking Fels."

The policeman looked personally affronted and immediately set off in the direction of the street corner that we had just come around. As the policeman walked away, the Fel who had tapped his shoulder stepped forward.

"Welcome to our troubled world, Toby Walsgrove," the stranger said. He was taller than most of the Fels I had seen and was dressed in a brown robe. His face was hidden in the shadow of his hood, and I could just see the glint of two green eyes.

"Grandpa!" Egil exclaimed.

The stranger pulled his hood back from his head. I saw a lined face the color of tanned leather with green eyes even more remarkable than Egil's. He had a light gray beard, his ears were a little pointed, and he had the same fragile smile as Egil.

"I am Doctor Felman," he said softly, taking my hand, "and I am so very pleased that you came."

Egil immediately hugged him and was about to lick his hand, but Doctor Felman cleared his throat and Egil thought better of it.

"We must hurry," he said, and he set off walking quickly into the red glow of the dark side. Egil's step was suddenly springier than it had been for the whole journey.

"Grandpa, where on earth have you been?" he said.

"I've been preparing for Toby's arrival," the doctor said softly, and he glanced at me as if this were some kind of private joke.

8

Doctor Felman's house was far from grand. He lived in a square block of gray volcanic slabs, stacked high to make a two-story house with windows made from very pale blue glass. Volcanic smoke puffed from the chimney, and hot lava rocks glowed in lamps on either side of the small front door. The house sat right in the heart of the dark side. As Egil, the doctor, and I walked up the shale garden path, Doctor Felman nodded a greeting to his next-door neighbor, a small Vellish-looking woman with her arms full of washing. She didn't nod back. Instead she glared at Egil's unruly hair.

Inside, lava rocks glowed in the fireplace, and the air was filled with the smell of coffee. A metal coffeepot hissed on a stove and looked to be on the point of boiling over. This made me suspect that someone else was already in the house.

Once inside his own home, Doctor Felman was unsure of himself, as if the humble surroundings were new to him. He fussed over the lava fire and burned his hand taking the coffeepot off the stove. There was very little light inside the front room since there were only three candles burning. A soft red light came from the lava stream outside, but the only sunlight was a distant shaft, bathing the other side in brightness.

He caught me looking around at his tiny room and smiled, reading my thoughts precisely. "I'm afraid that ever since Helva Gullkin took power in Langjoskull, I and other Keepers of the Arts have fallen on hard times."

"Grandpa, he doesn't know what Keepers of the Arts are," Egil said quickly, to prove he had obeyed his instructions to tell me nothing. Doctor Felman smiled and poured himself a cup of coffee.

"But he knows who Helva Gullkin is?" Doctor Felman asked softly. Egil cursed under his breath.

"He tricked me into telling him Gullkin's name," Egil said, and he poked out his tongue at me.

"I only know that Helva Gullkin wants me dead," I said firmly. "And if anybody tricked anybody, it was *you* who tricked *me*."

Doctor Felman looked at us both as if we were squabbling

children, and we both fell silent. He sipped his coffee.

"Coffee is one of my few pleasures now. I bring it back from the human world whenever I go. Would you like some, Toby?"

"No, but I would like you to explain why you brought me here," I replied flatly. I glanced at Egil. "So far I've just been given riddles."

"I have fended off his questions like a swordsman," Egil said proudly. "Jab, parry, jab, parry . . ."

Doctor Felman turned to me, and I felt his extraordinary eyes piercing my own. It was as if two hands were gently stroking the inside of my skull.

"Do you like *your* sword, Toby?"

I realized that in the safety of the room, my sword had shrunk away to the size of a dagger again.

"I put my own power inside the sword," Doctor Felman continued. "Whenever you are in danger, you can pull the sword, and it will help you do what must be done. But my power will only last so long. It is like a human car that after a certain number of miles runs out of fuel. Soon you must fill the sword with your own fuel."

Egil was licking his fingers, and I imagine the taste of salt brought back a memory.

"Oh—and Grandpa, I had to work very . . . quite . . . no *very* hard to stop Toby from turning into a big fat walrus the second he hit the seawater."

Doctor Felman studied me and looked impressed.

"Of course, technically that is because the clothes we gave him were soaked with Jerlamar power," he said. "But for them to work so well, Toby must be very responsive."

I didn't like them discussing me as if I were a specimen, and I didn't like the fact that I didn't understand what on earth they were talking about.

"The Jerlamar sounds like some sort of cake," I said loudly, being rude deliberately. "It sounds like some silly thing you eat."

Egil sucked in his cheeks at my irreverence. Doctor Felman turned to look up at the ceiling.

"I am aware, Toby, that you are owed an explanation, but we really don't have time to give the same explanation twice."

"What do you mean, 'twice'?"

"I mean that there is someone else who is in exactly the same position as you and who is just as eager to hear why they have been brought here. We will wait until you are both in the room before we explain."

It was only then that I heard footsteps above my head. I was an expert in drawing pictures of people from their footsteps. This was someone light and frail . . . a child, maybe. Both Doctor Felman and Egil both looked up.

"Do the police know that they are both here?" Egil asked. Doctor Felman nodded his head, still staring at the ceiling. After the footsteps stopped, I thought I could hear someone crying. It was definitely a child.

I struggled out of the armchair and got to my feet.

"Who is that?"

"That, Toby, is your sister," Doctor Felman said. My mouth fell open.

"Not in the human sense of the word, but in the Fel sense. I fear she is rather upset. Perhaps, before we talk, it would be a good idea if you went up and said hello to her."

I climbed the stairs with a mixture of terror and curiosity. My coat was thin and lifeless. Doctor Felman led the way up the winding staircase with his flickering candle. We reached a door, and the doctor knocked.

"Emma? It's the boy we told you about."

"Go away or I will punch you on the nose again" came a female voice. She spoke with a strange accent. Doctor Felman quickly touched the tip of his nose, evidently remembering a blow he had received.

"Please, Emma, he really wants to talk to you."

"I don't want to talk to him. Leave me alone."

Doctor Felman sighed and, with great reluctance, took out a key and unlocked the door. He gestured to me to go in.

"I will leave you young people alone," he said wearily.

"She has been very upset ever since she arrived here."

Doctor Felman pinched the tip of his nose again, then forced the candle into my hand and urged me to go inside. He turned and walked back down the stairs, and I watched his huge shadow disappear. In the flickering light I hesitated for a long time before speaking to the half-open door.

"Hello," I said. "My name is Toby. Are you all right?"

There was no answer, but I heard a match being struck and a candle began to flicker inside.

"They said you're my sister, but I don't believe anything they say," I said, and after a pause I heard her say softly, "Neither do I."

I waited a long time in silence, then spoke to the door again. "How long have you been here?"

"Almost two weeks. I think."

"I just got here today. It's bloody weird, isn't it?"

I heard a bed creak, then heard her footsteps.

"Are you . . . human?" I asked.

"Yes. This isn't a dream, is it?" she said.

"No. I don't think it is, actually."

I could tell that she was struggling with the same questions that I was dealing with. I just had to see her. I was about to ask if I could enter, but she beat me to it. "Do you want to come in?"

I walked into the bedroom with the candle in my hand. Emma was about my age. She looked African, with fragile bones, like someone who'd never had enough to eat. Her hair was tied into a tight bun on the top of her head, fastened with two pencils. She wore a calico dress and was barefoot.

Her face was pretty but her eyes were full of suspicion as I stepped inside. She didn't look like my sister at all.

I decided to be the grown-up one and held out my hand to shake.

"Pleased to meet you, Emma."

Her hand felt like a bunch of dry twigs that might snap at any moment.

"If you are here to fool me, I will roll you in the mud like a little dog, that's for sure," she said. "And just because I'm skinny, don't think I'm weak. Ask that doctor out there. I cracked his nose pretty hard."

I blinked quickly and stepped back a little. The candlelight caught a moistness in her eyes, and I could see she was hiding her fear with tough words.

"I don't think you're weak," I said. "And why would I fool you? We're both in the same boat, aren't we?"

"What boat?"

"Oh . . . it's just an expression. It means we are both in the same trouble."

The word *trouble* made her clench her small fists. She stared at me for a little while longer, then gestured at a hardbacked chair near the lava fire.

"At home I would offer my guest porridge," she said,

"but here I can't because I don't have any."

She sat down on the bed and it creaked. I put my flickering candle on top of the fireplace and sat down uneasily on the hard-backed chair. There was an awkward silence for a few moments. I forced a smile.

"So where *is* home?" I asked.

"A village called Kapoeta. It is in southern Sudan. Where are you from?"

"Boring East Finchley, I'm afraid," I said, hoping that by mocking the name, I wouldn't get a lump in my throat when I said it.

"Where is that?"

"London. England . . . Europe."

"I know where England is," she said, and at last she smiled. Her eyes lit up. I saw she had a small gap between her front teeth that made her look daring somehow.

"And I know where Sudan is," I said. "I used to have a nurse from Kenya. She showed me maps."

"Were you sick?"

"Of the nurse?"

"No, I mean if you had a nurse you must have been sick."

"Oh yes. I was sick."

"What was wrong with you?"

I thought about telling her a lie. I already wanted to impress her, and I didn't want to admit I had once been nothing more than a motionless *thing* in a chair. But there was something about her that made lying seem . . . disgusting.

"I was paralyzed," I said. "Totally. I couldn't move anything. I could just blink and swallow. I used to live in a convent with nuns. But then . . ."

My voice trailed away because I didn't really know where to begin with the story of the last two days. Emma nodded her head as if she understood completely. She decided to change the subject.

"We had nuns come to us," she said. "In the refugee camps. They gave us food. Some of them we called Momma."

"You were a refugee?"

She nodded.

"From which war?"

"All of them," she said.

She stood up and closed the door. She then came to the fireside and warmed her hands. She really was terribly thin, and her skin had a grayness to it that made it look like dry paper. She could not have been more different from me, but we both already knew that we had a most extraordinary experience in common. I didn't know how long we would have together, so I was eager to swap stories and try to make sense of what was happening as quickly as possible.

"I was told they had brought me here for the reading of

a will," I said. "They said there was some great inheritance." She stared into the red glow of the fire.

"They told me that too," she said. "They told me I would meet my brother."

We glanced at each other and quickly looked away.

"Did Egil bring you here?"

"Who is Egil?"

"A boy."

"No, it was an old lady who brought me. She told me a story. . . ."

"What story?"

"It is too, too wicked." She shook her head quickly and fell silent. Then she suddenly turned to me and bumped her fists together. "You do understand, don't you, that we have been stolen by witches."

Her voice was very firm, and she glanced down at the floor as she said the word *witches*.

"I don't think there's such a thing as witches," I said.

"Then you don't believe your own eyes."

"They say they are Fels. . . ."

"That's just another word for the same thing. The old lady who brought me here said . . ." She stopped talking and blinked at the enormity of it all.

"Please, Emma. What did she say? We must tell each other everything."

Emma bumped her fists together again.

"The old lady who brought me here said that for seven years she had been . . . *a dog.*"

She checked to see if I would laugh, but instead I nodded.

"And Egil said he had been a cat for seven years," I said.

"There," she said in a whisper. "They are shape-shifters."

She could see from my face that I had no idea what a shape-shifter was.

"Shape-shifters are witches who can change their shapes into animals. They are the very worst sort of witches. In my country, if they are caught, they are killed with sticks and fire."

She studied me for a moment, then knelt down by the bed and lifted the thin mattress. From underneath it she produced a small golden dagger.

"I found this on the street when they brought me here," she whispered. "They don't know I have it. The first chance I get, I'm going to use it."

The small dagger trembled in her bony hand. It seemed like a feeble weapon to use against a whole world of enemies. She saw the look on my face and slowly lowered the dagger.

"I'm not sure a dagger will be much use," I said. "There are lots of them, and they seem to have all kinds of powers."

Emma put the dagger into her lap and stared at it. I realized I had just carelessly robbed her of her only hope.

"Emma, perhaps if we tell each other everything we know about what's happened to us, we might be able to come up with a plan of action," I said.

I thought I sounded quite grown-up, and Emma appeared to think so, too. She laid the golden dagger aside, and I pulled my chair closer to the fire. I told her the whole story of how Egil had brought me to Langjoskull. When I had finished, I urged her to tell me her own story from the very beginning.

"I was lying in the animal pen, waiting to die," Emma said, her eyes fixed on the lava fire. The red glow reflected in her eyes, and I was drawn into them.

"When they are sure you are going to die, they put you in with the animals so that the other children don't hear you calling out. That is how it is. . . ."

She clapped her hands together like someone making flat bread.

"When your time has come, it has come. So, so. One less mouth to feed. Life is hard."

Her voice was melodic when she spoke, and even when she was describing horrible things, there was light in her eyes.

"For example, my only brother died because he stepped

off a path. Just a little step like this"—Emma rose and took a sideways step, still staring at the lava—"and *boom*. Land mine. They graze goats by the paths to set them off, but the goats have learned to step over them. Not my brother. *Boom*."

I was horrified, but Emma bumped her fists together again. It seemed she made this gesture whenever she decided life had to go on. She sat down again.

"In my part of Sudan there has been war forever. I lived with my mother and my brother until he died on the land mine. My father was killed when I was small. . . ." Emma choked a little on her father's death but continued.

"When this all began, my mother wasn't happy because the men were back in the village. There was a cease-fire for just a few days. They all still had their AK47 guns, and eventually, if they kept on drinking, they would all kill each other, which was fine, but in the process they would kill the cows, which was not fine because in my village, cows are life."

Emma then put the back of her hand to her forehead and shook it as if her hand were suddenly scalding hot.

"It was then that I got the heat," she said.

"What heat?"

She turned to me and pushed her head forward on her neck and widened her eyes.

"Malaria," she said.

Emma turned and touched the pillow.

"I got hotter and hotter until there was no cool place in the bed. On the second night, I thought I saw my father's ghost. He wore a leopard skin over his shoulders and he told me that soon someone would come to save me."

She got to her feet again and stamped her foot hard on the floor. A small vase on the fireplace rattled.

"I will *not* die," she said firmly. "That was what I said to myself. But I just got hotter and hotter and shook and shook. . . ."

She stretched out her arms and they began to tremble. Emma's story was a song and also a dance, and I began to feel ashamed of the dry way I had told my own story.

"The village doctor gave me some roots cooked in condensed milk, but they made me sick." Emma pretended to retch a little. "So soon they said it was over. My mother didn't even weep as she carried me to the animal pen and laid me down in straw."

Emma raised her hand high above her head, then gently stoked the side of her face.

"My mother told me we would meet again. 'Oh, my poor kitten,' she said."

Emma clutched her arms to herself and began to shiver.

"Then it was already nighttime. It was cold and the moon was shining when I felt cold fingers on my spine."

Emma reached around and clutched the back of her own neck in exactly the way Egil had taken hold of my neck. "It was like ice."

"Yes," I whispered without thinking, remembering the icicle on my own neck.

"Then I saw a small woman with a red face and a green tunic smiling at me. She was not African, so I thought perhaps she was a nun. But the woman spoke my language, and she told me to get to my feet and walk because we had a long journey ahead of us. When I asked her who she was, she told me something that almost knocked me off my feet. . . ."

Emma reached over and picked up the golden dagger to protect herself from the truth she was about to tell.

"She said that she was Shinti," Emma said in a whisper.

"Who is Shinti?" I asked.

"For seven years I had a dog I called Shinti. She was my best friend in the whole village. She walked into my hut when I was small, and I had loved her ever since."

Emma brandished the dagger. "Now this old lady with the cold hands told me that *she* was Shinti. My eyes were suddenly like this knife. *Ready*. I knew that the shape-shifters had come for me, and I wanted to fight."

Emma let the dagger drop onto the bed and spoke in a weary voice. "But I was too weak to fight. The old lady was small, but she picked me up easily and carried me out of the village. 'Hoo, hoo,' the owls said, and the men fired guns from the beer compound. No one saw us in the moonlight."

"A full moon," I said quickly.

"Yes, but even so, no one could see us. She said there was a boat waiting for us and we had to be on board before the moon set."

"They use the moon, I think," I whispered, but Emma was lost in her story.

"We found a boat on a great river, and the woman covered me in her shawl so I could sleep. She told me she was a professor and that her name was Professor Elkkin. She also said she was a Keeper of the Arts. I thought perhaps she was a doctor and that she had given me medicine. She told me she was from Iceland and I liked the sound of it because it sounded so cold after I had been so hot with the disease. There was no engine on the boat, but Professor Elkkin told me she was going to row us to our destination."

Emma opened her hands out and began to gently row the air around her.

"The shawl had blue circles on it, like eyes. When the wind blew cold off the river, the shawl grew thicker and kept me warm."

"Did she row all the way to Iceland?" I asked, and Emma shook her head.

"When I awoke, we were in Egypt, so far from Sudan. We left the rowboat and stowed away on a cargo boat. Still I was so weak, I had to be carried. Sometimes I thought I was dead. Sometimes I *hoped* I *was* dead. But other times being with Professor Elkkin was just exactly like being with Shinti, and she made me feel better. I saw with my own eyes ships as big as the sky." Emma waved her arms at the ceiling as if watching a ship sail across the heavens.

"The crew of our boat was busy and the men didn't seem to notice the professor or me. Then one morning the ship was close to a mountain of ice. There were lots of birds shrieking and calling. By now I believed Professor Elkkin was kind even if she was a witch, and she was very scared that the birds knew where I was. I held her hand, and we jumped into the water and swam ashore. My shawl kept me warm and helped me to swim, even though I had never swum before."

Emma's body deflated a little, and she looked down at her bare feet.

"It felt so nice to swim. To push and push and feel my feet . . ." She hesitated.

"You became like a sea creature," I said, and she nodded just once.

"It was then I knew that I was becoming a witch too. And I felt . . . so ashamed."

Emma stood with her head bowed. I got up and took her hand and squeezed it.

"There is nothing to be ashamed of," I said. "We are children. We were both sick. What else could we have done?"

A single tear dropped onto the floor from Emma's eye. It glowed red in the lava light as it fell.

"You don't understand. It is worse for me because of my father." She looked up at me defiantly.

"When I was small, my father was killed by the people of my village because they said he was a shape-shifter. All my life I have fought anyone who has repeated that *lie*. I have fought them with my fists." Emma bumped her fists together.

"But now perhaps I must believe that it is true. Perhaps I am here because my father was a shape-shifter too."

Emma took a sharp breath. She reached under the single blanket that covered her bed and pulled out a beautiful shawl. I realized it was the shawl she had been given by Professor Elkkin. She wrapped it around her neck like a scarf. It had the most beautiful blue circles woven into it, and they *did* look like eyes. She used it to dry her tears delicately.

I had no tears to shed. I wouldn't have admitted it to Emma, but I was still happier to be here under the ice than back at home in my chair. I could walk and talk and fight if I had to. I let go of Emma's hand and decided to try to cheer her up.

"Did you really punch Doctor Felman on the nose?" I asked, and she nodded and at last laughed.

"He said he understood how I felt, and I didn't believe him. So—*whack*."

I laughed too and glanced at the closed door.

"Emma, there are two of us now," I said. "So we will be twice as strong. Let's go and ask some sensible questions."

9

When we went downstairs, Doctor Felman had been joined by an old woman who he introduced as Professor Elkkin. Emma nodded at her with a shy look. Egil had disappeared.

Professor Elkkin looked to be about as old as a mountain and as tough as a walrus hide, but she had the eyes of a little girl. They were blue and twinkly and darted around when she spoke, as if she were following the flight of invisible hummingbirds.

"Ah, children," Professor Elkkin said, and drew on her pipe. "Are you making company?"

"We have shared our stories, if that is what you mean," I said, and the tone of my voice made the doctor and the professor swap looks. I could see they were preparing for an ordeal.

"You must have lots of questions," Professor Elkkin said, and the doctor gestured for us to sit in the two empty chairs in front of the fire.

Emma and I looked at each other. Now that our moment had come, neither of us was sure who should go first. My first question was really rather insignificant, but it was one that had been bothering me ever since I met Emma.

"How come we can all understand each other?" I said. "Emma tells me she can't speak English, and I don't speak her language, but we can talk to each other. And all of you seem to me to be speaking English, but Emma thinks you're speaking her language."

"You are speaking Dinka," Emma said firmly.

The doctor was pleased by the question, and he puffed himself up and stared at the ceiling, a physical assertion to the professor that this question was *his* territory.

"A very interesting point," he said, and folded his fingers together. "The truth is that none of us are speaking in any of those languages. We are all speaking Fellish."

"Dinka," Emma said again.

Doctor Felman glanced at her, then continued. "Fellish is . . . something more than a language. You will come to learn that fundamentally, all the Fellish arts are to do with naming. That is to say, the isolation of external phenomena as discrete entities through the attachment of symbols . . . in this case, words. . . ."

Emma and I glanced at each other, and I realized she had no idea what he was talking about either. Doctor Felman looked rather deflated when he saw our blank expressions.

"What he's trying to tell you is," Professor Elkkin said, "it's done by magic."

Doctor Felman tapped his pipe as if her interruption irritated him, but I could tell that nothing Professor Elkkin could ever do would really irritate him. I guessed that they had a very strong connection to each other.

The professor peered at Emma. "Emma? Are you happy with that explanation?"

Emma blinked in the red light of the lava fire.

"How can I be happy about anything here when I am imprisoned?"

Emma had a way of making simple statements sound like mighty winds, or earthquakes, or volcanic eruptions. Professor Elkkin reached out for Emma's hand to comfort her. Doctor Felman turned to me.

"Do you feel the same, Toby?" he asked, and I could feel his eyes searching behind my own. He seemed to know already that I was happier to be here than Emma was, but I didn't want to betray Emma by admitting it.

I wiped a cold droplet from my nose with my sleeve.

"Just give us some answers," I said firmly.

Doctor Felman nodded once, then crossed the room to an old trunk that stood near the door underneath a woven rug. He used a key from inside his shirt to open it, and from inside he took a large oil painting of a young Fel with handsome eyes and flowing brown hair that curled around his chin. He angled the painting into the red light of the lava fire.

"Do you see any resemblance?" Doctor Felman said softly.

"To who?" I asked.

"To you," Professor Elkkin said with a smile. "And to dear Emma."

Emma and I looked at each other. We were so dissimilar, it was impossible to imagine how *anyone* could look like both of us. Then I looked back to the painting, and the red light of the lava flickered on the face of the noble Fel. Suddenly the eyes on the canvas had the moist sparkle that I had seen in Emma's eyes. There actually *was* a resemblance, but it was more than physical. It was a similarity in the feeling behind the expression.

Emma was staring at my eyes, and I could tell that she had seen a resemblance between *my* face and the face in the painting. I had seen that face only in the mirror that Sister Mary held up for me when she cut my hair. My features had been slack and expressionless, but any life had always been in my eyes. Perhaps I saw a faint reflection of that life in the eyes on the canvas. Doctor Felman held the portrait up to the light a little longer, obviously pleased with the effect it was having.

"This, my dear children, is a painting of your great-great-great-great-great-great-great-great-*great*-grandfather. And even that is missing another nineteen *great*s for the purpose of brevity."

The eyes in the painting seemed to smile at me. I could feel a great kindness there, and they drew me in just as Emma's eyes had done when she'd told me her story.

"You mean . . . we are descended from a Fel?" I asked, and Professor Elkkin clapped her hands together twice.

"Not just any Fel," she said with delight.

"This is a painting of the great Will Wolfkin," Doctor Felman said. "He was king of the Fel for over two thousand glorious years."

Doctor Felman rested the painting against a table, carefully wiping dust from the edge of it.

"This is a painting of him as a young man," he said. "It was painted shortly before he became king, which was, of course, one hundred years after the death of his great-uncle, King Bearkin the Second, who ruled for one thousand and eight years following the reign of—"

Professor Elkkin jutted her chin and scolded Doctor Felman. "Enough," she said. "These poor children are not here for a history lesson."

"Indeed, indeed," Doctor Felman replied, and for the first time I realized that both the doctor and the professor were very nervous and anxious to present their story in a way we would comprehend. Professor Elkkin got to her feet and took up the tale.

"Will Wolfkin was the first king of the Fel to come to power after the Great Separation," she said, and she peered at us both.

"They are human," Doctor Felman whispered. "They don't even know what the Great Separation is."

Professor Elkkin thought for a moment. "You are right, of course. I often forget how little the humans remember. . . ."

"Perhaps a history lesson is not such a bad idea after all," Doctor Felman murmured.

"Perhaps," Professor Elkkin concurred.

At that moment Emma pulled one of the pencils out of her hair and snapped it in front of her face.

"That was my patience," she said. "It just snapped." She tossed the two ends of the pencil onto the lava, and they burst into flames. "Now please get to the point."

Doctor Felman looked at Emma with wonder. "So much like the great king in spirit as well as looks," he said softly.

Professor Elkkin reached for a shelf and pulled down a blackened kettle with a gold handle.

"Doctor Felman, why don't I make some tea for us all while you tell these good children who they really are."

"The Fel are a species that inhabited the earth long before humans beings existed," Doctor Felman said as the kettle began to hiss on the lava bricks. "Our chronicles tell us that humans came from the south. Now we Fels live in a place where no humans bother us. Here under the ice of Iceland."

Doctor Felman offered us both his pipe to puff, but Emma and I refused. The smell of the tobacco was sweet and reminded me of Sister Mary's smell on Sunday after mass.

"Humans now remember us only in legends and fairy tales. But many, many centuries ago, humans and Fels used to trade with each other. They even shared festivals together at midsummer and midwinter. They also . . . occasionally . . . fell in love with each other. And when they fell in love, then sometimes . . . naturally . . ."

Professor Elkkin giggled as she adjusted the kettle on the heat. "I'm sure they are old enough to know how babies come about," she said. Doctor Felman looked a little embarrassed and puffed out some smoke to hide behind.

"Such relations between human and Fel were by no means common, but they happened," Doctor Felman said.

"Usually there was no consequence; but sometimes, if the male was Fel and the woman human, children were born. As a result there are a number of humans alive now who have inherited tiny amounts of Fel blood from those times."

I already had lots of questions, and the more they talked, the more the questions piled up, like snow before a plow. But Doctor Felman was in his stride now, and I didn't dare interrupt. Professor Elkkin poured the hot water from the kettle into the teapot, and Emma placed four cups in front of the fire without taking her eyes off Doctor Felman. Emma seemed to be a very practical person.

"The Fel tended to live in the deepest part of the forests, in the rocky places, in caverns. We were good diviners and miners and had a nose for finding gold. We were also good herbalists and could cure many things human doctors couldn't. The humans, on the other hand, had an ability to fashion tools that the Fel needed. So the Fel and the humans helped each other. But after many years of peaceful coexistence, the Great Separation began."

I glanced over Doctor Felman's shoulder at the portrait of Will Wolfkin. In that uncertain red light it was possible to imagine many things, but I was sure that his face was now urging me to listen.

"Humans chose to devote themselves to . . . their inventions. We Fels, on the other hand, were busy with our *arts*, which you may also call *magic*. But there came a time when there was an imbalance. The humans became more and more greedy for our knowledge. In particular, our use of herbs to cure sickness and also our ability to shift."

Professor Elkkin was pouring the tea, and she spilled a little of it when Doctor Felman said the word *shift*. She looked up at Emma and obviously knew already how Emma felt about shifting. Emma simply narrowed her eyes. Professor Elkkin pushed a cup into Emma's hands, and she huddled around it.

"Humans began to kidnap Fels to make them share their magical secrets. They used their weapons and their traps to hold us. After many years of this, the Fel held a great council and decided to stop trading with humans. The humans became angry, and soon there was all-out war."

I sipped my tea for the first time and almost choked. It tasted horribly bitter and made my mouth feel numb. My spluttering made Doctor Felman stop for a moment.

"Fellish tea is an acquired taste," he said softly. I noticed that Emma was sipping her tea without a problem. Doctor Felman and Professor Elkkin noticed too, and it seemed to please them.

"The war between human and Fel was brutal and bloody," Doctor Felman continued. "Finally the Fel decided to end the bloodshed by migrating. In Iceland in those days there were no humans. Only fat gray seals to eat and glaciers to hide under. The Thrull lived here already, but they were our cousins and welcomed us."

Doctor Felman's eyes glistened. He lost some of that history-professor tone of voice and spoke as if suddenly imparting urgent news. "It was during that great exodus to Iceland all those years ago that *your* story begins."

The tobacco in his pipe glowed red hot because he was puffing so hard.

"One of the boats leaving Scotland was captained by the young Fel of noble birth named Will Wolfkin. It had already been agreed that he would become king of the Fel when we reached the new, promised land. But his boat was caught in a storm, and unusually for a Fel, he was shipwrecked."

"It must have been the Jerlamar's will," Professor Elkkin added confidently.

"Will Wolfkin swam ashore on a lonely island somewhere west of Orkney. A human fisherman lived there with his daughter. Her name was Gwendoline McShaffrey. She found the poor Fel washed up on the beach, barely alive, and she secretly nursed him to health in a cave with milk and herrings she stole from her father. She also fell in love with him. And he fell in love with her."

Emma had finished her tea and poured herself another cup. I was still recovering from taking just one sip. Already I was getting the uncomfortable feeling that Emma was more at home in this world than I was, even if she was less happy to be here.

"Soon Gwendoline McShaffrey was pregnant," Doctor Felman said. "Our chronicles say this was one of the last times in history that a Fel and a human mixed in this way. After the child was born, Will Wolfkin had to continue on his way to Iceland because the Fel needed him. He was forced to leave Gwendoline to bring up the half-Fel child alone. And in all the long years he reigned over the Fel, he never told a living soul about the child who had been born. . . ."

Doctor Felman was hit by a memory. He whispered, ". . . Until the night he died."

I could feel Will Wolfkin's eyes drilling into my head from inside the painting. Outside, the wind howled and the lava in the streets glowed more brightly. The collar of my coat bristled.

"You two children are here in Langjoskull because you are the only living descendants of Gwendoline McShaffrey and King Will Wolfkin," Doctor Felman said.

"And therefore you are part of a very important family," Professor Elkkin added.

The word *family* echoed in my mind. I had always been alone in this world, someone who had simply *appeared* inconveniently as the result of a clerical error. The idea that I had a family of any kind hit me hard. Doctor Felman appeared to understand the effect the word would have, and he was in no hurry to interrupt my thoughts.

In some ways I was overjoyed at the idea that I had a family, but like most people who have hard lives, I kick good news around and pick at it for a while to see if it's real.

"How can you be sure who we are if everything happened thousands of years ago?" I asked.

"A thousand years is nothing to a Fel," Doctor Felman explained. "I myself am three thousand nine hundred and eighty-nine years old. Egil is my youngest grandson and he has just turned five hundred. And besides, through two dozen centuries, you still have his eyes."

Doctor Felman turned to gaze at the painting of Will Wolfkin.

"I knew your ancestor very well. For many years I was his teacher of Fel magic and many other things. That is what I am, Toby. I am a teacher of Fellish magic. In my world we are known as Keepers of the Arts."

After a moment Doctor Felman turned directly to me alone. "It may help you to know that it is almost certainly because of your Fel blood that you were born with your unfortunate condition," he said quickly, to tidy the matter away.

"You mean my stillness?" I said softly. In my head I had always called my condition my "stillness." It was much more comforting than the medical version. Doctor Felman nodded gently.

"When Fels and humans mix, there is always something . . . *remarkable* about their descendants, though no one knows why. Sometimes it's good, sometimes it's bad. Often there is the loss of power in the limbs, or madness. But sometimes, Toby, *sometimes* the part-Fel child is brilliant beyond all explanation. If the beautiful Fel powers are stoked up, the child will create things that no pure human could ever hope to match."

Doctor Felman leaned on the fireplace and spoke in reverent tones. "After years of research I am convinced that none other than Wolfgang Amadeus Mozart was descended from a Fel. Also Lord Byron, William Blake, and—"

"All totally unproven," Professor Elkkin said, her voice ringing like a bell. The interruption irritated Doctor Felman, and the look on his face made me smile. He fussed with his pipe, which was now smoked out. I realized I was beginning to quite like these two old eccentrics.

"What about Stephen Hawking?" I said.

Doctor Felman refilled his pipe, lit it, and puffed. "I'd say he's one of ours, wouldn't you?" he said, glancing at Professor Elkkin.

Emma wasn't so easily charmed by them. She got to her feet.

"And because we are descended from this Fel person, we are due some great inheritance?" she said. Doctor Felman nodded.

"So what exactly is it that we are supposed to inherit?" she asked.

Doctor Felman suddenly hitched up his trousers and stepped into the fireplace. He then ducked under the chimney breast and began to climb. We could hear him gasping and struggling to get his footing. Professor Elkkin chuckled at his efforts as Emma and I watched.

The doctor reappeared with his face blackened and his clothes covered in lava dust. He had to arch his back to flip himself out of the chimney without putting his feet into the hot lava.

When he dusted himself off, I saw that he had retrieved what appeared to be a tube of walrus hide, tied with red sinew. He took it over to the oak table, where the portrait still smiled. Professor Elkkin lit two candles and urged Emma and me to come to the table.

Doctor Felman then very solemnly closed the curtains on all the windows and locked the door before beginning to untie the binding. He took out a walrus-skin scroll. The candle flames burned more evenly without the drafts.

"This document is King Will Wolfkin's last will and testament, written on the night that he died."

With the bindings undone, Doctor Felman began to very carefully unroll the parchment. The stiff hide crackled as he did.

"I have kept it hidden here because there are many powerful Fels who would wish to destroy it and its message."

Professor Elkkin used a set of golden jugs decorated with black wolf heads to keep it from rolling up again.

"I was the king's closest adviser," Doctor Felman said, "and on that final day, he sent everyone else from the room and asked me to bring him a quill, ink, and parchment."

Doctor Felman held his breath as he lifted the candle closer. We all instinctively leaned into the light. The portrait of Will Wolfkin seemed to be giving us his attention too. The walrus skin was ornately decorated, with depictions of wolves of all shapes and sizes all around the borders, some howling, some sleeping, some suckling. At the top of the scroll there was some kind of royal stamp that showed a wolf and a walrus at odds, and at the bottom there was a red wax seal, stamped with the face of a bear.

Doctor Felman put on a pair of golden round-rimmed spectacles. The royal seal and howling wolves were reflected in their lenses.

"'This is the will of King Will Wolfkin . . . ,'" he read aloud, but he evidently wasn't happy with the way he'd begun, so he cleared his throat and repeated himself even more grandly.

This is the will of King Will Wolfkin . . . and these words are written half by me and half by death itself.

A wagon and horses passed outside the window, and Doctor Felman looked up, ready to roll up the parchment if the hooves and wheels should stop. Professor Elkkin had her hand over her mouth. When the wheels rolled on, Doctor Felman continued:

All through my long life, I have kept a secret . . .

Doctor Felman was breathing hard, speaking each word as if it were precious.

When I was a young prince, at the time of the Great Separation, I was shipwrecked . . . and I met a human woman.

The candles flickered. Doctor Felman glanced at me and at the portrait.

Gwendoline was a kind woman, and she bore me a child in her human vessel on the Isle of the

Sunset. It is now three thousand years since that child was born. But upon my death, it is my wish that if any living descendants of our union can be found, then it is they who must be considered as the rightful heirs to the throne of Langjoskull. . . . And they must be considered before all other claimants and in preference to all pure-born Fel, no matter how noble their birth. . . .

Doctor Felman looked up from the parchment. Professor Elkkin urged him to continue with her eyes, as if the next part were the most important.

I wish this to happen because the Great Separation between Fel and human has gone on for too long. It is time for us all to come together in peace once more. To achieve this, I decree that the next ruler of Langjoskull should be part human and part Fel in order that our precious, shared earth . . .

The words had run out halfway down the page. Doctor Felman put the tip of his finger on the final word. "King Will Wolfkin died as he wrote the word *earth*."

I stared down at the royal wax seal on the parchment, then looked up at Doctor Felman. His face was filled with glory.

"Though the great king died almost one hundred years ago, it seems to me like only yesterday."

I glanced at the portrait of Will Wolfkin, looking so young and alive.

"He has been dead a hundred years?" I said with disbelief.

"It is Fel law that after any king dies, there is one hundred years of mourning before the heir takes the throne," Doctor Felman said. "It is now almost one hundred years since our great king died, and that is why the succession is now such a burning issue. The period of mourning comes to an end very soon. Just a matter of weeks."

Doctor Felman glanced at Professor Elkkin, who nodded quickly.

"Unfortunately, in the hundred years since our king died, not everyone has observed the law," she said. A spooked horse whinnying outside made Doctor Felman and Professor Elkkin look sharply at each other. Doctor Felman began to carefully roll up the scroll.

"Helva Gullkin is King Will Wolfkin's cousin and his closest Fel relative," Doctor Felman said. "Ever since the king died, Gullkin has been agitating to take the throne, and he has already begun to act like the new king," Doctor Felman said.

"He is pompous and vain and warlike," Professor Elkkin added, removing some of the golden jugs from the corners of the scroll. "He has moved into Will Wolfkin's royal palace, which is against the law, and he defiles it with his feasts and revelry."

Doctor Felman began to tie the sinew around the scroll once again with shaking hands. "What is worse, he enforces laws preventing the general populace from practicing the Fellish arts. The schools of magic are all closed. We Keepers are now allowed to teach only Gullkin and his henchmen how to shift. He wants to keep all the powers of the arts for his own household and his soldiers to prevent rebellion." With the scroll rolled up, he put it back into its walrus skin.

"The only thing that now stands between Langjoskull and an abominable tyranny is the Swearing of the Oaths."

Doctor Felman and Professor Elkkin both looked up at the same time, apparently checking the effect of the words *Swearing of the Oaths*. They looked quietly relieved when it was obvious that the words meant nothing to us. However, we could see that Doctor Felman felt he had said too much. Emma was onto it like a cat onto a mouse.

"What is the Swearing of the Oaths?" she asked.

Doctor Felman cleared his throat and glanced at

Professor Elkkin. "Perhaps you will explain," he said, and with the scroll under his arm he scrambled up the chimney like a cat with its tail on fire. Professor Elkkin took a breath and glanced at the portrait of Will Wolfkin.

"It is Fel law that when the hundred years of mourning is over, the new king or queen of Langjoskull is announced on a day we call the Swearing of the Oaths."

Doctor Felman reappeared with soot on his face. He mumbled a little exultation.

"On that day," Professor Elkkin continued, "all those who have a claim to the throne come together in front of the entire population and . . . *decide* . . . who has the strongest case to become the new ruler."

She hopped over the word *decide* as if it were a muddy ditch. With the ditch successfully cleared, Doctor Felman took up the explanation.

"As things stand, Helva Gullkin would take the throne without legal challenge. But on the day of the Swearing, our plan is to produce the will of Will Wolfkin, read out its message, and then present you two to the populace."

They both turned to us and saw us blinking with disbelief. Perhaps they had rehearsed this moment so often, they had forgotten how profoundly absurd it would sound. After a few moments of silence, Emma spoke up.

"You mean you want *us* two children to be your . . . king and queen?"

Professor Elkkin and Doctor Felman both nodded in unison. Emma laughed out loud. Doctor Felman suddenly looked angry.

"My dear girl, it has taken the professor and me almost seventy years of hard work to follow the blood line of Gwendoline and Will Wolfkin down the ages, using only human records and parish registers."

"I am not your dear *anything*," Emma said with one fist clenched. Doctor Felman met her stare.

"Professor Elkkin had to travel all over Africa for years and years to find you—"

The professor interrupted, trying to calm the doctor with interesting facts. "Emma, did you know you are descended from a certain Scottish soldier called McShaffrey?" she said quickly. "He traveled to Africa with the British army in 1887 and . . ."

Doctor Felman waved the professor into silence and turned to me.

"And *your* line was no easier to trace, with many oddities and gypsies and rogues," he said. "But we worked and worked and found you both just in the nick of time. We then spent seven years preparing you for this moment in magical ways. . . ."

"And I suppose we should be grateful," Emma hissed.

She had no fear of Doctor Felman's piercing stare. Professor Elkkin stroked the doctor's shoulder, and her touch made him take a deep breath and calm down.

"Children, we should explain," Professor Elkkin said. "We don't expect you to stay as king and queen for more than just that one day."

"Nor would we want you to," Doctor Felman said sourly, turning to face the portrait of Will Wolfkin to restore his mood.

"You are here purely to perform a ritual," the professor continued. "When the Swearing of the Oaths is over and you have been declared rightful heirs to the throne, you will immediately hand all the power you have inherited over to a new, free, democratic Fel parliament."

Doctor Felman repeated the word *parliament* as if just saying the word relieved some terrible inner pain.

"It was always King Will Wolfkin's wish that whoever succeeded him should introduce a democratic parliament," the doctor said. "We spoke of it many times during his life. If he had not died halfway through writing it, he would have mentioned the parliament in his will."

The doctor and the professor both began to speak with glory in their voices.

"The Fel parliament will take over the running of Langjoskull and will do it with justice and consideration," he said, "and you two will return to the human world, taking your ceremonial titles with you, since your work here will be done."

"Freedom will be restored under the ice," Professor Elkkin said with a finger raised to the heavens.

"And if you are agreeable," Doctor Felman added, "you two may act as messengers to the human race on behalf of the Fel, helping bring about an end to the Great Separation and thereby fulfilling another of King Will Wolfkin's dying wishes."

For a moment both Doctor Felman and Professor Elkkin stared up at the ceiling with the same smile, apparently having forgotten that we were even in the room. Perhaps if you keep a grand plan in your mind for long enough, it begins to seem inevitable. From the outside it seemed *incredible*.

"And what happens if we don't *want* to help you?" Emma asked.

It took a while for Doctor Felman and Professor Elkkin to descend from whichever heavenly cloud they were sitting on.

"Don't *want to?*" Doctor Felman repeated with some disbelief in his voice.

"This stupid bird person Helva Seagull or Seava Gullkin, or whatever his name is, isn't going to give up his throne without a fight," Emma said. "And he already knows we're here."

"Your existence is known to him, but your location is a secret," Doctor Felman said quickly.

"And if he finds us he'll kill us," I said. "It doesn't look as if you have any big armies of tough soldiers around here to protect us. So what's to stop us from turning around and saying . . ."

Emma finished my sentence.

". . . we want to go home."

Doctor Felman glanced at Professor Elkkin, who nodded firmly. "We have of course thought through this possibility," she said.

"And there are some things that we can offer you as rewards in return for your cooperation," Doctor Felman added. "To begin with—" There was a dramatic pause. Doctor Felman allowed Professor Elkkin to fire the cannon he had loaded.

"Gold," she said with a wicked twinkle in her eye.

"You will have noticed that there is an enormous amount of gold here," Doctor Felman continued. "Gold to us is like iron is to humans. It runs in giant seams under the Blue Volcano to the east. If you agree to help us, you can take as much of it away with you as you wish when this business is finished."

He turned to Emma. "In your homeland this amount of gold would buy food and clothes for your people. Your whole village . . . your whole tribe would never have to be hungry ever again," he said. "You could build schools and hospitals and dig wells." Emma looked up at him, and I saw her big eyes softening in the doctor's hypnotic gaze.

Then Doctor Felman turned to me. "And if gold is not

enough to induce you, we are also offering to give you the most thorough and comprehensive education in . . . the forbidden Fellish arts."

There was now a darkness in Doctor Felman's eyes and I began to feel their swirling power.

"In these exceptional circumstances, and given your ancestry, we will break the law that forbids the teaching of the arts to part humans. We will give you both abilities you have never dreamed of. Even you, Toby, through all your battles on the moon with Egil, could never have conceived of the powers you will be given. You will fly, you will read minds, you will acquire magical weapons of enormous strength, you will escape whole dreary universes, you will . . . *transform yourselves from within.*"

I could see that Emma had become a little overwhelmed by the talk of gold, just as I was becoming intoxicated by the idea of flying and fighting magical battles. We both stood speechless as Doctor Felman came close and put a hand on each of our shoulders.

"What I am saying is that we are offering you both nothing less than *everything you ever dreamed of,*" he said, "in return for fulfilling our own dreams."

He spoke with the authority of certain knowledge, like someone who knew our private dreams intimately. The lava fire hissed on a stray moth, and he lowered his voice to a whisper.

"And add to that, children, the fact that we Fels are your true family."

I thought something inside me was going to burst. Doctor Felman took his hands from our shoulders and stepped back. Emma and I were left dazed, hardly knowing where we were.

There was a brief moment of silence before I asked my final question. "Why have you chosen us?" I said. "If our ancestor was born thousands of years ago, there must be millions of descendants."

Professor Elkkin shook her head. "When Fel and human mix, the family tree is not like an ordinary tree," she said. "It is like a tree that has been struck by lightning."

"Only the rarest buds grow to bloom on its dark branches," Doctor Felman added. "So . . . children . . . when you have time to reflect on all this, I'm sure you will agree to stay and help us."

Neither Emma nor I made a sound. I wanted to sit alone with Emma in a quiet place and go through all that we had been told. But then I heard footsteps coming fast. I knew from experience that these were the footsteps of someone who was scared.

I turned toward the window sharply, and Doctor Felman read my thoughts. Suddenly there was a heavy thud against the door. Someone was breathing hard and scratching at the door with their fingernails. Doctor

Felman ran to the door and unlocked it. Egil fell inside, his body shaking with anxiety.

"Egil, what is it?" Doctor Felman said. Egil took a huge breath.

"Helva Gullkin's police are coming and they're looking for Toby and Emma!"

10

Emma and I stood frozen in the darkness for a long time. We were in the cellar of Doctor Felman's house, and the only light was the glow coming down from the street through the ventilation grill. We could hear voices in the living room and furniture being scraped along the floor as the policemen began to search the house. Then we heard the heavy thump of boots on the stairs. The voices became louder, and occasionally we would hear Professor Elkkin or Doctor Felman speaking softly, trying to calm the policemen down.

Egil had pushed a heavy bookcase up against the door of the cellar after we had hidden. Now we heard the same bookcase being shoved aside, and the voices outside became twice as loud.

"Why has this door been concealed?" a policeman said.

Emma and I instinctively held hands in the darkness.

"It is where I keep valuable books," Doctor Felman said. "On the dark side you have to hide your valuable things."

"Give me the key."

"I really can't quite remember where I put it . . . ," Doctor Felman said, and then we heard a heavy kick against the cellar door. There were a dozen blows, and I knew that with a few more it would fly off its hinges.

Emma reached into her calico dress. She produced her tiny golden dagger.

"I'm ready for you," she said.

At that moment, my fur coat came to life. I had forgotten about it as we sat by the fire because it had become as light as cotton. Now it shivered and began to ripple all around my body, growing back into the mighty fur it had originally been.

Emma's shawl responded at the same time, slithering around her neck like a reptile. In the half-light I saw that the pattern on the shawl resembled the tips of peacock feathers. The shawl smothered the dagger in her hand and seemed to be telling her it would be no use. As the shawl began to move, I could swear that some of the "eyes" in the pattern began to blink.

The left sleeve of my coat began to twist itself around

my arm, holding it in a tight grip. I knew the coat was telling me to turn to the left. I looked across the cellar toward the far wall, which was carved from volcanic rock. The policemen were now almost through the door. I ran toward the rock wall, and since I had Emma's hand in mine, she was dragged along with me.

I punched the wall with the hardened fur around my arm. The first shaft of light became visible through the disintegrating cellar door. I saw a policeman's boot kicking at splinters. I reached to my waist and put my hand on the handle of my sword. I hardly had to make a wish. We needed to get out of there.

The blade began to glow with a soft blue light that was also like a gentle hum. I knew I had to use the sword to hack against the wall. At the same time, the blue eyes on Emma's shawl began to glow with a similar blue light. The eyes blinked, and Emma hissed. "The eyes can see a doorway."

The lights from the eyes and the blue light from my sword concentrated into a beam that illuminated a small area on the wall. I struck the wall where the light was brightest, and there was a shower of rock. We both saw a handle.

I grabbed the handle and pulled with all my might, but it wouldn't budge.

Emma grabbed the handle too. As we pulled, the first policeman appeared in the shattered doorway. I turned and saw that the roof of the cellar was held up by a wooden beam. I swung my sword around, slicing through the beam. Plaster and bricks began to crash down, and I thought we were all going to be buried. However, Emma's shawl billowed up and formed a kind of umbrella that was as hard as a tortoiseshell over our heads.

Debris rained down on our covering. Then my sword took over once again, and with four lightning-fast strokes I scored out the edges of the hidden door as if the wall and door were a child's drawing. I put my sword back in its sheath, and Emma and I grabbed the door handle again and began to pull. Bricks and wood were falling in an avalanche behind us. Her arms may have been skinny, but she had the strength of terror, and between us we managed to pull the door open. There was only darkness on the other side, but we had no choice. First Emma and then I scrambled through the opening. Her shawl sucked itself up into something no larger than a silk scarf and flew back around her neck.

I looked back to see a fat policeman in a green uniform and a pyramid helmet covered in dust and debris rolling forward into the darkness of the cellar. Once we were on the other side, I pulled the door closed behind us.

The darkness now was total, and in the confusion Emma and I fell backward away from the door. We immediately began to slide down a steep slope, something like a water chute at an amusement park but without the water and without the amusement.

We picked up speed but still couldn't see where we were going, banging our knees and elbows against crunchy volcanic rock. It was hard to tell up from down, but after a while I sensed that gravity was now working to slow us down rather than speed us up. Emma and I tumbled and rolled on for a few more moments, then came to rest. The incline was more shallow now, a manageable gradient, but there was still no light.

"Emma, are you all right?" I asked.

"Just a few cuts," she said, and we reached out for each other. I felt softness, then the bones of her fingers. We clutched each other tight.

"Where do you think we are?" she whispered.

"I'd say we rolled a long way down."

We used our hands to feel our way along the rough-hewn walls of the tunnel. The gradient became more gentle and we could walk easily, though the lack of light was unbearable. Emma and I kept talking to each other, saying pointless things, just to be sure that the other was still there.

"Back at home when there was no moon, I used to be good at walking in the dark," she said softly. "Perhaps I should lead."

I didn't like the idea of putting Emma ahead of me and replied with a firm voice. "It's okay, I think I know where I'm—" I banged my nose on hard rock. The tunnel had reached a dead end.

We felt all along the rock face in front of us, but there seemed to be no way through. I scraped away at the rock with my fingers and could feel volcanic dust crumbling in my hand. Suddenly the air felt hot and stale. The walls seemed to be closing in, and I heard the unmistakable sound of bubbling water, an obscene gurgling sound somewhere to our right. I had begun to feel my way toward it when without warning I was plunged into scalding hot water.

"What's happening?" Emma cried. "Are you okay?"

My coat immediately wrapped itself around me to protect me from the heat. I was now floating on top of a bubbling cauldron of water with my face pointed upward. I could feel bubbles bursting all around me, and the gas they emitted smelled of rotten eggs. My magical coat soon became almost like a raft, and I managed to call out to Emma.

"I think it's some kind of underground hot spring," I said. "This place is full of them."

In the darkness the feel of floating on the water was almost pleasant. I had no idea what was rock, what was air, and what was water. Then, as I tried to find a ledge to haul myself out, I saw a glimmer of light reflecting on the water a few feet away from me.

I used my feet to paddle toward the light, my coat now slick as seal fur. When I looked up, I saw a circle of yellow light high above my head. I was at the bottom of a deep well, the surface a hundred feet above me.

"Emma, come quick," I said, knowing that any light was better than darkness.

"The water's too hot," she said quickly, and I realized she had already dipped her fingers into the spring.

"Wrap your shawl around yourself and you'll be okay," I said.

I waited a few moments, then heard Emma slipping into the water. She yelped and for one horrible moment I thought she might scald, but soon her shawl had worked its magic and she floated to my side on a dazzling raft made from bright blue eyes. Her face was peeping at me through the steam. We even smiled at each other. Then I pointed upward toward the light.

"Too far to climb," she said.

Suddenly the water around us erupted in a large bubble, like a burp inside a giant stomach. The air that emerged from the water smelled even more strongly of rotten eggs. Then there was another burp, even bigger, and then another. Finally the air was boiling with a dozen bubbles.

A horrible realization struck me. This wasn't just a hot spring.

Suddenly a jet of water drove us both up and up toward the light at terrifying speed. We clung on to each other for dear life, my coat and Emma's shawl swelling around us to protect us from the rough rock walls of the geyser. Since we were at the top of the jet of water, our upturned faces were saved from the scalding spray, and instead of being afraid we both whooped with exhilaration at the feeling of being shot out of the earth like two pebbles from a volcano.

The few seconds we spent at the mercy of the water seemed to last an age, but soon we were flung out into the daylight and tossed in opposite directions to splash into the warm sulfurous pool at the base of the spray. I was submerged for a long time by the cascading water, but when the geyser eruption finally died away, I floated gently to the surface. The water was warm and strangely calming. Emma was sweeping her wet hair from her face and blowing water from the tip of her nose.

The moment our eyes met, we both burst out laughing. But when we looked around and saw where we were, we fell silent.

There was one shaft of sunlight coming at a low angle from a distant ice window, but it was much thinner than the light I'd seen above the marketplace. I knew straightaway that we were now deep in the dark side.

All around there were ramshackle dwellings made from pumice and shale, some arranged as longhouses. Washing hung between the houses, and hundreds of Thrull children played around the lava flows that edged the streets.

Emma and I stayed in the warm water and put our elbows on the bank, studying the throng of Thrulls going about their business in the street. Neither Emma nor I spoke. The

Thrulls I'd seen in town looked to be heavy, ungainly creatures, and when they walked the ground shook. Here they seemed to move more elegantly, and their expressions were more benign.

Suddenly there was a deep, gravelly voice behind us. "Who in the name of Jerlamar are you?"

A Thrull was standing at the edge of the geyser pool, his fists clenched, his jaw jutting forward.

"We got lost," I stuttered, dripping warm water. "We fell down a hole."

The Thrull studied us and sniffed the air. He analyzed the smell for a long time.

"You have come from Doctor Felman's house," he said with certainty. "I smell the idealism and the books. And you are human."

We both nodded.

"Come," he said. "There are no secrets here anymore. The police will be here soon."

The Thrull introduced himself as Arthur. He said he had been given the name by his new master, who was a Fel blacksmith on the light side. He took us into his home and boiled some sulfurous water on a lava stove. A few minutes later he gave us a cup of bitter Thrull tea that was even more disgusting than Fel tea. Even so, Emma drank it without a word while I secretly tipped mine onto the dirt floor.

Arthur's home was a tiny rectangle of shale enclosed by lava bricks. There were a couple rooms and only half a roof, and the spray from distant geysers meant that there was a constant shower of fine warm water falling onto his poor collection of belongings. He had a bed made from pumice and a boulder for a table. He appeared to live alone. Even in the few minutes I'd known him, I sensed that he was not used to visitors—and not in any hurry to become used to them, either.

However, he began to break warm bread for us, which he took from an oven chiseled into a lava flow. It tasted of grit and smoke, but Emma and I ate it anyway so as not to be rude.

"So you two *kids* are the great hope of the Blue Volcanoes," Arthur said with a snort as he tore at his hunk of bread with sharp teeth.

"The blue *what?*" Emma asked, and I thought I saw a look of pity pass fleetingly over Arthur's face.

"They haven't even told you who they are?" he said, and swallowed a dry lump of bread, which he washed down with bitter tea. He got to his feet and poured himself some more.

"The Blue Volcanoes are Langjoskull's most terrifying revolutionary organization," he said with a huge dollop of irony. "Assuming, of course, that you are terrified of intellectuals, professors, academics, and teachers."

He came back to the table with more tea.

"They dream of a Fel parliament. They dream of freedom and liberation for themselves and for poor, ignorant Thrulls like me."

He snorted, tore off some more bread, dipped it into his tea, and stared into my eyes. "Of course, the truth is they are more interested in preserving their precious Fellish magic than they are in helping the poor," he said, challenging me to disagree. I didn't.

There was a knock on Arthur's door, and Emma and I froze. Arthur didn't bat an eyelid.

"Come," he said with a giant yawn. A young Thrull boy came in and was about to deliver a message, but he stopped when he saw us.

"It's all right," Arthur said; "they just fell down with the last shower of rain."

The Thrull boy fidgeted nervously. He stared at us for a long time. "Police patrol coming," he said at last. Arthur carried on eating regardless. After the boy had delivered his message, he stood awhile waiting for thanks or acknowledgment from Arthur, but when Arthur said nothing, he left.

"How do you even know about us?" I asked.

"There have been rumors on the dark side ever since Helva Gullkin seized power. The Blue Volcanoes promised that two human children were going to appear under the ice to liberate us and install a parliament," he said.

He obviously thought the idea was amusing somehow and picked his teeth with his giant knife.

"They promised us that you would be able to defeat Gullkin on the day of the Swearing of the Oaths." He peered at me over the blade of his knife. "You'll forgive me, but we were expecting something a bit more . . . formidable."

I wanted to give him some encouragement to believe Emma and I weren't totally hopeless.

"The Swearing of the Oaths is the day when the Fel choose their new king and queen," I said.

Arthur stared at me blankly. "The Swearing of the Oaths is a battle to the death," he replied with expressionless eyes. Straightaway he saw the look of shock on my face, and he turned to Emma with curiosity.

"So they didn't tell you that either," he said.

Emma was beginning to get angry, and she bumped her fists together quickly. "Tell us what they didn't tell," she said.

Arthur chuckled. "It is true it is a ceremony. On a lake of ice. Inside a giant volcano. Where the contenders shift from shape to shape and claw and bite and stab each other."

He could see that each new piece of information was more alarming than the last, but that only served to add color to his language and turn his voice into a menacing hiss. "The crowd bay for blood, and they get it by the gallon. The fighters turn themselves into bears and tigers and beasts from the darkest parts of their imagination. And only when one or the other of them lies dead and frozen on the ice is the winner declared and the new king sworn in."

I cleared my throat and saw that Emma now had her golden dagger in her hand. Just talk of battle had made her ready to fight. I realized she had been fighting all her life and that she was already a formidable warrior. I, on the other hand, was a formidable dreamer. I reached out and put my hand around Emma's to hide the weapon.

"I think we're talking about a different thing," I said.

Arthur dunked his bread into his tea and shook his head. "Nope," he said, and slurped. "You are here to challenge Helva Gullkin for the throne of Langjoskull by engaging in enchanted combat. You will fight to the death."

Arthur was someone who evidently enjoyed shattering illusions the way some people enjoy popping bubble wrap. However when he looked up and saw the murderous look on Emma's face, he retreated a little.

"Sorry," he said. "My old friend 'the truth.' He always shows up when you don't want visitors. The Blue Volcanoes were probably going to hide it from you until the last minute. Good people tell good lies."

Emma fixed Arthur with her fierce stare. I thought she was angry that we had been lied to, but she surprised me, as she often would.

"It seems to me the Blue Volcanoes just want justice," she said.

"And what would you know about justice?" Arthur asked.

Emma didn't answer, and Arthur picked up Emma's cup and began to lick it clean with his big tongue. His sharp incisors looked lethal.

"Maybe they just want things to change," Emma said. Arthur carried on licking.

"And maybe the moon will come crashing through the ice roof and hit Gullkin on the head to save you two the trouble," he snorted.

"So you are happy being a slave?" she said with her head at an angle.

Arthur stopped licking and stared at Emma so hard, I felt the collar of my coat bristling. Her shawl stiffened too. Arthur laid the cup down slowly, then gestured around his crumbling room.

"Once this was a home. I had a wife and two fine sons. When Gullkin took power, my wife was taken to serve in the castle. My sons fought back. . . ."

He stroked the cold boulder that served as a table. "They are under the rocks now." When he looked up, I thought I saw a younger face and gentler eyes just for a moment. Then the memory of his wife and sons flickered and died.

"No. I am not happy to be a slave," he said softly. He

turned to me, and I imagined he was taking in my puny chest and my thin arms. "But I do not believe anyone on this earth can free us."

At that moment I heard the flapping of wings above our heads. I heard it long before Arthur or Emma, and I was already looking up through the large hole in Arthur's roof when the seagull landed at its edge. I saw the tail feathers and then the large white and yellow head. The bird peered down at us and blinked.

Arthur had seen the bird too, and he grabbed a long iron blade that had been concealed behind the kitchen curtain.

"Police patrol!" he hissed. "Your jabbering made me forget!"

My fur bristled and bulked up more quickly than ever.

Arthur was now swinging the blade around his head like the blade of a helicopter. The seagull let out a vicious scream. Its wing feathers emerged through the hole and caused a shower of volcanic dust to fall down onto the table. A few moments later another six gulls flew down through the hole in the roof, and the room seemed to be filled with gray wings beating around our heads, making the air throb. Emma had fallen backward onto the floor, but as she fell her shawl turned into two elegant butterfly wings that flapped and pulled her away from the swirl of seagulls. I pulled my sword from its scabbard, and it executed defensive movements all on its own. I saw the blade zipping through the air in front of my face and over Emma's head.

The kitchen window was smashed by a punch made up of wings, beaks, and bones, and more gulls were sucked inside. Then I saw a white mist swirling near the door. Two of the gulls that had flown in first were consumed by the mist for a moment, and then I saw the faces of two Fel warriors staring at me. The gull wings were turning into arms that carried flashing golden swords, their beaks turning into hooked noses.

Arthur was filled with terror.

"They are shifting!" he yelled. "You must run!"

He flew toward the back room, and we followed. I kept my sword in my hand, and it vibrated in my grip. I felt there was suddenly so much power in it that I could hold on to it and command it to fly if I wanted to. In the absence of a door, Arthur demolished part of the back wall with his shoulder, and we were suddenly in the dark alley at the back of the house. There was a small stable with a door made of hides. He pulled the hides aside, and in the half darkness I saw two pairs of eyes.

Arthur stepped into the darkness and emerged holding the manes of two black Iceland ponies. They bucked and reared, but he was so strong that he could hold them steady with one hand each.

"Ride them," he said. "They know where to go."

I grabbed the mane of the nearest pony and hauled myself

aboard. I had never ridden a horse before, so I just wrapped my arms around the pony's neck. Emma was having trouble getting on her pony because it had begun to kick, so Arthur lifted her with one hand and dropped her onto its back.

"Now fly!" he yelled.

He stepped out of the path of the horses, and they took flight. A moment later we were emerging onto the street, sending children scattering as the hooves of our mounts kicked up gravel and dust.

The horses were heading for the light side of the city, which I thought was madness, but we had no control over their direction. They ran side by side, matching each other stride for stride. I could see that Emma was gritting her teeth to stop her jaws from smashing together. Walking for the first time was nothing compared to my first ride on horseback. I felt the solid ground beneath my horse's hooves with every bone in my body. Then my coat tightened around my back, and I saw Emma's shawl gently easing itself into the shape of a saddle.

The riding grew easier, and Emma glanced over at me from the neck of her galloping horse. She smiled. I saw the gap between her teeth, and she looked like a cheeky child. I'd felt lots of new feelings in the last few days, but the feeling I had when she smiled at me was the best of all.

That's my baby sister, I thought.

11

The ponies slowed and stopped as we reached the white pumice building of the university. Emma and I slid to the ground in a small alley that was hidden from the street by a fountain and a statue. The ponies appeared to have chosen the hiding place deliberately.

I felt as if I had been put under a tea towel and bashed with a wooden mallet.

"Are you all right, Emma?" I said.

"No. I think I've broken everything except my tongue."

We looked into each other's eyes. In all my wild dreams in my chair, had I ever dreamed of having a sibling, or even a cousin? Had I ever imagined what that might be like? I began to wonder if she was thinking the same thing.

"Hello, Toby. Listen, I've had some thoughts about your name. I really don't think Toby works at all."

Egil emerged from the shadows, chewing on a reindeer bone. He was wearing a bright green tunic with silver stars sewn on it, but even that wasn't the most surprising thing about him. The *really* surprising thing about Egil was that he had now teased his unruly black hair into two thick horns that protruded from his head. He looked like a young, underfed buffalo.

"I thought your new name should be Brythnold," he said. "What do you think? Smells of wood varnish and big tables."

"I've told you I don't want a new name," I said. "And anyway, Brythnold sounds like somebody trying not to sneeze."

Egil shrugged, then turned to Emma and bowed. Her face was half hidden in shadows. "Hello, Emma," he said, with his charming green-eyed smile. "We didn't really get a chance to talk at Grandpa's with all those policemen around. I'm Egil. Ex-cat. In recovery."

Emma shook his hand warily, and then Egil walked over to our weary little ponies. In a very matter-of-fact voice, he spoke to the horse I had ridden. "Well *done*, Gletta," he said. Then he turned to Emma's horse. "And you too, Kolaa." He blew into their noses and they blew back. "Now go back home and tell that big brute Arthur to take better care of his guests in the future."

With that, Gletta and Kolaa turned and began to trot back in the direction they had come, just as if they had understood every word Egil had said.

"This is the boy who used to be a cat?" Emma said, looking Egil up and down.

"Emma, it's okay," I said, remembering her fear of shapeshifters. "Egil is just a bit . . . you know . . . well, actually he *was* . . . *my* cat. My best friend. Once."

Emma was staring at Egil with deep suspicion. I could see that her hand had moved toward the pocket inside her dress where she kept her dagger. Egil stared back at her with his superior cat expression.

"Has something frightened dear Emma?" Egil said.

"Where Emma comes from, people who can turn into animals are considered evil."

Egil found the idea amusing and rotated his face around. "Emma, you are *so* mistaken," he said softly. "You have no idea what *fun* life can be if you have a rough tongue and night vision."

"How come you've got horns?" she said.

"Sweet, aren't they?" Egil grinned. "But sadly just an artifice."

Emma suddenly pulled her tiny dagger and brandished it.

"I don't trust this one," she whispered. Egil stared at

the dagger with interest.

"Emma, Egil helped me," I said. "He's a little odd but he's okay. He makes shape-shifting seem harmless. Like origami or something."

"What's origami?" Emma and Egil both said in unison.

"It doesn't matter," I said. "I think we just have to take Egil at face value."

"'Face value,'" Egil repeated with a curious smile. "I like that. What does it mean?"

Emma stared into his green eyes, then slowly put the dagger back into her dress. Egil watched the dagger intensely.

"Sweet Emma has only been here for the blinking of an eye, and already she has her own magic weapon," he said.

"It's just a knife I found on the floor," she said.

"*It* found *you,*" Egil said mysteriously. "Bravo. Take good care of it."

Once again I felt that Emma was more equipped to be in this world than I was and that she did well without any effort. It would have been annoying if she hadn't been so unaware of it.

"Egil, please, the police are looking for us. Where are we supposed to go?"

Egil finally blinked and turned from Emma to me. He took my hand in his bony fingers and clawed at them.

"Egil Catkin to the rescue," he said, and with that he

turned and disappeared through a small wooden door I hadn't even seen a second ago.

The door opened into a dark corridor that led into the university. A uniformed policeman stood guard in a small cabin at the end of the corridor, but Egil had a plan. Those bizarre buffalo horns had grabbed the guard's attention, and while he questioned Egil, Emma and I were able to slip past unnoticed.

I now understood why Egil had made an effort to look so unusual and began to suspect that perhaps he wasn't really as silly as he made out.

The same routine worked at the second checkpoint inside the university building. Egil took the curiosity and the questions while Emma and I strolled past. Above the arched central hall were words written in a language neither of us understood, along with an engraving of a gull and a raven.

Inside the hall, the walls were made from polished obsidian that shone a rich dark chocolate color. The floor was made from black and white hexagons of chalk and shale, and corridors led away in all directions to halls lit by glowing volcanic lamps. The air smelled of books and hot stones, and the halls echoed with the sound of busy students hurrying between classes.

Egil bounded around us, grinning.

"You can relax now," he said. "After the checkpoints, there are no police allowed inside the university. That's how the great Will Wolfkin decreed it should be. But who knows how much longer it will be before Gullkin gets rid of this rule too?"

Egil gestured up at a giant statue that appeared to be made from solid gold. The figure was an impressive-looking warrior with a shield and sword, his face looking up toward the central dome of the hall, where a particular ray of sunlight entered from a window in the glacier above. The shaft of light made the statue sparkle, and I suddenly recognized his features.

"King Will Wolfkin," Egil breathed. "Your great-great-great-great-great times twenty-seven grandfather. And guess what—he really was that great. I have a strange urge to lick his golden feet."

"Please don't," Emma said, and we both stared up at the face of the statue. I could see that Emma was impressed, and I had to tug her hand to get her to follow.

As we approached an ivory staircase, I called out to Egil and my voice echoed. "Why didn't your grandpa tell us the truth about the Swearing of the Oaths?" I said, and he turned sharply.

Emma and I simply stared at him, and he rippled his shoulders a little.

"Perhaps he didn't want to scare you," he said with a languid smile.

"We're supposed to fight some horrible monsters to the death," Emma said.

"On ice. In a volcano," I added.

Egil put his finger to his chin and peered up the spiral of the staircase with a deeply thoughtful expression. "That sounds pretty much accurate," he said at last.

"So how are we supposed to do that?" Emma said. "We're just children."

Egil turned to me and twirled his buffalo horns between his fingertips. "Perhaps you can save your really *difficult* questions for the grown-ups," he said.

Egil turned and began to leap up the spiral staircase two steps at a time. Emma and I had to hurry to keep up, and we'd climbed six flights of stairs before we both had to stop to catch our breath.

"Altitude is power," Egil said, leaning over the railing above our heads, "and we are going right to the top."

We had to climb as far again before we reached the top floor of the university. We emerged onto a pure white floor made from smooth tiles that looked like whalebone with black stepping-stones. We followed the path of the stones to a large wooden door with antlers and horns nailed above it. There was writing on the door that I couldn't read. The letters looked like insects, and they swarmed rather than followed a straight line.

"You are about to meet the chancellor of the whole of Langjoskull University," Egil said in a voice filled with awe. "He is so clever, it is as if the rest of us are just pages and he is an entire book all to himself."

Egil straightened his tunic and then grabbed his buffalo horns in his fists. In one short jerk he pulled his hair loose, and he once again had the familiar scattered black mane. I imagine he thought this looked more dignified, even though he looked like a tree under water.

When he was happy with his hair, he knocked on the door.

The door creaked as it opened very slowly. A small, unhappy Vellish face appeared in the doorway. The woman had gray hair pulled back into a bun, and her forehead was marked with a large red birthmark that looked a little like a map of Great Britain.

"No," she said immediately, even before any of us had said anything.

"No what?" Egil said, a little bewildered.

"He's busy," the doorkeeper said.

"But we have urgent business," Egil whispered.

"He has no business with you," she said, and her voice sounded almost identical to the creaking of the large wooden door. "He's busy conducting an experiment and must not be disturbed."

"We are here to see Earl Hawkin regarding a private matter," Egil said reverently.

"The chancellor does not concern himself with students unless they are dead or very brilliant," snapped the door-keeper. "And he is very, very busy."

Egil looked left and right before whispering, "It is . . . *geological* business." The weight he gave to the word *geological* seemed to be deliberate. The effect on the Vellish doorkeeper was instant. She poked her head out of the doorway, looked left and right, then hurriedly ushered us all inside.

We were now in a long, wide corridor that had oak panels and lava torches hanging from the walls. The dark red light inside made my stomach turn over, and my coat hardened immediately, though I couldn't see any danger. The Vellish doorkeeper was walking so fast, Emma and I had to run to keep up with her.

"Where are we?" I whispered to Egil.

"We are in the inner sanctum."

"The inner sanctum of what?"

"Of knowledge and everything," Egil said.

"What is *geological* business?" Emma asked, breathless from keeping up.

"It is a code word, silly," Egil said. "Geology as in *volca-noes.*"

"Shhhhhh," hissed the Vellish doorkeeper, and she

turned around sharply. We all fell silent. She set off running, and after a few moments we had reached a large oak door similar to the first. She produced three iron keys and proceeded to unlock three heavy locks before pushing the door open.

Suddenly, pure white light flooded the dark corridor and made us all shield our eyes. The doorkeeper turned her back on the light before urging us to walk on. As my eyes grew accustomed to the brightness, I saw that beyond the doorway there was a vast expanse of snow stretched out beneath a gigantic glass dome. The snow was as smooth as glass and sparkled in the pure light coming from above.

I was about to step forward, but Egil grabbed my arm.

"Wipe your feet," Egil said softly.

Emma and I began to wipe our feet, but the doorkeeper hissed at us to hurry. She dragged all three of us toward the threshold, then pushed us through it. I heard the door slam behind us and then stared all around as the three locks were locked again.

We were in an area the size of four football fields, knee-deep in pure white snow. The space was oval, with the glass dome reaching a hundred feet above our heads. In spite of the snow, the air was warm and smelled of the ocean. I could see that Emma was just as startled as I was at the size and serene silence of the place.

"This is Earl Hawkin's laboratory," Egil said softly. "It is different every time. He is a very unusual and brilliant individual."

Emma had bent down to grab a handful of snow. She looked at me curiously.

"It's warm," she said softly. "I was always told that snow was cold." I reached down and picked up a snowball of my own, and it felt like the warm body of a small animal in my hand. I could almost feel a heart beat inside it.

Egil had grabbed a snowball too. He sniffed it and then licked it.

"It's sweet!" he said. Emma and I checked with each other before timidly licking the snow. Egil was right. It tasted like sugar.

"He truly is a genius," Egil breathed.

"It's just a silly experiment," said a booming voice.

All three of us leaped into the air in surprise. We turned to see a Fel dressed in green tweeds, with a Robin Hood–green hat perched sideways on his head, climbing out from a snow hole just behind us. He sported a beard that was just beginning to gray and a mustache that he had teased into handlebars. His eyes glistened beneath his green hat, and I smelled the pleasing essence of cinnamon.

He dusted snow from his clothes and smiled.

"Would humans find warm, sweet snow amusing?" he asked. Emma had already dropped her snowball, but I looked down at mine, then back at the smiling face.

"Y-yes," I stammered.

He chuckled before marching off across the snow toward the center of the dome. "What a silly idea it is," he said, his voice trailing away, "but fun nevertheless." We turned to Egil, who urged us to follow. The snow grew cold around our legs as we disturbed it.

"That is Earl Hawkin, the finest Keeper of the Arts of them all," Egil said, quickly licking as much sweet snow as he could between words. "He is also without doubt the . . . (lick) . . . cleverest . . . (lick) . . . Fel in . . . (lick) . . . Langjoskull."

"Nonsense!" Earl Hawkin suddenly boomed without turning his head. "Doctor Felman is cleverer than I. And so much more practical."

Finally he stopped and turned to beckon us forward. Earl Hawkin had the warmth of a log fire and made you want to be near him. We all hurried to where he was standing. As we approached, he cleared a patch of snow with his foot and revealed a gate, similar to the one I had seen under the snow on the roof of the glacier. He used a golden hook to lift the door, and as it opened we saw a small wooden staircase that led down into candlelight and half darkness.

"Come into my office," Earl Hawkin said, and he took Emma's hand to help her walk down through the hole in the warm, sweet snow.

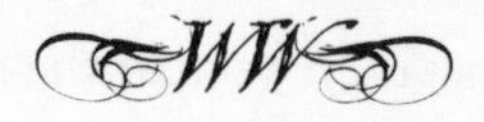

The descent was easier and shorter than the descent from the roof of the glacier into Langjoskull, but I could see that Earl Hawkin had re-created some of the details of the ice staircase, including the landing and the walrus-fat candles. Perhaps he wanted to create the gateway to Langjoskull in miniature. As we all descended the steps, he dismissed the experiment we had seen up above as "just some playful possibilities that I hope to present someday to the human race as a gift from the Fels. . . ."

He turned and grinned at us.

". . . When the Great Separation is finally over."

He said the "snow" was actually made from a fungus that grew in the deep volcanic fissure beneath Langjoskull. "It is a very primitive form of life that I have purified to resemble snow. I understand that humans like things that exist for no reason. Music, for example. Well, we Fels like music too. We are not so different."

His office was circular and resembled a cave, with a warm lava fire glowing in the grate. He had a large desk made from oak and more carved whalebones, and above the fireplace there was a portrait of the man I now recognized as King Will Wolfkin. In Earl Hawkin's warm office, with the light flickering, I imagined that the resemblance between the king and me was even clearer.

"I am given a free hand with my experiments at the university"—Earl Hawkin chuckled—"because I am of royal blood and related to Helva Gullkin." The mention of the name made my fur coat writhe at my throat, and I saw Emma's shawl tightening around her shoulders.

"Gullkin believes I am on his side. But in truth I secretly threw in my lot with the Blue Volcanoes two years ago."

He glanced at Egil, who bowed his head.

"It was a glorious day for our cause," Egil said, and Earl Hawkin growled as if he wasn't so sure.

"I could not stand by and watch that ignorant bully destroy our civilization and our magic, even if he is my cousin. And like everyone else on our side, I am impatient to get to work with the human race on the many problems we all face. I have been waiting for the arrival of you two children with great, great anticipation."

I felt a great weight on my shoulders. Earl Hawkin took note of my writhing fur coat and Emma's stiffening shawl with interest as he continued. "I have never concerned myself with practical things before because I am not a practical sort of Fel," he said, and lifted a large, upturned silver bowl from its place on the desk. "My interest is in particles and forces. Energies and orbits. The space between visible and invisible. However, Gullkin has made me devote my full attention to the fight against tyranny and the subsequent quest for peace with humanity."

To my surprise, underneath the silver lid there was a small stove with a blue flame heating a gold pot of water. When he lifted the lid, steam rose in a great cloud, and Earl Hawkin leaned in to study the contents.

"In a single pot of boiling water there are all the secrets of the universe," he said, his face almost lost in steam. "But sometimes I have to be reminded that it can also be used for making tea. Do you want some?"

He turned to us all, and his smiling eyes glistened. We all nodded in unison, even though my hatred of Fel tea was now personal. He fussed over some cups and saucers, and I was delighted when he finally handed us cups of ordinary tea that smelled like the kind Sister Mary used to make. He even had a jug of milk on hand and a golden bowl of sugar. I'd never tasted tea before, but when I did, it reminded me of Sister Mary's smile.

"Doctor Felman often brings me back things from the human world," Earl Hawkin said. "I like to keep abreast of scientific developments among our old enemies. It seems that their science and our magic are becoming more and more similar."

As I poured milk for myself and Emma, Earl Hawkin squeezed past his desk to his bookcase, where I saw a hundred old texts all tightly packed into the shelves. I wanted to open them all up and smell their musty pages, but the book Earl Hawkin pulled out was almost brand-new.

"Developments like this," Earl Hawkin said.

I was astonished to see the crooked smile of Stephen Hawking staring at me from the cover. It was a copy of *A Brief History of Time*, which Sister Mary used to read to me. It was like staring at the face of an old friend. Earl Hawkin saw my astonishment.

"This fellow is very instinctive for a human," he said. "But may I say in all modesty that in terms of research I am ten years ahead of my . . . distant relative."

I gulped my hot tea. I wanted to ask if it was really true that Stephen Hawking was part Fel, but Earl Hawkin read my mind and nodded with a big grin on his face.

"I even visited him once to swap notes, but I imagine he remembers it as a dream," Earl Hawkin said.

Egil was shifting on his feet, and he cleared his throat nervously. "I know I don't know everything," he said in a very grown-up way, "but who are we talking about?"

"Oh, no one important," Earl Hawkin said, and he winked at me before trying to push the book back into the bookshelf. Of course, in a bookshelf as tightly packed as that one, the gap that existed when the book was removed had now closed up. Earl Hawkin began to work up a sweat trying to find a space among the heavy textbooks as he spoke.

"Now, children, perhaps we should get down to business," he said with a gasp. "I understand you were chased from the dark side by Gullkin's police."

He turned to us and we nodded. He then took a teaspoon and tried to use it as a lever to make a space in the bookshelf. Emma glanced at me and smiled behind her hand.

"In that case, we need to get you both to a safe place straightaway."

The teaspoon finally bent, and he dropped it with a clatter and a curse. His face was flushed, and he tugged his jacket straight before giving up on the book and placing it in a drawer. He turned to Egil.

"I suggest you take them to Doctor Felman's house."

"The police came there already," Egil said. "Doctor Felman himself has had to flee to the most secret place."

Earl Hawkin clutched his chin and nodded gravely. "Then why don't you take them to the most secret place too?"

"That is what we plan to do," Egil replied, "but there are police everywhere. They are searching every cart and carriage. We would never make it out of the city."

Earl Hawkin thought for a moment; then his eyes lit up. "We could disguise them as Thrulls. Or as one single Thrull. The girl could ride on the shoulders of the boy, and they could wear a long coat."

Egil blinked quickly at the absurd idea, then looked down at his shoes and cleared his throat. It was quite clear that Earl Hawkin had been correct in stating that he wasn't very practical. Egil allowed a polite silence before speaking up.

"My grandfather suggested that perhaps you could put them in a university laboratory cart," Egil said. "The driver will say it is harmful waste being taken to the eastern caves to be dumped. No policeman will dare search it. Also, you can put your royal seal on the carriage to make the passage easier."

Earl Hawkin considered the idea for a few moments and sighed. He sat down heavily in his chair and peered up at his bookshelves.

"Now, why didn't I think of that?" he said softly.

"Your mind is busy," Egil said.

Earl Hawkin reached into his desk and began to sift through a pile of paperwork before signing two sheets of paper and handing them to Egil. "I suppose I have my uses," he said.

"When we need you, my grandfather will call for you," said Egil.

Earl Hawkin peered at the gold pot. The remains of the water had now almost boiled dry. He reached forward and turned off the blue flame. Then he looked up at Emma and me. His crinkled blue eyes were piercing.

"I may not be much use to our noble cause in practical ways," he said, "but the Jerlamar has blessed me with an ability to see directly into people's hearts. It is my most profound magical accomplishment."

Egil nodded confirmation and whispered, "He is unequaled."

Earl Hawkin got to his feet and wandered around the desk. He peered at Emma and me. "I can see that you are both afraid of what will happen on the day of the Swearing of the Oaths." The words already had the power to chill my blood. Now he peered at Egil for a moment and smiled. "I see that Doctor Felman wanted to keep the truth from them. That was a mistake."

Egil shrugged his shoulders and ran his fingers through his hair.

I could feel Earl Hawkin's gaze on my face like a kind of heat. It was a very odd sensation, and when Emma squeezed my hand, I could tell that she could feel it too.

"But I also see that you are brave," Earl Hawkin said softly. "I am a Fel of royal blood, and *I* will tell you the truth. At the moment you are just frightened children, but within you there are two mighty warriors. Doctor Felman and I will give you all the strength you need. We will see to it that you are given the education and the weapons to win the great battle. The Jerlamar knows that you are fighting for justice, so the Jerlamar will flow mightily inside you."

"We still don't even know what the Jerlamar is," Emma said. Earl Hawkin turned to her.

"You don't need to know. You know what justice is," he

said, and Emma nodded her head just once, but firmly.

"You will be remembered forever among the Fel as our greatest heroes, and the great king himself will honor you in spirit."

Earl Hawkin pointed toward the portrait of King Will Wolfkin, and I imagined I saw the portrait smile at me. Then, to my astonishment, the painting suddenly blew open like a door. Behind it there was a hidden passageway. The portrait smashed against the wall on its hinges, and a powerful wind began to swirl inside the room.

Egil had shrunk back into the shadows, but he arched his back and shook himself as the wind began to blow. He stuffed the papers Earl Hawkin had given him into the inside of his strange tunic and led us both toward the passage.

As I helped Emma climb into the hidden doorway, I turned back to see that Earl Hawkin had his face turned up to the ceiling.

"Let the Jerlamar take you and bring you victory!" he said.

PART TWO

Gold

12

We were bundled under wolfskin in the cart, moving at great speed through the darkness. On the side of it Egil had attached a golden sign with words I didn't understand written on it, and a depiction of a skull. He had then tied up the cover tight. The whole carriage had rocked from side to side as the driver clambered onto the perch and flicked the reins.

We traveled in silence for a while, and then we pulled up. I heard a voice outside.

"What are you carrying, Thrull?"

"Casks of poisonous vapors from the university" came the reply from the driver's seat. "I've got special gloves and masks for you if you want to search. Also an inventory from Earl Hawkin himself."

There was a brief silence followed by a nervous call, "Drive on."

As we pulled away, the red light of the police lava torches penetrated the cover of the carriage. I closed my eyes and shrank into the shadows. When I opened my eyes briefly, I saw in the torchlight that the mountain of metal that was concealing my position was in fact a huge stack of solid gold bars.

The cart rocked and rolled over a bumpy road, and I began to hear the sounds of the Fel city. It was market day again, and there was the loud drone of the odd Fel instruments, and cries of the market stallholders. I also heard children playing. I envied them as the cart rolled through their imaginary worlds.

As the noises of the city died away, Emma decided it was safe to whisper, "Where do you think they're taking us?"

"No idea," I whispered back.

Then Emma lifted the cover a little to peek out. In the shaft of light she saw the gold bricks, and her eyes widened. She clambered over the gold and came to sit beside me, our heads just touching the walrus skin that concealed us. The cart rattled over some deep potholes in the road.

"So what are we going to do?" Emma asked, and began to pick at stray hairs in the walrus skin. "Are we going to try to escape?"

"Escape where?" I said. "Even if we got to the surface, we'd be in the middle of a glacier."

Emma examined a walrus hair, and I glanced at her.

"I actually quite liked Earl Hawkin," I said softly.

"I liked Arthur the Thrull," Emma said. "He reminded me of my uncles. They pretend they don't think things can change, but they know they can."

Being inside the cart was like hiding under the bedcovers. It made me want to reveal secrets. I decided I needed to tell Emma the truth about how I was feeling.

"Emma, when I was in the chair, I used to wonder who I was," I said in a matter-of-fact voice. "I used to wonder where I came from. And I used to wonder . . ."

I stopped speaking and the cart rattled over some particularly rough ground.

"I used to wonder what was the point of being alive at all."

Emma peered at me.

"And in the end I didn't want to live anymore."

"But now you do," she said, reading my mind.

"Now I want to live like . . . like a firework," I said, even though I didn't quite know what that meant.

"I know this Swearing of the Oaths thing sounds scary, and I know we've been tricked, but I'd rather fight and die here than go back to the human world and live for no reason."

I turned to her. Ever since we'd met, she had been more angry about what had happened to us than I was. I just wanted her to know that I was actually having the time of my life. She was silent for a few moments, then spoke softly. "When I was in my village, I always thought it was unfair," she said. "It was unfair that my mother had to walk three miles to fetch water. It was unfair that bad people with guns ran everything. I used to have dreams. . . ."

She bumped her fists against each other and laughed and shook her head.

"In my dreams I gave hell to those bad people. I became a tiger—"

"I was a tiger too," I whispered excitedly.

"I made the water flow and made the food tins grow on trees. I made the men with guns suck their thumbs."

"I was a hero on the moon." I laughed.

"I was a hero too," Emma said.

We looked at each other. I began to think about the whizzing weapons and the amazing powers that I imagined might soon be given to us if we were taught the Fellish magic.

"Emma, I have decided I want to stay here and fight."

Emma thought for just a moment. "I think we should do a good thing and stay too," she said. "My mother would say to me you should do a good thing. I think we should fix *this* world because our world can't be fixed."

I reached out my hand to her, and we shook to seal our agreement. Together our hands felt strong.

As if by magical command, the rattling cart suddenly came to a halt.

When Emma and I peeked out from under our cover, all we saw was a plain with a semicircle of small stables in the near distance. A fire was burning nearby, and the air smelled of tar and the ammonia of horse manure. A few tough-looking ponies grazed on the mud and frosted grass.

"You can come out now," shouted the Thrull driver. It wasn't until I poked my head out of the covers that I saw the driver was Arthur. Emma poked her head out as Arthur freed the horses from their traces. I recognized the horses too. They were Kolaa and Gletta.

"What are *you* doing here?" Emma asked.

Arthur turned and growled at us. "I'm here because of you two," he said. "Thanks to you, I am now a fugitive too."

When he looked up at us, to my surprise, his growl turned into a huge grin, with his giant incisors poking out over his bottom lip.

"But at least now I am *something*."

Emma and I jumped down into the mud where the cart wheels had cracked the frozen surface of the moorland. The wind was sharp as a hunting knife. I guessed this was the most secret place that Egil and Earl Hawkin had talked about.

"So where are we?" I asked as Arthur slapped Gletta's rump and sent her trotting away to freedom. Kolaa blew steam into the frosty air and soon followed.

"If you have any questions, ask him," Arthur said, gesturing. We turned toward the stables. Suddenly a geyser erupted. It blew scalding hot water a hundred feet into the air, and a fine warm spray blew into our faces. A rainbow formed in the thin sunlight, and it arched right over our heads.

At the other end of the rainbow stood Doctor Felman. Arthur stumped away across the mud toward the stables.

"Good-bye, children, and good luck," Arthur called out with a wave of his hand.

"You truly are the chosen ones," Doctor Felman said at almost the same time, walking toward us through the mud. He was dressed in a rough brown sackcloth robe with a hood that half concealed his face. He chuckled. "Even the rainbows point you out—and why wouldn't they, indeed?"

Emma and I didn't speak as Doctor Felman pulled the walrus-skin cover off the cart and began to examine the solid-gold cargo. The spray from the geyser was now falling as rain and it made the gold glisten.

"We had to fill the carriage with something," he said. "So we filled it with gold."

Doctor Felman seemed to be making a fast count of the bars in his head and finished it before he turned to us.

"There are seven hundred and fifty bars of gold here," he said, and to our astonishment he pulled a plastic calculator from the pocket of his robe. It looked so out of place that Emma and I stared at it as if it were enchanted. Doctor Felman knew the effect it would have but looked up at us with mock puzzlement.

"What?" he said. "I picked it up when I was in London. It runs on sunlight. The humans are becoming very resourceful. Almost as if they know of the disasters to come."

He began to do a calculation and examined the result by holding the calculator up to the light from the ice roof.

"There," he said. "According to my calculations, using the price of gold I saw in the London *Times* on the day we left England, in the human world this cargo is worth thirty million British pounds. That's more than fifty million U.S. dollars."

He smiled and put the calculator back in his pocket.

"And it is all yours," he said casually. "You will receive half each. After the Swearing of the Oaths and the creation of the new parliament, we will put your gold aboard a small ship with a good Fel captain who will sail it first into the

Thames to deliver your half to you, Toby, and then down the River Nile to deliver the remainder to you, Emma. After that you can do with it whatever you please."

Emma spoke loudly above the wind. "We have decided to fight for you. But not because of the gold."

"We are doing it because . . ." I felt strangely embarrassed. ". . . Because it is the right thing to do."

The wind blew Doctor Felman's hood from his head, and I could see his face clearly for the first time. I thought I saw a moistness in his green eyes. All the air left his body, and I knew that many, many years of work had been devoted to making this moment come about.

"But you lied to us about the Swearing of the Oaths," Emma said firmly. "Please don't ever lie to us again, or we might change our minds."

Doctor Felman composed himself quickly. "I promise," he said, and he had to clear his throat. "I promise we will never again . . . protect you from the truth."

"Call it what it is," Emma said firmly. "A lie is a lie. You lied to us but we have forgiven you. So"—she bumped her fists together—"let's get started."

Doctor Felman smiled. "We have many bridges to cross together," he said. "Let us begin with the bridge that leads to your new home." He gestured toward the stables.

"There are some citizens there who will be rather pleased to see you."

Behind the semicircle of stables there was a ramshackle tree house made from oak logs, except it was a tree house built on ground level. The logs had been leaned against the trunk of a dead oak tree stump to make a kind of slightly sad-looking wooden tepee. Smoke was curling up from inside, but even so, it didn't look particularly warm or inviting.

"Now that you have agreed to fight with us," Doctor Felman said, "I can introduce you to our most important and secret stronghold, known to us as the Grove of the Holy Trusted Oak."

My feet were getting stuck in the mud where the warm water of the geyser had drenched the churned-up earth. There was a lot of mud, and boulders and sprigs of heather all around, but no grove of oak trees.

"I can't see any oak grove," I said, pulling my foot from the ooze.

Doctor Felman chuckled. "We cut the oak trees down to build our headquarters."

"'We' being the Blue Volcanoes," Emma said.

"Yes. The Blue Volcanoes," he said. "We named ourselves after a particular volcano to the east. It is dormant and looks harmless, but someday it will erupt in a great big *whoosh*."

As he walked, I noticed that his feet didn't sink into the mud the way ours did. We had reached the pitiful little door of the small tree house, and Doctor Felman held it open.

"Is this your hiding place?" I said, a little incredulously. It looked like a place you might hide in a game of hide-and-seek. Doctor Felman just smiled and urged me to duck inside. I went first and Emma followed. What we saw when we entered made us fall back in astonishment.

What from the outside had looked like a tiny hovel was, on the inside, a magnificent longhouse, made from giant oak beams carved and jointed with incredible precision. The house was over a hundred feet long and thirty feet high, with an oak floor and giant stone fireplaces every fifteen yards. In all the fireplaces oak logs burned, and the flickering light of their flames illuminated the polished wood all around. On the walls there were animal skins and the heads of bears, elk, wolves, and what appeared to be a woolly mammoth.

The longhouse was filled with Fels, Thrulls, and Vela of all kinds. Even more shocking was the noise. When we were outside, just a pace away, there was silence and the occasional moan of the wind. Now the sound of industry was deafening. The nearest open fires were being used as forges, and blacksmiths pounded away at golden blades on iron anvils. Some of the Fels wore warriors' armor; others were dressed in the robes of students. All their clothes were made from exquisite silk, woven with depictions of planets and wild animals. And every tunic had the same single blue eye woven into the back of it, identical to the ones in Emma's shawl.

Everyone seemed to have their task. Apart from the blacksmiths, some were sharpening weapons on grindstones that gave off showers of golden sparks. Some young warriors were practicing their sword skills, and the clashing sound of gold on gold gilded the rumble of a hundred conversations.

We stood at the threshold of this cacophony for a moment.

"Behold . . . the Blue Volcanoes," Doctor Felman said softly. Emma and I stared at the miraculous hive of industry. I wanted to step outside and come back in again, just to repeat the effect.

"These are the brightest and the best of all the Fel," he said. "We are all united in our belief in a free Langjoskull and in the ultimate goal of an end to the Great Separation. During your stay with us, they will be your bodyguards and your servants until the day of the Swearing of the Oaths."

Already some heads were turning toward us and looking at us with curiosity. Doctor Felman dragged a chair close.

"This is the moment they have been waiting for these many, many years," he said. "I would ask you in advance to please forgive their emotion."

Doctor Felman stepped up onto the chair and clapped

his hands. Miraculously, the small sound was enough to bring instant silence. Now *every* head was turned.

"My friends . . . comrades," Doctor Felman pronounced, "I have news."

Word spread from Fel to Fel as the industry died. Some Fels jumped onto workbenches to get a closer look at Emma and me, and already speculation was riding on whispers.

"As you all know, for almost one hundred years," Doctor Felman said, his voice thick with feeling, "I and other Keepers of the Arts have been working in great secrecy to find the human heirs of the great Will Wolfkin. We have been doing it in order to prevent the illegal tyranny of Helva Gullkin ever becoming legal."

As people stared at Emma and me, the whispers turned into a great buzz of anticipation. Some mouths fell open. Hats were swiped from heads in disbelief.

"We ventured into the human world. We walked many miles. We read many registers in many churches in the dead of night, disguised as ghosts. We hoped beyond hope that before the Swearing of the Oaths we could find the descendants of our great king and present them to the populace. Many doubted us. Sometimes we doubted ourselves. . . ."

The crowd was now a hundred years ahead of Doctor Felman, and he was having to hold them back as if they were wild horses pulling a carriage. Weapons and tools were dropped in amazement as the crowd began to realize who we were. Emma must have felt the great wave of hope and grabbed my hand to squeeze it tight.

"What have we *done?*" she whispered with fear and excitement mixed.

Doctor Felman's chest was swelling now and his voice grew louder. "In the past few days, you may even have heard rumors that human children were under the ice."

The rumble from the crowd grew louder. Some of the Fels and Thrulls began to hug one another. Some wiped tears from their eyes.

Doctor Felman began to speak quickly, like a sprinter racing for the finish line. "Well, the truth is that by the grace of the Jerlamar, our dreams of freedom have become reality. No lies from Helva Gullkin can deny them. Behold, citizens of Langjoskull!"

Doctor Felman turned and gestured at Emma and me with a sweep of his arm.

"Fels, Vela, and Thrulls equally, I present to you the mighty Toby and the mighty Emma—

A huge roar went up, and Doctor Felman had to yell at the top of his voice. "The rightful heirs of the will of Will Wolfkin have been found and delivered!"

Amid the uproar a hundred swords were raised and waved, some of them still glowing hot from the forge.

"All hail the future king and queen of Langjoskull!"

Doctor Felman took our hands and raised them above our heads as if we were punch-drunk boxers. The crowd then all began to chant in unison. "Long live the king! Long live the queen! Long live the king! Long live the queen!"

"And long live parliament!" Doctor Felman exclaimed.

Just a few moments before, Emma and I had been alone on a wind-blasted wasteland, squelching in mud. Now we were engulfed by the love and hope of an entire army. When I turned to Emma, I saw a look of deep determination on her face. Her expression gave me strength, and I turned back to face the crowd.

"Now we must make sure we don't let them down," I said.

Doctor Felman led us away from the cheering throng through a heavy velvet curtain, decorated with the same unblinking blue eye, and headed down the length of the longhouse. The sound of the excited voices behind us disappeared, and our footsteps echoed on the floor.

Emma stopped walking. She was looking up in wonder.

"The entire ceiling is made of gold," she said. I looked up and saw a vast expanse of hammered gold that dripped amber light onto the walls and deadened the firelight.

"We mix the gold with certain minerals taken from meteorites that make it harder," Doctor Felman said. Then he grabbed a flaming torch from the wall to light our way.

"The magical oaks we used to build this house are very clever," Doctor Felman said. "Those who are not welcome can't even see the house or the stables. They see only a shack, some stumps, and some petrified logs, covered in volcanic ash. The wood of those old oaks is visible, invisible, flexible, inflexible . . . it is whatever you want it to be. The fires made from this wood not only give off heat, they also give off wisdom and strength . . . and visions. This wood is still alive and happy to be worked by those who respect the Jerlamar inside it."

Finally we arrived at an enormous dining table. There were at least a hundred chairs around it, with a giant carved throne at each end. The wood looked to have been well worn with age, and in places the edges had been carved into the shapes of animal heads. As we walked, the smell of bread and roasting meat grew stronger. I could see a massive fireplace at the far end of the room where a giant fire was burning. The more we walked in this place, the bigger it seemed to become, as if it were being stretched by our perception of it.

"Just there, to your left, Toby, is where you will sleep." I saw a small chamber, like a hermit's lodge, with an arched roof and a stained-glass window. There was a bed and a fireplace with a roaring log fire. It looked incredibly inviting.

"And to the right, Emma, is where you will sleep." There was an identical chamber on the other side of the long table, a mirror image of my room. By now we were close enough to the big fireplace at the end of the room to feel its heat. Doctor Felman pulled a large silk curtain across the back of the table to give us privacy.

"And this," Doctor Felman said, "is dinner fit for a prince and princess."

On the table was a golden cauldron with a lid. Doctor Felman hooked the lid handle with a golden dagger and lifted it off. The most incredible aroma of roast meat filled the air. He then unrolled a white cloth to reveal two loaves of steaming bread. In the firelight we could see that two places had been set, with golden plates, golden knives and golden forks, and golden goblets, already filled with dark wine.

"I cooked the stew myself," said a voice, and we turned to see Egil standing by the fire. He was now wearing a white tunic and had his hair twisted into a thousand tight spirals. "I used a really, really happy reindeer so you can taste the happiness."

Doctor Felman smiled at Egil and urged him to step closer. Then he turned to me. "Prince Toby Walsgrove," he said with sudden reverence, "for the rest of your stay with us, my grandson will serve as your royal butler."

"In that case the deal is off," I said. Then I smiled and

Egil blinked quickly.

"Your highness makes a joke at my expense," he said. "Perhaps he should remember that if it weren't for a certain individual, he would have been eaten alive by seagulls like a crust of moldy bread before his adventure even began."

"Doctor Felman," I said, "will our butler always be so disrespectful?"

"Cats are not easily trained," Doctor Felman replied, straightening our cutlery.

"So get a dog," Egil said with a smile.

I turned to Emma and saw her serious expression. I spoke softly to her so that Egil and Doctor Felman couldn't hear. "Emma, will you be able to tolerate a shape-shifter so close? I'm sure that if you want, we can send him away."

Emma studied Egil, who was smiling warmly at her from across the table.

"In this new world there are new rules," Emma said. "Perhaps I should leave my fears behind."

At that moment Egil stepped forward and fell to his knees.

"I cook, I clean, and I also flatter."

Emma stared at him for a moment and finally smiled. Doctor Felman studied her reaction and appeared to be relieved. He bowed to take his leave.

"When you have eaten, children, perhaps you will get some rest. Your education begins tomorrow."

As he walked away, the unblinking eye woven into his robe stared at us.

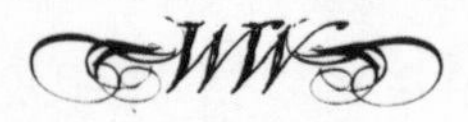

Emma and I ate in silence at first. The sounds of swallowing, of putting down cutlery and serving from the cauldron, were deafening. Egil was standing at attention, still as a statue beside the fire, and he was making Emma and me feel distinctly uncomfortable. He was obviously taking his new role extremely seriously.

"Egil, are you not hungry?" I said.

"Servants do not have feelings," he said evenly.

His stomach rumbled.

"Egil, just sit down and eat something. This is ridiculous."

"Servants are made of gold," he said. "Unfeeling. Enduring. Untarnished by age, reflecting only their master's face—and besides, I know that Princess Emma does not care for my kind."

"Oh, just sit down and eat," Emma said, clattering a golden bread plate in front of the chair beside her. Egil quickly sat down at the end and helped himself to stew. Emma and I smiled at the way he shoveled the food onto his plate and then into his mouth.

"It is such a wonderful relief not to have to eat mice and bats," he said, to explain his eagerness to fill his plate.

"Where I come from we very rarely ate meat," Emma said.

"And where I come from all I ever ate was white goo," I said, and we all smiled at our silly competition to have had the hardest life.

"So there," Egil said, breaking himself some bread. "We are all happier to be here. And I imagine, Toby, that I am now forgiven for rescuing you from the chair."

"That depends on what comes next," I said.

"What comes next is your education," he said.

"And what will our education be like?" Emma asked.

"I don't know exactly," Egil said, spooning gravy. "My own education was very short because I am a prodigy."

"Who will teach us?" Emma asked.

"I believe Earl Hawkin is the first teacher on your timetable," Egil said.

I was glad to learn Earl Hawkin was to be our teacher. I already felt a connection with him through his musty old books. However, what I was really looking forward to was the bangs and the whizzes of battle.

"They said something about giving us weapons," I said casually, and Egil shrugged. I could see he wanted to lick his hands, but he controlled himself.

"What kind of weapons will they give us?" I asked, and he glanced at me.

"The Jerlamar will decide what weapons you are given," he said. "Some go fizz and some go pop and some go bang and some hiss and some shoot fire and some are just the size of a fingernail and are the worse for that. Some are open and loud and some are sly. And of course, one weapon you have already."

Egil gestured at the pocket in Emma's calico dress that contained her golden dagger.

"Everyone here is amazed that one so new to the Jerlamar should have been given a head start," he said, and Emma looked a little embarrassed.

"You don't realize it, but your little trinket is one of the most mighty weapons there is, and it found you the moment you came under the ice."

I felt uncomfortable again. I was bottom of a class of two already. Emma still looked dubious.

"It's just a knife I found under an old cart wheel when Professor Elkkin was leading me to the dark side," she said.

Egil wiped his mouth of gravy with his sleeve.

"Nevertheless you filled it with hope. You trusted it even though it was obviously too small to be of any real use. You gave it power by believing in it. That showed us you understand that using belief is an important part of the Fellish arts."

Egil looked at me and smiled. "But now look at poor Toby, all upset that he doesn't have a knife too. Here, take this one. . . ." He offered me the knife he had been using to cut his meat. I thought he was teasing me. He stopped eating and gave me a piercing look. His big green eyes blinked, and I saw the reflection of the fire in them. I was expecting him to say something silly, but he spoke in a deadly serious voice. "Toby and Emma, now that your education is about to begin, you must both understand you are in a serious place, and you must learn from everything that happens."

He then turned the knife around and suddenly stabbed it into the table. Emma and I gasped in shock. The knife stuck fast.

"The weapons themselves are not important. It is what is inside that is important. The power comes from what you believe things to be," he said. The stabbing of the table was like a full stop. Something had changed. Egil suddenly looked more like his grandpa than he had before.

He continued to stare into my eyes as a giant crack suddenly appeared in the thick wooden table, starting where Egil had stabbed it with the knife. The crack soon ran the full length of the table, and Emma and I leaped to our feet and jumped back to avoid the two halves that fell to the floor with a crash. Half the table lay in front of Emma, half in front of me. Egil was still sitting at the head. The dishes had all crashed onto the floor, and the stew was pooling at our feet.

With that Egil wiped his mouth with a napkin and got to his feet. His silly grin suddenly returned, and he waved his long bony hand with a flourish. "From now on," he said, "expect the unexpected."

13

Our education in the Fellish arts began early next morning with a short introductory lecture from Doctor Felman. We sat together near a hot spring. There was a boulder nearby that had been shaped by the wind to resemble a man on his knees. As Doctor Felman talked, the water in the hot spring bubbled blue and black, and steam rose in thin clouds that smelled of rotten eggs and hot rocks.

Doctor Felman told us very solemnly that the kind of knowledge we were about to be given was normally forbidden to humans. Humans who had no Fel blood at all would be unable to master the arts anyway, but they might be able to learn certain techniques such as casting the evil eye or learning certain spells to do with falling in love. However, humans with Fel blood could be introduced to the whole world of Fel magic and, if they had the correct spirit, could even become Keepers of the Arts.

Doctor Felman said he was one of only seven Keepers of the Arts who retained the Fel knowledge, and there were never more than seven Keepers at one time. Doctor Felman, Professor Elkkin, and Earl Hawkin were the three Keepers who were all secretly in favor of the new parliament, while the other four Keepers were loyal to Helva Gullkin.

"Those old fools are lost to themselves," he said wearily. "They are for tradition and silly crowns worn under yew tree boughs. They do not understand the knowledge they have or what it really means."

When I asked about Egil, Doctor Felman said he was a very talented apprentice who, for all his silliness, would one day be a great practitioner of the Felllish arts.

He warned us that we would see and do some incredible things while we were learning the arts, and also warned us that dealing with this kind of power could be extremely dangerous if we didn't approach it in the correct spirit.

"Now, before we begin, children, do you have any questions?"

Emma raised her hand and asked the question we had wanted answered for so long. "What is the Jerlamar?"

Doctor Felman smiled. "That is a very big question to

ask on this first hour of the first day of your education," he said, but I could see he was pleased that Emma had asked it. He scooped up some hot water from the spring and held it in his cupped hand. "The Jerlamar is"—he sipped the water like a wine taster savoring a fine vintage—"a great mystery."

I thought he might leave it at that, but he urged us to move closer to the edge of the spring and peer down into it.

"The Fel believe that the Jerlamar is the force that controls every geyser and volcano, every lava flow and hot spring in Langjoskull. It is the energy that runs through the earth, giving us heat and light and also power."

Through the steam Emma and I saw our own reflections in the water, troubled by rising bubbles.

"But we Keepers know that it is more than that," he continued. "The Jerlamar also runs through every living thing. We are all hot springs with deep roots below the surface. We are all volcanoes. We all have the power of the whole earth inside us—we simply need to learn how to control that power. And also allow that power to control us."

Emma and I glanced at each other.

"Whoever learns the mysteries of the Jerlamar will find that there is no shape or size to things, and that you can choose to be whatever you wish to be. If you learn to harness its power, then the Jerlamar will do wondrous things for you."

Doctor Felman got to his feet and stood at the edge of the hot spring.

"Wondrous things . . . like this. . . ."

He bowed his head for a second, looked down into the steaming water, and opened his arms wide.

"Jerlamar . . . *erupt!*" he said.

A huge blue bubble burst onto the surface of the spring, and then a gigantic tower of water shot up a hundred feet above our heads. Emma and I were about to duck for cover, but Doctor Felman yelled to us above the roar of the eruption.

"*This* is the Jerlamar welcoming you, children," he said with a laugh in his voice. "Embrace it. The water won't harm you."

It took a while for the first drops of water to land, but when they did they were fat and hot. At first the water made my skin sting, but then the heat turned into a feeling of well-being. I slowly got to my feet as the water drummed on the top of my skull, driving out some upsetting thoughts and driving in happier ones. Emma got to her feet too, and we looked at each other as the cascade of hot water drenched us. The feeling of well-being turned into a surge of strength that I felt through all my muscles, and I could see that Emma was feeling it too. My fur coat was swelling up in the rain, and I could see that Emma's shawl was glistening in a hundred different colors. The blue eyes that were woven into her shawl seemed to blink away the warm water like fresh tears.

"Can we drink it?" I yelled.

"Of course you can drink it!" Doctor Felman cried back.

We opened our mouths, and I drank the water as it splattered against my teeth. We both stretched out our arms to feel as much of the power as we could, and soon a rainbow formed directly between us.

The jet of water fell back into the spring with a splash, and there was silence. My fur coat shook itself like a dog. Doctor Felman wasn't even wet.

"You will know that your education is complete when you are able to make a hot spring erupt at your command," he said. "But that day is a long way away. Now I must introduce you to your first teacher of the Fellish arts."

Earl Hawkin came to us with a sack of his snow and offered it to us to eat. Emma said it was better than the condensed milk the nuns gave out in her village. I thought this was a fine way to begin school. Earl Hawkin explained that he had taken a week's holiday from the university and had told his superiors he was on a hunting expedition. As we munched the sweet, warm snow, he assured us that since he wasn't at all practical, his lessons would be playful and dreamy instead.

Like Doctor Felman, he didn't sink into the mud when he walked, but when he saw us struggling in the slush, he kindly took us to a patch of dry ground under a rock overhang in the middle of a circle of white mushrooms.

A little way away from us, members of the Blue Volcanoes stood guard discreetly, armed with bows and golden swords, which had embedded in them pieces of meteorite to give them a hard edge. I even saw golden blades glinting in the sunlight on distant hills. From that moment on, every lesson we had was guarded by these warriors, searching the horizon for strangers, scanning the glacier roof for the unusual flight of birds, especially gulls. I also suspected in darker moments that they were really there to stop Emma and me from escaping. Most princes and princesses are also prisoners in some ways.

Earl Hawkin told us rather modestly that among other things he was a professor of intuition, and that learning to read minds and talk to flowers were to be our first lessons.

"When you are at war, it is essential that you know what your enemy is thinking," Earl Hawkin said. "And reading someone's thoughts is also great fun because it is dangerous."

His eyes twinkled.

"Emma . . . what do you think of Toby?" he said suddenly,

and she blinked quickly. She hesitated and glanced at me.

"I think he is nice."

"*Too* nice," Earl Hawkin snapped. "You think he should be a bit ruder, a bit sharper, a bit more like a knife than a spoon."

Earl Hawkin angled his head at Emma, and she looked embarrassed.

"That isn't true," she said softly.

"Yes, it is," Earl Hawkin said, "because I can see it behind your eyes. How do I see it? That is what you are here to learn. And *you*, Toby . . ."

He turned to me and stared at me with his piercing eyes. I tried to shut my mind down completely and think about nothing, which of course made me think about everything I shouldn't think about.

"You think Emma is too reckless. She is always picking fights she can't win. Did you know, Emma, that Toby feels he must protect you?"

"Wait, this isn't fair," I said. "You can't just sit there and say personal things about—"

"Look out, Toby!" Earl Hawkin suddenly yelled. I stared at him, but then I saw that Emma had leaped to her feet.

"Behind you, Toby!" she cried. I turned and saw that one of our Blue Volcano guards was standing just twenty yards away with his bowstring pulled tight and with an arrow pointed directly at me. I instinctively jumped to my feet and leaped forward as an arrow whizzed past me just a few inches from my right shoulder.

"And there!" Earl Hawkin said, also scrambling to his feet. He was pointing to our right, where I saw two more of our guards with arrows strung and pointed directly at us.

"What's happening?" I yelled.

"Education!" Earl Hawkin yelled back with a laugh.

I saw one of the bows snap and knew the arrow was heading for Emma. I leaped onto her, and we both fell to the ground. Two arrows whizzed over our heads and thudded into a stunted oak tree. When I looked up, I saw that Earl Hawkin had his hands on his knees and was laughing.

"You must learn to *feel* the arrows that are pointed at you," he said, "just as you must learn to feel the hurt in someone's heart, or the anger, or the betrayal, even if you aren't expecting it."

"That was a really idiotic trick," I snarled. I stood up quickly and helped Emma to her feet. "We could have been killed."

"Emma felt the first arrow coming," Earl Hawkin said. "Two points to her. You, Toby, knew where the second arrow was heading, two points to you. Come, let's go pick some flowers."

With that Earl Hawkin marched off toward a small hillside beyond the stables. I had mud on my trousers and sleeves, and Emma was pulling straw out of her hair. We glanced at each other.

"Some school this is," Emma said, but she was first to turn and follow Earl Hawkin through the mud.

On the other side of the hillside there was a small forest where lots of flowers were growing. These flowers grew purple and looked like sad little footballers with their heads bowed. Earl Hawkin asked us to pick a flower and take it away to a place on our own where we were to tell the flower our entire life story. We had to tell the flower everything we could about ourselves, tell it things we wouldn't even tell our best friend. Afterward Earl Hawkin would hide our flowers in the forest. It would then be my task to find Emma's flower and try to "hear" all her secrets. Emma would have to do the same with my flower. It sounded like an odd thing to do but a pleasant way to spend an afternoon.

I picked a flower and took it to a place where a shaft of sunlight filtered through the ice and treetops and formed a warm island of damp grass. At first I was embarrassed about talking to a flower, and after telling it my name I gave up. Then I thought I might as well tell it the story of the nurses who named me after a cat, and after that the whole story came out. I had a hard time getting through my description of Sister Mary without choking with emotion, and I began to ramble on about my mother who I had never met.

Soon I was telling the flower things I hadn't even been sure of myself until that moment, and after a couple of hours I wasn't certain if I was telling the flower things or if the flower was telling *me* things.

Finally I heard Earl Hawkin calling my name through the trees. His voice sounded like the call of a large wild animal. I walked back to the clearing where I had left him and found Emma already waiting with her flower in her hand. Her eyes were red, and I thought she had been crying.

"Excellent," Earl Hawkin said. "Now give your flowers to me."

Emma and I handed him our flowers. It was obvious that we were both reluctant to part with our secrets. Earl Hawkin held one flower in each hand and put one to each ear. It was as if he were listening to beautiful music, and a warm smile appeared on his face.

"Now I will hide these flowers among their brothers and sisters," he said, and he walked toward the part of the forest where the flowers grew thickest. He disappeared from view behind a stand of trees, and Emma and I were left alone.

"Pretty strange, huh?" I asked.

"Yeah, pretty strange."

"I don't think this will work at all."

"I sort of hope it doesn't," she said, and glanced at me. "I told it so many things."

"Me too," I said.

Earl Hawkin returned and clapped his hands. "Your secrets are lost in the forest. Now, go and find each other."

Emma and I set off in separate directions. I followed a narrow path that led into a deep glade and began to wander aimlessly around. For a long time I succeeded only in getting my feet and the hems of my trousers soaking wet among all the flowers. My coat was thin and light, and I began to feel cold. There seemed to be more flowers now than there had been before, and I became convinced that I had already trampled on Emma's flower without realizing it.

I was sure I would fail at this test and just as certain that Emma would succeed.

At one point I got angry and called out. "Earl Hawkin, this is ridiculous—all the flowers look the same!" There was no reply. Just a forest of identical flowers shivering in the wind.

I sat down on a fallen oak log and rested my head against the tree beside it. My coat thickened to keep me warm, and the fur collar made me feel drowsy. I closed my eyes, and a pleasant dreaminess swept over me.

I was woken by the sound of a child sobbing.

When I opened my eyes, I saw Emma's calico dress on the other side of some bushes. I got to my feet and approached. There, sitting among the flowers, was a girl who looked exactly like Emma but five years younger. She had the same dress and the same gap in her teeth and the same eyes, but she was a small child, and she was weeping quietly into her hands.

"Emma?" I said, and she turned sharply to me. She appeared not to recognize me, but she didn't appear to be afraid either.

"What's the matter?" I said, stepping closer.

"My brother," Emma said softly.

"What about him?"

She sobbed some more and put her face into her hands again. I saw she was holding a flower between her fingers.

"I was supposed to be looking after him, but I wanted to play with my dog. I let my brother wander away. He stepped off the path. There was a land mine. . . ."

Her body shook with sobs, and I knelt down beside her to comfort her.

"It's okay, Emma."

"It's not okay, he's dead," she said. "He's dead and it's all my fault."

I squeezed her bony little arm and spoke softly.

"Emma, it's not your fault. You mustn't blame yourself. . . ."

"From now on I will only do the right thing," she said firmly, and bumped her fists together. "I will make it right somehow."

I studied her face and her look of determination. I had

no idea that listening to a flower would actually be more like a vision. I wasn't sure if I was awake or dreaming, but Emma looked real. Egil was right: I should expect the unexpected.

At that moment I heard Earl Hawkin's booming voice echoing through the trees once more.

"Time's up, children!"

I turned to look for Earl Hawkin, and when I turned back, Emma had disappeared. Instead of a little girl, I saw the flower she had been holding, lying on top of all the other flowers, shivering in the breeze.

That night Emma and I ate alone. Egil had very wisely excused himself, and I suspected he knew we would have things to talk about.

Earl Hawkin hadn't asked us any questions about what the flowers had told us, but I think he could tell by our thoughtful silence that his lesson had been a success. Emma and I didn't speak until I ladled the first helping of stew onto Emma's plate as we sat at the table, which had either been replaced or mended while we were away.

"Did you ever find my flower?" I asked, trying to sound unconcerned, and she nodded.

"Did you find mine?" she asked in return, and I nodded too.

She looked up at me, and her eyes were enormous in the candlelight. "Well?" she asked.

I put my spoon down and took a breath. "I think you told your flower that you blame yourself for your brother's death."

Emma looked down at her lap sharply. I wished I hadn't spoken, but then I decided I should try to make her feel better.

"You really *shouldn't* blame yourself," I said. "Blame the idiots who planted a land mine in a crowded village."

She nodded to her lap. I waited for her to look up, but she didn't.

"It's okay to cry, you know," I said, and she nodded again but still didn't look up.

"So what did you find out about me?" I asked.

Emma finally looked up at me. She smiled. Then she reached across the table and held my hand.

"You were in the forest. You were completely still," she said softly. "You were about five years old. You couldn't move at all. You were sitting on the ground with your hands curled up."

I was embarrassed that Emma had seen how I once looked.

"Did I speak?" I asked.

"Yes. You said you wanted power. Power like a king. You wanted a big army, and you wanted to fight battles."

I could feel my face reddening.

"I was always dreaming of stupid wars," I said.

"You were very sweet."

"Hardly. I was a tyrant. Was that all I said?"

Emma shook her head and looked at me sadly. "You also said you thought you were born to fail," she said. "You thought it was your destiny because of how you were born."

I immediately picked up my spoon and began to eat, just to prove to Emma I didn't care what she had found out. She studied me.

"And what did you say to that?" I asked.

"I told you it could be different here. I said it was your choice to be different in a different world. I told you not to be afraid. . . ."

I suddenly banged my fist on the table.

"I *hate* school," I said firmly.

Emma was still smiling.

"I suppose it's never easy when a brother and sister are in the same class," she said, and then she picked up her spoon to eat.

14

The next day school became much more fun.

Earl Hawkin was in a jolly mood, and he gave Emma and me bows and arrows. The bows were made from willow wood and sinew, and the arrows had real tips made from gold mixed with meteorite metal "to help them fly through space," Earl Hawkin said.

The idea of the lesson was that Emma and I would hunt each other. He instructed us to behave as if this were a real battle to the death. First Earl Hawkin sent Emma into the forest, and I had to track her down. Earl Hawkin told us to use the lessons we had learned the day before about flowers. Emma was told to pick flowers and tell them the direction she was headed. I had to somehow find the flowers and "listen" to their directions. Then, when I found Emma, I had to sneak up on her and point my arrow in her direction. Emma had to "feel" the arrow being pointed at her and yell, "Arrow!" at the top of her voice.

Then I would have to run and Emma would have to chase.

It was great fun to play in the woods like this. In the morning the flowers told me nothing, but by the afternoon I began to get "feelings" coming into my head about where Emma had gone, and I guessed these were coming from the flowers she had picked. After failing to find her six times, I finally succeeded on the seventh. I saw her hiding among some dog roses. She had her back turned, but when I pointed my arrow, she leaped to her feet and yelled, "Arrow!" Earl Hawkin suddenly appeared from nowhere and applauded us both.

"Two points to Toby for finding your quarry," Earl Hawkin said. "Three points to Emma for feeling the intention of the arrow."

Emma was a far better hunter than I, and she had her arrow pointed at my back for ten seconds before Earl Hawkin again appeared from nowhere and growled, "Must try harder," at me for not feeling it.

For the moment Earl Hawkin's chuckling disapproval didn't matter. It felt so good to be out in the wild woods with muddy hands and knees and with leaves and twigs tangled in my hair. Emma and I played our hunting game for a whole week, and by the end of it we were both fast and strong. The muscles that pulled the bowstring grew powerful, and our aim became sharp. Earl Hawkin said we both had a facility for these games because of our Fel blood and that at last our Fellish powers were being exercised.

"You're using parts of your mind that have been stuck in a cage," he pronounced to us both at the end of a long day of hunting.

"Did we have these powers anyway, or are we learning them from you?" Emma asked.

"A bit of both," Earl Hawkin replied. "The Jerlamar cannot be learned, and yet it cannot be acquired without learning."

The second week we had to learn how to feel each other's thoughts without the use of flowers. Emma would stare into my eyes and think of an object, and I had to guess what the object was. I found I could do this easily with Emma and she could do it easily with me. Emma's mind was filled with invention, and it was an exciting place to visit. She was always thinking of strange African animals and birds and spiders that I couldn't name but only describe. I, on the other hand, usually thought of objects from the convent like bowls and cups and door handles, or the faces of particular nuns. I think Emma grew bored of my mind, but she didn't show it.

Then we had to learn to use trees and bushes to get information about our enemies. Earl Hawkin assured us that when Fels or humans talked to one another as they walked through the forest or as they sat at a campfire, their words were heard by the plants around them, and that if you had the ears to hear, you could persuade the trees and the bushes to divulge their secrets.

Earl Hawkin would walk ahead of us along a path and talk all kinds of nonsense. It was Emma's and my job to follow and see if we could "hear" the words he had left behind among the leaves and branches.

Slowly we learned how to piece together whole sentences from words that seemed to be whispered by the breeze as we followed in Earl Hawkin's footsteps, brushing our hands against the leaves. I was good at this game because it reminded me of how I used to "feel" the words Shipley the cat had licked onto my skin when I was in the chair.

Earl Hawkin would say silly Fel nursery rhymes or pieces of profound wisdom, depending on his mood.

"The moon is the grease that greases the wheel that turns the handle that works the world and eases the strain on the moon-filled brain" was the first sentence we worked out in full. Once we became proficient, he used the game to give us pieces of useful information that we would hear being whispered among the foliage.

"The gray and white mushrooms are good to eat, but

the crimson flowers are poison."

"Make your arrowheads by the light of the moon for greatest accuracy; make them by the light of the sun for the greatest power."

After a long walk with lots of messages, he would test us on the facts he had given us, just as if were learning geography or chemistry in a real school.

This game was just as much fun as the others until one morning when Earl Hawkin split Emma and me up to see if we could "hear" the leaves on our own.

Earl Hawkin had us all walk in a big circle through the forest. He led the way and Emma followed, trying to pick up the words Earl Hawkin had said and saying them out loud. I then followed Emma and tried to hear the words Emma had said. Then, since we were walking in a circle, Earl Hawkin would be behind me listening to see if the words I picked up were the same as the words he had said in the first place. It was supposed to be a sort of telephone game, and Earl Hawkin said it was always funny to hear how the words got changed as they were passed on around the circle.

Earl Hawkin was a long way ahead. Emma was just visible on the path in front of me. I was hearing the words of an ancient song about the Fels' journey to Iceland that Earl Hawkin was singing and Emma was repeating. Then suddenly the singing in the trees stopped.

I very distinctly heard the words "I will betray you" coming from a boulder behind the leaves of a big dark oak to my left. The voice sounded like Emma's voice.

A chill went through my body and I yelled out, "Wait!" without thinking. Emma could now sense my thoughts easily from quite a distance, and she knew something was wrong. She turned to hurry back down the path.

"What's the matter, Toby?" she asked.

I stared into her eyes. She began to read my thoughts, and I decided I shouldn't hide anything from her.

"I heard a voice from that big boulder," I said. "It said something about betrayal. I heard the words 'I will betray you.'"

"*Who* will betray you?" Emma asked.

Her eyes narrowed. I looked down at my feet, and Emma spoke softly. "You mean *me*?"

I didn't reply.

Earl Hawkin suddenly appeared from behind a tree as if summoned from thin air. "Come along, children, don't break the enchanted circle. No dawdling, please," he said, but then I imagine his intuition sensed the dark feelings surrounding us. Earl Hawkin walked around us as Emma and I both stared down at the ground.

"What did you hear?" Earl Hawkin asked.

"Nothing," I said. I could feel Earl Hawkin's eyes on the side of my face.

"Something about betrayal," he said softly.

"I must have misheard," I said.

I suddenly regretted ever having said anything, but Earl Hawkin obviously found this horrible moment utterly fascinating. He turned to peer at Emma and mumbled, "Well, well, well," under his breath.

"You may have heard a voice from the stones," Earl Hawkin said. "The leaves and trees pick up words that are said. Rocks and stones can sometimes pick up deep feelings from those who pass by. You must have heard a rock that had heard something coming from dear Emma."

I glanced at Emma. Suddenly a geyser hidden by foliage erupted, and a fine shower of water fell onto our heads. A rainbow appeared between Emma and me.

Earl Hawkin studied the rainbow for a moment, and at last he smiled. "Hearing the voices of the stones is very advanced Fellish art," he said. "Very good, Toby. Ten bonus points. You are indeed progressing well. Class dismissed."

I lay awake in silence that night. The fire in my chamber crackled and spat. I really wished I hadn't said what I had said, and I was sure it was utter nonsense. I wondered why Earl Hawkin had seemed so fascinated and why Emma hadn't said anything at all. These thoughts rolled around endlessly in my mind, like barrels in the hold of a ship in a storm. Then I heard Emma's voice on the other side of my curtain.

"Are you awake, Toby?" she said.

She pulled open the curtain. Her hair was tied back and held in place with a golden comb. She wore a silk robe with the unblinking blue eye and a procession of golden wolves dancing around the sleeves.

"I'm sorry I said such a stupid thing," I said.

Emma suddenly looked furious, and I thought she was furious with me. But she wasn't. She sat down heavily in front of the fire.

"Well, don't be sorry," she said, "because the stone was right."

"Please, Emma, it's just a silly game. . . ."

"No, Toby. I've been thinking about it. And it's true. I have thought about betraying you."

"Emma, what are you talking about?"

"Every time I do something better than you, I wonder if perhaps I'm more of a Fel than you are."

"That isn't betrayal," I said.

"And I think about all the gold here. If I had the chance to escape, I might just steal lots of gold and take it back to my home and leave you here alone."

My intuition told me she had been lying awake, worrying. I smiled at her.

"These are just thoughts anyone would have," I said. I stood up and wrapped the deerskin on my bed around myself. The fire crackled, and I stepped close to it.

"So what did the voice mean, then?" she asked.

"I don't know," I replied. "Because if anyone is going to betray anyone, it would be me."

"If we became king and queen, which one of us would be in charge?" I asked. "Can you believe I have even *thought* about that? It's exactly as you found out from my first flower. I have always dreamed about power because I used to be powerless."

Emma took hold of my arm, but I pulled it free.

"All those years, I was in a chair at everybody's mercy. Sometimes at night I imagine going back to the convent and getting revenge on anybody who was ever horrible to me or laughed at me. I also want to find my mum who abandoned me and say really horrible things to her."

I couldn't speak anymore. Emma pulled her robe tightly around herself.

"Perhaps the voice was a warning," she said. "Maybe the voice was actually telling us that we must *never* betray each other."

When I turned to Emma she lowered her eyes, then walked back through the curtain to her chamber.

It was probably no coincidence that the intuition lesson that caused the trouble was our last. Earl Hawkin told Doctor Felman he had taught us all he could for now, and he returned to the university since he had already extended his holiday by far too many days. His warm snow was cooling down.

Next day Doctor Felman woke us both and told us he would be conducting the second part of our education in person. When he told us it would involve the making of weapons, I felt my heart leap.

Doctor Felman took us to a sheltered place behind the glacial boulder. Guards from the Blue Volcanoes patrolled the hills all around, staring upward toward the sky, and Iceland ponies grazed all around us. Doctor Felman built a fire from twigs that were taken from the Holy Trusted Oaks. He said the heat the twigs gave off was enchanted and was perfect for forging magic weapons.

The flickering flames lit Doctor Felman's face, but the light from the enchanted twigs was different from ordinary light. It seemed to glow on the inside of my skull, filling my mind with a powerful energy.

"Earl Hawkin tells me that you two have a very strong connection as Fel brother and sister," he said. We both nodded.

"But he also said there is now a question as to whether or not you can trust each other."

I was about to protest loudly and could see that Emma was about to do the same, but Doctor Felman raised his hand.

"The Jerlamar travels through time both forward and backward. Sometimes it knows things that do not seem possible. The stone spoke, and that is unusual. We learn from everything that happens."

I could feel my fists clenching. I hated the idea that there was mistrust between Emma and me, and I thought it was all my fault that the suggestion had even been raised. I could see that the smoke was getting in Emma's eyes, but maybe there would have been tears there anyway. We glanced at each other, and in an instant our intuition confirmed that we trusted each other totally, no matter what Doctor Felman or the Jerlamar might believe.

"As a result of this, the weapons we give you will be joint weapons. That is to say, they will work only if you are using them together. On the day of the Swearing of the Oaths, this will make your weapons twice as powerful." Doctor Felman's eyes darkened. "It will also ensure that you can never use these weapons against each other."

I shook my head in disgust at the thought. If this was the will of their precious Jerlamar, then it was utterly wrong.

"Emma, I must ask you to give me the dagger that the Jerlamar gave you."

Emma's lip curled, and she bumped her fists together.

"Please, Emma, do not be angry. The future is an unpredictable country full of temptation."

"I don't care about the stupid knife," she snapped, and I could see Doctor Felman wincing a little at her irreverence. She pulled the golden dagger from her inside pocket and gave it to him without looking at it.

Doctor Felman took the dagger and tossed it into the fire.

"By Jerlamar's will, the weapon that was given to one will now be given to both," he said softly.

The flames flickered, and my face burned. I felt that as well as causing all this mistrust, I had now stolen Emma's weapon from her. Doctor Felman felt my turmoil and whispered, "You must be still, Toby, for the flames to work. Look into the fire."

Doctor Felman stared into the flames, and Emma and I did the same. The golden dagger had already begun to melt.

"The flames are like moonlight," he said in a low voice. "We use the power of moonlight to change things. The flames also change things. There is moonlight in the flames as well as sunlight."

As Doctor Felman spoke, I felt I was falling into a trance. When I tried to focus on Emma, I saw that she had disappeared in the smoke.

"Now look into the flames very hard," Doctor Felman said softly. "Your weapons bring with them important visions."

Suddenly the fire exploded into a ball of colors, but the explosion was silent. The smoke got into my eyes, but when I opened them, inside the fire I saw blue, green, and white patterns that formed themselves slowly into the surface of an ocean.

I was gliding over the ocean very fast until I came to an outcrop of rocks, then a long sandy beach. A man was washed up on a beach by a furious surf. He looked to be dead, but then one mighty wave delivered him onto a rock. As the waves withdrew, a young woman in a long black cloak climbed onto the rock and dragged the man away from the next wave. She laid him down on the beach, and the sand was the color of flames. She bent down to listen for his breathing, and her long black hair covered his face. When she lifted her head, the man opened his eyes.

Except he wasn't a man, he was a Fel. He looked up at the sky, past the woman, and saw me flying over his head. I was hovering like a bird, and there was another bird beside me that I somehow knew was Emma. I saw she had blue wing tips and blue forked tail feathers. We were both vibrating in a strong wind that was holding us up like kites. When I looked back down to the rocks, Will Wolfkin stared into my eyes and smiled . . . and then the vision vanished. The spell of the fire was broken. The smoke made me choke for a moment, and suddenly Emma was coughing too. I realized our heads were almost inside the flames.

Doctor Felman was using a stick to rake the ashes. I saw two glints of gold. I couldn't see what they were at first because they were covered in ash, but Doctor Felman separated them on the embers.

"You must remember every detail of your vision, because everything has meaning," Doctor Felman said. "The Fel you saw in the flames was the great Will Wolfkin himself as a young man. That is a very good omen. It means your weapon will have great power. The Jerlamar is very strong with you because you have both spent so many years dreaming, and dreams are the Jerlamar's kingdom."

The ash was red-hot and still smoking, but I could see now that the single golden dagger had turned into two identical daggers.

"Now pick up the gifts the Holy Trusted Oak has forged for you," Doctor Felman said firmly.

I looked up at him. "They are still hot," I said.

"Pick them up now or the moment will be lost. You must take them while they are still filled with the power of the Holy Trusted Oak."

I hesitated.

"Which one is mine?" I asked.

"Whichever one you pick up."

I saw Emma's hand reaching out. She picked up the

burning dagger nearest to her and squeezed it tight in her hand. There seemed to be no pain. Doctor Felman gave her a half smile of pride, then turned to me. He urged me with his eyes to hurry. I hesitated, but Emma looked at me, and with my intuition I heard her telling me that it was all right to take half of the weapon that had once been hers alone. It was her gift to me. I reached down and picked up the red-hot dagger and squeezed it in my fist.

"Now look," he said.

We both opened our hands. In my palm I saw that the simple golden dagger had been transformed in my grasp. It was now a beautifully crafted knife with a thin blade and a handle decorated with gold lace as thin as a spider's web. It also had a single emerald at the base of the blade. In Emma's hand the dagger had turned into a smooth oval pebble of gold the size of a bean.

Neither item looked like a particularly formidable weapon. But beneath my dagger I saw to my astonishment that the skin of my hand was now marked with a blood tattoo. It was in the shape of a wolf, its head raised, its mouth open in a silent howl, the contours etched out using my heart line, my life line, and my head line. When I looked at Emma's palm, I saw she had an identical tattoo.

"The marks on your skin are proof that you are *kin* of the wolf. They are called clan signs and will be with you for the rest of your lives," Doctor Felman said. "They have great power, and soon you will be taught their purpose."

We peered at each other's hands, then clenched our fists tight again.

"Brother and sister Wolfkin," Doctor Felman said. "Together you will be formidable."

"Very human," Egil said softly as he served us an elaborate roast dinner involving puffins and elk. Emma and I were sitting at the table, staring dumbly at the wolf tattoos on our hands.

"Do you want gravy?" he asked wearily for the third time. Neither one of us answered, so absorbed were we by the marks on our hands.

"Egil, please, give us a clue," I said, not looking up from my palm. "What do these things actually *do?*"

"Do you think for one moment that I would go against Grandpa's strict instructions and tell you *anything?*" he said.

"He doesn't know," Emma said breezily, and I knew instantly that she was trying to trick him into telling us something.

"Yes, I do," Egil said, placing a bowl of gravy on the table with a clatter.

"No, you don't," Emma said, and turned to me. "It's magic that is far too advanced for Egil. We've gone beyond his level already."

"That is just such utter—" He leaped into the air and scratched at nothing. "Air knot," he said.

"Yes," I said, joining Emma's game, "it's an air knot because you're confused by the wolves on our palms. You've never seen anything like them before."

"They are just clan signs," he said. "I have one myself, a cat. Look. . . ." Egil held up his hand, but neither Emma nor I looked up.

"That's just a drawing you did yourself," Emma said, cutting herself some meat. "Ours are special."

"They are not special; they are basic, simple clan signs."

"Which are what?" I asked quickly.

"Which are doorways into—"

"Egil," came a sharp voice. It was Doctor Felman, who had suddenly appeared from behind the silk curtain that led to our chambers. Emma and I both cursed a little under our breath. As Doctor Felman approached the table, Emma began to smile secretly at Egil's discomfort.

"Please be careful with our dear prince and princess," Doctor Felman said to Egil. "They imagine themselves to be terribly clever."

Doctor Felman leaned over my shoulder and helped himself to a piece of roast meat. He nodded at Egil. "Egil, you really are an excellent cook," he said.

"But he is easily tricked," said Emma.

Doctor Felman thought for a moment. Then he put his hand on my shoulder and smiled across the table at Emma. "That is no way to speak about your next teacher," he said, and Emma and I stopped chewing at the same time. "I have decided. Tomorrow Egil will take your class."

I turned and stared at Doctor Felman with disbelief.

"If you want Egil to tell you something, then you must allow him to do it properly," Doctor Felman said. "The Jerlamar takes tricks and turns them into truth. Tomorrow Egil will teach you all about your clan signs and what they are for."

With that Doctor Felman turned and walked back through the curtain. Egil angled his head like a cat to smile at us both.

"That backfired on you, didn't it?" he said. "Now, once you've eaten, straight to bed. Professor Catkin believes in long days with lots of homework."

15

"*You?*" I said. "A teacher?"

Emma and I met up with Egil by the hot spring beside the boulder that looked like a man on his knees. He had dressed up for the occasion and was wearing a flowing black robe that made him look like a bat. He had combed his hair back and greased it flat. He still looked like Egil, though.

"Yes, *me* a teacher," he said. "Silly idea, isn't it? Still . . ." He bowed like a virtuoso preparing to perform.

"As I think I told you, I actually *do* have . . . certain natural talents. And Grandpa has asked me to teach you about one of them. So today's lesson, children, is about the use of clan signs . . . and the related art of shifting."

The word wiped the smile from Emma's face. I glanced at her as Egil continued. "You see, the signs on your hands are gateways into the world in which you can change your shape. For me, changing shape is as natural as breathing." He jutted his chin. "Let me show you. . . ."

"Wait," I said firmly.

Egil peered at me, then at Emma. "Is there a problem?"

Emma bumped her fists together, but I spoke for her. "Yes, there is a problem."

"No, there isn't," Emma said firmly.

I turned to her, and she spoke loudly enough for Egil to hear and for half the glacier to hear. It was an announcement to the world of her new intention. "When I told my life story to the flower during our intuition classes, I realized something," she said. "I have always loved my father. My father has often visited me in my dreams, and I realize now he has always been helping me. The people who killed him were ignorant fools. I am proud of my father. Shifting can be good or bad."

Egil looked a little confused and a little annoyed that his performance had been delayed. "So . . . may I continue now, class?" he said.

Emma nodded firmly. "Yes. Teach us."

Without further invitation Egil leaped into the air and twirled around. His outline became blurred, and then the air was filled with a strange buzzing sound. As his spin began to slow, I saw that it was no longer Egil before us. Huge paws emerged first, then tusks, then tufts of wild striped hair, and then deep green eyes and a roar that made the ground shake. The spinning figure fell forward toward the ground, and when it landed . . . it was a saber-toothed tiger!

I leaped back. The creature roared at me again, showing off his massive saber teeth. They distorted the mouth and made the eye sockets bulge painfully. Sister Mary had shown me paintings and drawings of these prehistoric creatures, but this was something beyond the imagination of any book illustrator. He was as magnificent as a cathedral, with stripes of burning gold all along his back and down his gigantic tail. In my imaginary wars on the moon, Shipley had often transformed into a saber-toothed tiger, but in my dreams he was nothing as grand as this.

No sooner had I taken in the awesome sight of the tiger than he lifted himself onto his hind legs and began to spin again. This time the paws and striped legs stretched out and became wings, and the saber teeth melted into one to become a bright yellow beak. From the fizz and swirl emerged a black-and-white eagle that pounded the air around me and screeched to the heavens.

I stared with wonder as the eagle turned and became a bear and after that an elk. The display was so dazzling that I could hardly keep up with the changes. Finally, there emerged the small black cat I knew as Shipley. A few moments later, Shipley arched his back and stretched his legs, then began to turn once again into Egil. Egil the bizarre. Egil the suddenly magnificent.

He took a short breath and dusted himself off.

"Easy when you get the hang of it," he said softly.

Emma was staring with wide eyes, but to my surprise, I could see that she wasn't afraid. Indeed, she appeared to be quite overwhelmed by the performance. I took a moment to get the courage to go near to Egil. I touched him to make sure he was real.

"How do you *do* that?" I asked softly.

"You know already," he said. "You just don't know you know. And knowing what you know is more important than knowing."

He turned to Emma and held out his hand. His smile was beguiling, and his green eyes glowed.

"Of course, Emma, it seems a great big business at first," he said gently. "You need lots of pots, pans, and saucers banged together in your head. And you wonder if it is . . . not quite natural. But of course *everything* is natural. And unlike doing bad things, it gets easier. In the end the trouble you have is with staying as one thing. That really can get to be a headache."

Egil angled his head, and I could see Emma being drawn into those warm green eyes. Egil wrinkled his nose and Emma smiled.

"So, Toby and Emma," Egil said, "why don't we start with a little bit of theory. Just for fun. Promise, no horrid surprises."

I hesitated and looked through the steam at Emma. She stepped across the spring, and Egil took her hand to help her. When she was by his side, he clapped his hands.

"Very good, children," he said. "Let us begin."

Not surprisingly, Egil was a very bizarre teacher.

He began our lesson in how to shift into the "infinite varieties of imagination." His mind seemed to wander as *he* wandered round and round the kneeling boulder, strolling in and out of earshot as he rambled on and on about things as remote as far universes or as close as the fly on your nose.

"To begin with, you will shift into your kin creature," he said, pointing to his heart. "Your kin creature is the animal that is naturally in your soul and from which the Fel take their names. Professor Elkkin is kin of the elk, Hawkin is kin of the hawk, and so on. I am fortunate enough to be a cat. With you two, of course, it is the wolf, so that will be your first and easiest shift. That will . . . break the seal, so to speak. Then, with the easy part over, we can begin to . . ."

He disappeared behind the boulder at this point, and

his voice was just a droning sound. When he reappeared, things that had been complicated before became utterly indecipherable.

". . . It really becomes interesting only when you start on the infinite varieties of your imagination. You pick a creature that isn't your kin creature, and you study it and study it. You can picture it in your mind. The mist, you see, is deep underneath the picture, probably too far sometimes, so you have to just . . . dangle down and get in it. It's sort of wet, like new thoughts . . . old thoughts are dry and are prone to crack . . . but this mist isn't thoughts; it's more like itching in a place you haven't got. . . ."

Emma and I shook our heads at each other, totally confused, as he disappeared around the boulder again.

". . . Ninety-nine percent of any object is actually the space in between things. Mostly a thing is nothing. That's a fact. So you have to feel the in-between with a part of your body that doesn't exist and let it itch. Let it drive you mad . . . then you grab it! And you've got this bit of your body that is just . . . mist, and you squeeze the mist and this stuff drips out . . . like wet clay . . . and you shape it with your memory . . . and then . . . hey, presto. Before you know it . . . you're a marmoset."

"Egil, do you think you could stand still?" Emma said as he passed by.

"Was I walking?"

"Yes. Round and round. We didn't hear half of what you said."

"Oh. Anyway, shall we give it a go?"

"Give *what* a go?" I said.

Egil angled his head at me and smiled. "It's all right, you're not supposed to *understand* it anyway," he said, "because it's not really you I'm talking to. I'm actually talking to your little pets."

Egil sat down gently on the mud. We both sat down with him.

"Our what?" I said.

"Take a look at your hands," Egil said. Then he lay back on the mud to stare at the ice roof. I waited a moment, then looked down at my palm. The red wolf clan-sign tattoo on the palm of my right hand was moving! It was sitting up and howling silently, its head rippling on the joint of my forefinger, its tail sweeping the base of my thumb. I was so shaken, I could barely move.

When I looked up, I saw Emma staring at her hand.

"Toby!" she exclaimed. I hurried to her side and saw that the wolf on her palm was running through a dark landscape with low hills in the background. The images on our hands were like exquisitely detailed projections but somehow deeper than that and totally alive inside some silent world. We looked first at each other, then at Egil.

"Egil, what is happening?" I said. We both held our hands as far from our faces as possible.

Egil sat up and smiled. "And *you* thought I didn't know what they were for. How *wrong* you were."

He got to his feet and began to stroll toward us.

"Egil, this is badly, badly unusual," I said, staring as the wolf on my palm sat down to lick its foreleg.

"The Jerlamar and Grandpa drew those wolves from inside your souls and brought them out onto your skin," Egil said, picking his teeth with a thorn. "I have simply completed the second stage, which is to bring your clan signs to life. That's what teachers do. I woke them up with all the words I spoke behind the boulder. Words you didn't hear and wouldn't have understood anyway. Of course, the third stage is the really interesting part, and because it's interesting it is also difficult."

The image on my palm was noticeably slower and less active than Emma's. It was only now that I realized my palm had been itching ever since Egil had begun his lesson.

"Egil, they look . . . really, really real," Emma said.

"They *are* real," he replied.

"And . . . so beautiful!" Emma said, and Egil peered at her.

"Yes . . . quite beautiful," he said. "And they're not at all frightening, are they, Emma?"

Emma didn't hear. She was lost in amazement as she stared at her hand.

I clenched my fist, then opened it, but the wolf was still there. I dared to touch the image with my finger, and the wolf turned and snapped at it. I jumped with shock, and Egil giggled. Then he stood between us and studied our palms.

"Mmmmm," Egil said, "Emma's wolf is very alive, so I will give her five points. Toby, yours is looking a little bit not-really-there. I think two points is the best I can do. Please don't be offended; it's the Jerlamar that decides these things."

He scratched at an air knot, then turned his back to burp very loudly.

"So what is the third stage?" Emma asked, fizzing with excitement.

"The third stage is very complex," Egil said. "The bit of you that is a wolf gets bigger, and the bit of you that isn't a wolf gets smaller, until *you* become the wolf and the wolf becomes *you*."

I looked up at Emma, afraid of how she would react, but it seemed that nothing now could drag her attention away from the dancing creature on her palm. Egil gazed at her and seemed quietly satisfied.

"Okay, children, enough fun for today; class dismissed."

That night I hardly slept. I couldn't help checking my palm to see if the crazy thing was moving. Sometimes when I looked, the red wolf would be howling, but most of the time it was sleeping. It got more drowsy as the night wore on. The only way I could make it walk was to hold my hands to the fire made from the wood of the Holy Trusted Oak. The heat seemed to wake it up again.

I was surprised Emma didn't visit that evening. However, all through the night I could hear her laughing, like a child who has been given a brand-new toy to play with. I became annoyed that *her* thing was obviously far more entertaining than mine.

When I thought that envious thought, the wolf on my palm stopped moving altogether.

Egil came to our chambers early next morning and said he was going to take our "little pets" out for a run because they needed exercise. Emma walked through the longhouse staring at her palm and smiling at the tricks her wolf was doing all along her wrist and forearm. Her creature was evidently full of life. I kept my fist clenched because I didn't want Emma or Egil to know that mine had apparently died in the night. Killed, I thought, by skepticism.

We set off running through the mud, with Egil yelling,

"Yik, yik, onward to the mountains!" to encourage us. The idea was that if we ran, the wolves on our palms would run too, and by running together we would form a pack, the way that wolves do. He said we should free our minds of human thoughts and begin to smell and taste the world instead of looking at it. Eventually, he assured us, our shapes would shift and we would become the animals in our souls.

Our breath clouded in the frozen air as we ran. Egil called out to us that we had to feel the wolf scratching our palm and then try to feel the feeling from inside the wolf itself.

Running through the woods with a bow and arrow was one thing. This was different, and soon the relentless pace became a test of endurance. Emma had been walking and running great distances all her life, fetching water, herding cows, escaping from endless wars. I lagged behind Emma and Egil as we headed for higher country. Also, the wolf in my fist wasn't moving at all. Emma and Egil had to slow down and sometimes stop to allow me to catch up.

Finally I sat down on a rock and grunted with frustration. I dug my fingernails into my palm to spite the stupid wolf. Egil and Emma circled me. Egil peeled open my fingers and stared at my palm.

"Toby, there seems to be a blockage," Egil said, staring at me with his big green eyes. "Perhaps you should—"

"Egil, please don't start going on about the bloody mist again, because I have no idea what you are talking about.

Emma, do you have any idea what he is talking about?"

Emma shook her head, but my intuition told me she was lying. I stared at her.

"Actually," she said, "when I was running, I closed my eyes and . . ."

I could feel that Emma was pulling away from me, leaving me behind, and I didn't want to hear what happened when she closed her eyes. But I also wanted to hear every word.

"I saw . . . I felt"—she glanced at Egil, who urged her to continue—"a kind of white mist . . . like a memory. I was inside it. It was like having a memory of something that never happened. Except it was happening now."

"Beautifully put, Emma," Egil said softly, and they looked at each other like members of some secret club.

"Toby, I'm sure it'll come to you," Emma said. "You just need more time."

I got to my feet and turned my back on them. I really didn't want them being "nice" to me, especially not Emma. I felt a familiar sinking feeling and a voice inside my head telling me that those who are born broken stay broken, even in mad new worlds like this one.

Egil came close and spoke softly. "Toby, I don't want to put you under any pressure or anything, but if you can't learn to shift your shape, then there will be no point you carrying on, and Emma will have to continue on alone and will probably die a horrible death at the hands of Helva

Gullkin, and Langjoskull will endure three thousand years of tyranny and slaughter."

"Thanks, Egil," I snarled, "that's a great help."

"Sorry, Tobes. But what I'm saying is . . . try harder."

"I'm trying as hard as I can!" I yelled, and my voice carried across the windswept moor. "I just don't feel any mist, or spaces between things or anything! It's all twaddle! Okay?"

Egil peered at me, then jumped backward and clawed his hands.

"Sorry," he said, "you made the most disgusting air knot." I think he was just trying to make me smile, but I glared at him and then at Emma as if my failure were somehow their fault.

"Egil, let me speak to him alone," Emma said.

Egil bowed and walked a little way away to scatter some finches feeding on top of the mud. I didn't even look at Emma for a long time.

"Toby—"

I didn't let her speak. "Emma, for someone who not long ago thought shape-shifting was the worst, most wicked thing in the world, you're a pretty keen student," I said. "Or perhaps you just like the teacher."

I looked at her and saw the hurt expression I was hoping for.

"Toby, grow up."

"No."

"You have to believe this thing works. You have to believe we can change our shapes."

"Oh *yes!*" I said loudly enough for Egil to hear. "We just turn into bloody . . . birds or something and fly away."

"Why not?" Emma said, and I stared at her in disbelief.

"*Why not?* Because it's impossible. It's ridiculous. People don't just suddenly—"

"We're not people," she said flatly, and it sounded like some strong strap snapping somewhere far away. We looked away from each other for a moment. There was a horrible silence, broken only by the sound of our teacher yelling, "Yik, yik!" to some frightened birds.

"It's like sometimes in the moonlight a branch can look like a lion, or a monster," she said. "This is just making the half-truth come true."

"How do you *know* that?" I asked.

"I don't know," she said. "I just know."

"Well, good for you," I snapped.

"Just hold my hand," Emma said. I hesitated, then took her hand, and she squeezed mine tightly.

"If I can do the one thing I've always feared, then you can do it too," she said.

"Tell me how," I said, and added quickly, "without using the word *mist*."

Emma thought for a moment. "I think it is like . . . *imagining*," she said.

"That already doesn't make sense."

"When you say *imagine,* after you have said it, whatever comes next around it, there is a—"

"Mist?" I said flatly.

"Things that are solid wait for you to make them not solid. You can know something isn't real, but you can feel it in the palm of your hand—"

"Twaddle," I said.

"Also, Toby, those things I am remembering that never happened . . . they are all to do with my father. I seem to be remembering things he told me that I didn't remember before. He told me it's okay to search your soul."

"Well, I didn't have a father!" I exclaimed. "There. You have the advantage. You come from a long line of . . . shape-shifters. I come from a long line of people who don't exist."

"Toby, there is a memory inside you of a time when you shifted."

"What are you talking about?" I said.

"My intuition is telling me something. You *know* how to do this, but you are fighting against it."

She spoke with such authority that I sensed that she was moving beyond me in her power to read my mind.

"I'm not fighting anything," I said.

Emma opened her right hand and peered down. Her wolf was howling silently, its back traced by her heart line, its head defined by her life line, and I could see it was now much bigger than before.

"I don't know how I know," she said. "I just know that inside me something is breaking open. Something I thought was solid. It feels as if everything is just . . . *painted on.*"

I didn't like the distant look in her eyes and took my hand back.

"I have no idea what you're talking about," I said.

Egil was walking back toward us with a small sparrow in his mouth. When we turned to him, he dropped it quickly and coughed with embarrassment.

"Listen, we should be getting back," he said. "We've already gone much farther east from the longhouse than we should have. Grandpa said we mustn't stray too far without your bodyguards."

He looked at the distant mountains and mumbled a surprised little "yik, yik" to himself.

"In fact we're bloody miles away," he said.

We walked back in silence. I didn't even want to look at either of them, but I sensed that as we walked, Emma was trying hard to think of ways to explain all the things that were happening to her.

It was strange that when we had been running I had hardly noticed my surroundings, but as we returned I saw the most amazing sight on the horizon that I couldn't believe I had missed before. Past the ragged hills and valleys, there was the ghostly outline of a gigantic mountain that seemed to have had its head cut off. I stared at it as we walked, and Egil broke the silence.

"That is the Blue Volcano. The source, some say, of all Jerlamar power."

The volcano was lit by a hundred shafts of sunlight, and the steep outer slopes were indeed shining blue. A rainbow appeared above it.

"It's magnificent," Emma said in a distant voice.

"Does anyone ever climb up it?" I asked.

Egil laughed. "But of course," he said. "The Blue Volcano is where the Swearing of the Oaths takes place. When the great day comes, that is where you two will do battle with Helva Gullkin."

Emma and I stopped walking and stared at the mighty, majestic funnel of rock with sudden foreboding. The rainbow faded as quickly as it had appeared. I reached for her hand and held it tight to give her courage, but she didn't seem to need it.

"Inside the crater," Egil said in a distant whisper, "there is a lake, a mile across. It is frozen over with ice three feet thick. That will be the arena where you will fight Helva Gullkin. The inner slopes of the crater will be filled with Fels, Vela, and Thrulls who will witness your battle. Their roars will echo inside the volcano. And when the battle is won, you will stand on the rim and stare down as king and queen of Langjoskull. Then at last the Fel will be at peace."

Egil had become unusually somber. Suddenly the earth rumbled, and the ground beneath our feet shook. The volcano on the horizon looked like death or separation or both. It also looked like an awfully important place to die.

"Forgive me—it is traditional when passing the volcano to give thanks to the Jerlamar," Egil said, and he stepped a few yards away from us and fell to one knee, staring in the direction of the volcano. Emma and I glanced at each other. We spoke with our intuition and also with words, which were much more clumsy.

"I'm sorry," I said.

"For what?"

"For not being very good at turning into things."

"Toby, we stick together," she said. "Remember, we must never betray each other. I'm not going anywhere without you."

I was about to argue with her or blame her or even apologize again, but I didn't get the chance. Suddenly we heard a scream above our heads. Emma and I looked up at the same time to see twenty giant herring gulls flying toward us fast in V formation from the light in the east. The first scream must have been a signal that set off a hundred more.

Egil cut his prayer dead and got to his feet. He stared up

at the sky, and all the blood drained from his face.

"Helva Gullkin's warriors." He grunted.

My sword was in my hand before I knew it, and my fur coat writhed around my throat. The eyes on Emma's shawl all blinked at once, and it began to ripple in a wind none of us could feel.

"My eyes tell me it's an ambush," Emma said with great authority.

"And my intuition tells me Helva Gullkin is here in person," Egil said in a deadly whisper. "He has come to kill you himself."

Then, suddenly, just a yard away from us, there was a rainbow that touched the earth almost at our feet. And sliding down the rainbow came the feet, legs, body, and then gold-helmeted head of a huge Fel warrior. His hair flowed long around his shoulders, and his whiskers were greased to a shine. His nose was hooked, and his cruel eyes blinked quickly. In his hands he held a broadsword and a dagger, and his golden armor glinted in the ice-filtered sunlight.

His face was composed into a half smile, and his shining armor made him shimmer like an apparition. The rainbow around him slowly disappeared.

"Hello, cousins," he said. "It's Uncle Helva."

Egil spoke hoarsely. "Helva Gullkin, my lord. Have mercy."

My coat snarled and snapped around my shoulders. The

eyes on Emma's shawl stared without blinking.

"And why would you need mercy?" Gullkin said softly. His voice was hoarse, as if he had been screaming.

Egil was evidently terrified, and he tried to smile. "Quite right. We are just travelers."

"I believe you."

"We are just out strolling."

"Yes, yes," Gullkin said, and he suddenly pulled his golden sword. The emeralds, diamond, and rubies in the hilt flashed like lightning bolts. The air throbbed with power, and the blade glowed with a blue light.

"You are just travelers who are out strolling," he repeated. "Traveling to the throne of Langjoskull, strolling at the head of a rebellion."

The flock of seagulls above our heads was growing bigger by the moment, and as they circled they stared down silently, barely flapping their wings. Their movement was beginning to create a slow, powerful whirlwind.

"Lord Gullkin, you must speak to my grandfather," Egil stammered.

Gullkin was studying Emma and me with his head angled this way and that, looking at us like a curious bird. His sword suddenly rent the air, which fizzed.

"You mean your grandfather, the king of the conspirators?" he said.

"Please . . ."

"These *children,*" Gullkin snapped. "These sweet children . . . are human. I smell human. I *taste* human."

Gullkin suddenly bit the air, and his nose and mouth extended in an instant to become the horny beak of a gull. He screeched at the top of his voice, and the sound was unearthly. The ground shook, and for a moment my vision trembled.

It took a while for the echo to die. The gulls were circling just above our heads now, close enough for us to feel the draft from their wings.

"Yes, you are right," Emma suddenly said. "We *are* human. And also Fel."

Egil turned to her, astonished at her courage. I too was astonished. She was staring up at Gullkin, who towered above her. Gullkin twitched his head.

"You spoke to *me,* human mongrel?"

"I am no mongrel."

"You look and smell like a mongrel," Gullkin snarled. I suddenly felt a surge of anger run through my body and into my sword, which grew long at my hip.

"She is no mongrel, and neither am I," I said.

Egil stepped forward, his hands clasped together. "Lord Gullkin, please, there is a law," he said. "You *know* the law. You must respect it. If there is to be combat between you and these children, then it must take place on the day of the Swearing of—"

Gullkin suddenly screeched again, and this time the sound was so mighty that it created a wind blowing Egil, Emma, and me off our feet. We fell back into the mud.

Gullkin cut a diamond shape in the air with his sword and then came to stand over us. "A little bird tells me that these two mongrels are making fast progress," he hissed. "One of them is even hearing voices from the stones as well as the leaves. It would be foolish of me to allow them to finish their education."

He smiled and spoke softly. "So therefore the pupils must die now. In full public view. So that the hope of the rebels will be ended once and for all."

Emma and I scrambled to our feet, and Egil leaped to our side.

Gullkin twirled his golden sword around his head fast, three times, causing the whirlwind around us to speed up. A hundred gulls began to spin to earth, ripples of dark energy transforming them quickly. Within a few seconds they were gull warriors, their armor gray and gold, their swords curved like the beaks of gulls.

"Seize the children and kill the scarecrow," Helva Gullkin ordered.

"Run!" Egil yelled.

Emma, Egil, and I turned on our heels and ran. We scrambled over a line of boulders and struggled up a slope of volcanic shale. The line of pursuing gull warriors slid on the soft shale in their heavy armor, and soon we were far ahead of them on the brow of the hill. We dared to believe there was hope of escape until we saw another squadron of gulls landing and transforming on the other side of the hill, cutting us off.

I turned to Egil. "Egil, you can shift," I said. "Save yourself."

"No. I can't let you be captured. Use your weapons."

"What weapons?"

"The ones Grandpa gave you!"

Emma turned to me, and we both reached inside our shirts. Doctor Felman had given us reindeer-skin pouches to keep our golden weapons in, and they hung around our necks on gold chains.

I grabbed my dagger and Emma produced her golden pebble. They looked like feeble trinkets in our hands as the gull warriors began to charge at us.

"Egil, no one told us how they work!" Emma yelled.

"Put them together and release their power!" Egil cried.

We quickly clasped our palms together, and I felt an enormous surge of power coming from Emma's hand. I glimpsed a ferocious wolf's head snapping and snarling inside the cage of her fingers. The dagger and the pebble touched, and a blue lightning bolt flew toward the approaching warriors coming from the south and struck them in a crackling arc of electricity. The gull warriors were knocked from their feet, and some were thrown high into the air. Their golden suits of armor cracked like eggshells, and some pulled their helmets from their heads because the metal was glowing hot. The gull warriors fell back in confusion, and Emma and I looked at each other with open mouths.

"Wow," Emma said.

"Wow," I replied.

"Behind you!" Egil cried.

We turned to see another line of gull warriors charging toward us. Emma and I fumbled our hands together, and the effect was the same. A bolt of power flew from between our fingers like an electric-blue whiplash and hit the attackers with full force. The second wave fell back too.

Emma and I shouted with delight to see the power we had unleashed. A third line of gulls came at us, and we clasped our hands together again. This time the gull warriors transformed themselves back into gulls before the bolt of power could reach them. The defeated gulls took to the air and screeched.

"Egil! This is amazing!" I yelled.

Then Emma cried, "Arrows!" We both turned to see what looked like a heavy black rain in the air. We realized that it was a volley of arrows coming in our direction, and the bowstrings of the archers were still snapping. We touched our weapons together again, and the blue lightning swatted the arrows out of the sky. They fell in a burning bundle into the mud.

My intuition whispered a warning in my ear. I pointed to the left. "They are massing behind that hill," I said, and Emma nodded agreement.

"Let's go and get them," I cried. I could tell that Emma was enjoying this fantastic feeling of power just as much as I was. It felt like all my battles on the moon were rolled into one. I could smell burning feathers and see bodies lying in the mud, but they were demons and we were heroes, and of course we must triumph.

Then I saw Egil's face contorted with fear.

"Toby, look," he said. "He is inviting you to an enchanted combat."

Egil pointed in the opposite direction from the hill. Helva Gullkin was staring at us with his arms folded, a broad smile on his face.

"Do you dare?" he said.

Egil came close. "Gullkin has the power of four Keepers at his disposal," he said. "Your weapons are new, and your education is not complete. You will never resist him."

Emma and I were drunk on the power in our hands. Our intuition was in instant agreement. We would fight him.

"Run," Egil whispered. "I will become a lion and delay him."

"No," I said. "We fight."

Gullkin raised his arms. As he did they transformed into two wings that he beat against the air. A pulse of power burst forward. Emma and I touched our hands together, and our thunderbolt met Gullkin's invisible wave. There was a loud crack, and time seemed to stand still. In that moment Gullkin flapped his huge wings again, and another surge knocked Emma and me to the ground. Egil leaped above the wave and landed gently.

"Very heroic, Tobes and Emma, but please, listen to reason. You must live to fight another day."

He dragged us both to our feet and we began to run along the brow of the hill with warriors swarming toward us from both sides. Arrows began to rain down on us, but my coat had hardened into armor and Emma's shawl was like a cloak of steel.

I felt the weight of my sword at my hip and pulled it. I slashed at the nearest attackers, putting myself between Emma and the gulls to stop them from reaching her.

The sword clattered against their armor, but it felt less heavy and less powerful than when I was first given it. I realized Doctor Felman's power had almost drained away, and my intuition told me my own power was growing.

I managed to dispatch three of the gull warriors with one blow from the sword, clearing a path for Emma and me to race down a small slope. Then a giant gull flapped and landed directly ahead of us. It soon shifted and turned into Gullkin himself.

"Come, cousins, try your weapons on me again." He opened his arms and smiled.

"Emma, Toby!" Egil cried. "There is no other way to escape! You must shift or die!"

Egil threw himself between us and the gull warriors who were coming in pursuit to give us some time.

Suddenly Egil was lost among fifty flashing golden blades. But a moment later, a white mist gathered among them. The mist began to spin, and when it slowed down, I saw Egil had transformed into a gigantic snow leopard that began to tear into the feathers and flesh around him. His fur was thick and white, his paws the size of cart wheels, and he bounded across the helmets of his attackers, spreading mayhem and confusion as he made his escape.

With Egil gone, the gull warriors then turned their attention to Emma and me. In the few moments we had left before they reached us, Emma held out her hand and implored me, "Shift, Toby! You can do it!"

"I can't," I yelled.

The first of the gull warriors was upon us. Then Emma disappeared inside a cloud of white mist. There was a lightning flash inside the mist, followed by a terrifying howl. I saw electricity and flame. Shale pebbles were kicked up by a vortex of energy, and when the mist was blown away, there stood among the terrified warriors a huge, snarling red wolf.

Emma had shifted.

There were a dozen more gull warriors upon me, but I was too stunned to fight them. The flame-colored wolf reared up onto two legs, then hurled herself forward toward the line of warriors. I heard Gullkin yelling, "Seize her," but the raw fresh power of the new creature was too much for his warriors. The wolf bounded through the attackers, and with a snapping of straps and crushing of golden helmets, she was free. I saw her galloping across the hot earth and leaping over a lava stream toward a dark place where the snow leopard was waiting. I dropped my sword to the ground, and the warriors began to drag my coat from my back. The writhing fur fell limp. A warrior took my golden dagger and tugged the reindeer pouch from around my throat. A dozen golden swords were raised over my head.

As I waited for the first blows to land, the only thing I could think about was Emma, snarling and powerful and free.

16

When I came to, clawed hands were handling me roughly. I opened my eyes and saw golden helmets, hooked noses, and the unfeeling gull eyes of six warriors, some of them screeching in triumph.

Ropes were being wound around my body from my ankles to my chest. They were pulled tight, and then the biggest warriors took the ends of the ropes between their teeth. They began to run forward fast through the mud, and I was thrown to the ground, dragged at speed by the charging warriors with my head scraping violently against loose rocks. Within seconds, I felt myself being lifted. The gull warriors had changed into birds. They beat their wings in unison and pulled my ropes tight. I was soon flying high over the barren wastes of Langjoskull.

The pain of the ropes made me lose consciousness again, but I felt that we had been in the air for an hour or more when the Fel city became visible in the distance.

We flew around the outskirts of the city, and I saw heads raised below as Fels and Thrulls looked up at us. I had no idea if they knew who I was. They shaded their eyes for a few moments, then went back to their business.

After we had left the Fel city behind, I saw the distant outline of golden towers and wind-carved walls and realized we were heading for a huge castle. I guessed it was the castle of Will Wolfkin that Professor Elkkin had told us about and that I had seen in the distance on my first day under the ice.

As we drew near, I could see it was a mighty edifice that looked to have been carved out of smooth stone, rivers of red lava flowing all around it as a burning moat. The roofs of the palace swept elegantly into turrets and towers. The lemony shaft of sunlight that came from above made ice and metal sparkle in intricate patterns. The geysers inside exploded with blue water, which then turned yellow, then green, then golden.

When we were above the castle, I could see a network of streets laid out in concentric circles to form a pattern similar to a spider's web, or perhaps the iris of an eye, staring up at the ice roof.

There was no mistaking the ancient beauty of the castle. And there was no mistaking the ruination of that beauty, which first manifested itself in the dreadful stench of rotten fish and meat that rose in a cloud above the turrets.

Gulls had nested in every crevice and in every eave. All the concentric streets were littered with the trash of feasting, seal bones and the skeletons of other sea creatures piled high. Our giant shadow rippled over rooftops and crowded streets, where our progress was greeted with a deafening screeching from the gulls and gull warriors.

I also saw long lines of Thrulls in chains, being led away from the sunlight, pushed along by gull warriors using whips and canes. Meanwhile gull warriors sprawled beside the steaming hot springs, feasting and shrieking.

From my position high above the castle, I saw a vision of how the entire Fel city would someday look if Helva Gullkin ever came to full power.

There were chambers all around that were dug into the softer sandstone, with layers of rock forming roofs. The sandstone cliff was two hundred feet high, and there were maybe a thousand cells cut into it, all with prison bars made of gold. Gullkin's warrior guards flew to their positions in golden sentry boxes. I was dropped in a courtyard where the light was dim, behind high granite walls, and the force of the fall must have knocked me out again.

When I woke up, I was in a large dungeon shaped from

sandstone. The ropes that bound me had been cut. Water dripped from the granite roof, and I managed to drag myself under a regular drip to wash some of the dust from my mouth. The ropes had left deep impressions in my flesh, but the pain was far less troublesome than the feeling that I was now truly alone.

I looked through the golden bars across the castle. I could see straight lines of flowing lava that gave off a pleasant yellow light. The only thing I knew for sure was that in this world, just like in the old one, I was now a prisoner. Did I miss my old life? At least there was the kindness of Sister Mary, and Look and Leave to stare at. Here there were just shrieking gulls. Finally, I got up and walked the length of the cell, feeling the strength return to my legs. I scraped my hand along the rough walls just to feel something.

Even pain is better than no feeling at all. Finally I lay down to sleep.

I was woken by a spear poking into my back. When I opened my eyes, I saw Helva Gullkin himself standing over me. He had three warriors in attendance, and they angled their heads and blinked at me as I sat up, stiff from a night on hard stone.

Gullkin stood with his hands on his hips and his legs

apart, covered from head to toe in golden armor. His helmet had a spur of gold that covered his nose. His yellow eyes peered out from shadows.

"You have failed, cousin," he said.

"I'm not your cousin," I replied, stretching out my palm into the drip of water from the roof. I sucked some of the water into my mouth.

"You carry in your veins the blood of Will Wolfkin," Helva said. "The great Wolfkin would never allow himself to fail at *anything*. And yet here you are. A prisoner."

"Just tell me what you are going to do with me," I said as calmly as I could.

Gullkin's head drooped on his shoulders. Then he opened his mouth and let out one of his mighty shrieks. I fell onto my back up against the cell wall; the magnitude of the sound was so overpowering that for a few moments I was deafened.

Gullkin peered at me with his yellow gull eyes, which blinked quickly. He used the pointed toe of his boot to lift my chin.

"Tell me where the Blue Volcanoes are hiding."

"The Blue *what?*" I said, trying to buy some time. Gullkin gave one of his warriors a signal, and I was pulled roughly to my feet and pinned against the wall. The gull warrior had a blade to my throat.

"Tell me about the girl," Gullkin said.

"What girl?"

"The girl who succeeded where you failed."

Gullkin's head suddenly stretched again, and the visor of his helmet became a yellow beak. I feared another mighty shriek, but instead he simply twisted his head violently to expel his anger before silently returning to his Fellish form.

"I'm told you heard a voice, cousin."

"What voice?"

"A voice from the stones. Talking of betrayal."

I stared into his eyes.

"How do you know about that?"

"I have Keepers. The leaves and trees tell them things. You heard a voice from the stones. It said your little friend will betray you. And so it has come about. She abandoned you. She is free and you are in prison. What do you owe her?"

"I don't know what you're talking about," I said.

"If you can hear the voices of the stones, you are dangerous. Too dangerous. But I will do a deal with you, cousin," Gullkin said, turning his back on me, then twisting his head around to pierce me with his eyes.

"I will spare your life and make sure you are carried safely back to your human world if you tell me where the Blue Volcanoes are hiding."

"No deal," I snarled.

Gullkin jutted his chin, and one of the gull warriors pulled a sealskin parchment from inside his golden armor.

He unrolled it, and I saw a map of Langjoskull picked out in gold leaf on a deep blue background. I saw the land divided into light and dark, with the Fel city and the Blue Volcano glowing. I didn't understand the words that were written, but I saw an exquisitely drawn oak tree in the place I knew to be the Grove of the Holy Trusted Oak.

I realized quickly that wherever I looked on the map, the features came to life so that Gullkin could tell where I was looking. I knew that I mustn't look at the Holy Trusted Oak but neither must I *not* look at it. Gullkin grabbed the back of my neck and pushed my face toward the map. He hissed in my ear, and his voice was like razor blades. "Look at the place where you were taken by the Blue Volcanoes. Just look at it. You don't even have to speak."

I closed my eyes tight. Gullkin growled; then I felt his fingers turning into sharp claws as he began to squeeze my neck. Blood trickled onto my face, and I heard it dripping onto the map below my head.

"Unspeakable treachery," Gullkin growled, and I thought he was going to kill me there and then. Instead he shoved me with all his might against the wall. It took me a while to get my breath. Gullkin's claws had cut my neck in several places.

"I will never tell you anything," I said.

"Then you will die," he said.

"I don't care. I have lived a hundred lives in just a few days."

Gullkin shrieked again, and this time even his gull warriors were thrown off their feet. I shrank down against the wall. His screech was as powerful as an explosion, and the walls pulsed with it for several seconds.

"My power," he yelled in the echo, "is absolute! You will be killed so that everyone will know that the rebellion can never succeed!"

He stood over me, his feet either side of my knees as I cowered against the wall. I looked up at him with eyes wide and blood smearing my face.

"My only regret is that I won't live to see Langjoskull freed from your tyranny," I said.

With one sweep of his mighty arm, he lifted me from the floor and hurled me against the barred window in the far wall. I remember my head crunching against the rock, and I saw a flash of lightning before everything went black once more.

When I came to, I was standing on the back of a two-wheeled cart pulled by two black Iceland ponies. My hands were bound with ropes and I was being led out of the castle. We were heading in the direction of the Fel city, escorted by a squadron of gull warriors.

The market square was cleared when we arrived. Stalls were being dragged away and turned over by Gullkin's soldiers. Crowds of Fels and Thrulls had been pushed back by the guards, and others were arriving from every direction, summoned by royal decree. From my position up on the cart I could see all across the light side into the dark side of the city.

Hundreds of citizens were hurrying to get a better view, some of them laughing, others whispering and looking grave. It seemed that some were coming to celebrate my death, but many more were coming to mourn me. I saw shutters being closed in upstairs rooms by Fels or their Thrull servants, who gave me gentle, pitying looks before they disappeared.

Gullkin arrived in a golden chariot a few minutes after the market square had filled up. He was helped from his carriage by two warriors. His thin lips curled into a smile as he walked by and waved his glove in my face.

A scaffold of oak logs had been hastily built, and I thought it might be a gallows, but I soon saw that it was a speaking platform, with gold and gray flags draped across it. I then saw a huge rounded rock, like a millstone, being rolled into the center of the market square. A large gull warrior with an axe stretched his muscles nearby.

The crowd had now gathered and had divided themselves informally into two groups, according to their sympathies. The largest group was made up of an equal mix of Fels,

Vela, and Thrulls who watched the proceedings in silence. The other, smaller group was made up of wealthy-looking Fels and gull warriors, and they were talking excitedly and congratulating one another by shaking hands.

Then there was a drumroll, and Helva Gullkin climbed up onto the scaffold. He raised his hand and the crowd fell quiet. Mothers put their hands over the mouths of their children.

"Citizens of Langjoskull glacier!" Gullkin announced loudly. "I have summoned you all here today to celebrate a very happy occasion."

A ripple ran through the crowd. Gullkin stepped forward on the platform. He had a breathless, forceful way of talking, and no one in the crowd could take their eyes off him as he paced back and forth. He removed his helmet and swept back his hair.

"There is to be an execution today. This boy. This boy you see before you, the one you have heard rumors about, this . . . *human* boy." Gullkin gestured toward me. "This outlaw. This mongrel, this . . . offense against nature. Today he will die before your eyes. And you will cheer!"

The smaller portion of the crowd set up a huge cheer. The bigger mob stayed silent, and Gullkin studied them. He strode across the stage to be closer to them.

"You," he said, pointing at the mixed Fels, Vela, and Thrulls, "seem less than pleased that we are to be rid of this creature. Indeed, you seem . . . unhappy altogether. Sad, almost."

There was silence except for a loose shutter that banged in the wind above my head.

"Very well," Gullkin said. "You are then, I take it, supporters of the unrest. Believers in uncertainty. Followers of whoever may take the lead for whatever reason they might give. You are the ones who have been secretly hoping these past hundred years that you would be rescued somehow by outsiders and that some new world order would be put in place. You are, in a word . . . parliamentarians."

The silent mob began to shift uneasily. There were hundreds of gull warriors standing at attention around the market square and more waiting in the side streets. Gullkin sneered the word *parliamentarians,* and his face almost shifted into the face of a gull, but he contained it with a fierce smile.

Gullkin was staring only at his opponents.

"You are the ones who think, perhaps, that the mob can decide the fate of the mob," he said. "You think that the flood knows when to stop itself, that we should all share equally in the decisions concerning the future of our world."

Gullkin wandered across the platform toward his supporters and appeared to give the idea of sharing equally a moment of reasonable consideration. Like everyone else in the crowd, I found myself being hypnotized by Gullkin's performance. As he continued to speak, I almost forgot that my hands were bound with ropes.

He stopped pacing and smiled. "Who here likes roasted puffin meat?" he asked. "Come. Raise your hands."

Some of his supporters raised their hands. Some of the children among the group Gullkin had called parliamentarians raised their hands too, but their mothers snatched them down.

"And who here prefers to eat reindeer?" Gullkin asked, shading his eyes from the sun to get a better view of the vote.

Words were exchanged behind cupped hands among the parliamentarians. Some hands were raised among Gullkin's supporters.

"I only ask to prove that we all prefer different things," Gullkin said. "Myself, I prefer puffin. But as your king, I say those who like reindeer should eat reindeer. Those who like puffin should eat puffin."

Gullkin suddenly turned on his heels and pointed directly at the silent ones. "However, the parliamentarians disagree. They say . . . take a vote. And whoever gets the most votes wins. So if more voters prefer puffin, then *everyone* must eat puffin. Puffin for breakfast, puffin for dinner, and puffin for supper whether you like it or not, because that is what the mob has decided you like."

There was a single cry of protest from among the

parliamentarians, but the voice was stifled.

"And who exactly is it who is introducing this *human* idea of mob rule?" Gullkin asked as he strode across the stage to be nearer to the cart where I was standing. "Why, it is a *human,* of course. And what is more, these humans who are now among us also have other plans. Do you know what those plans are?"

Every head in the crowd followed Gullkin as he came to stand beside me.

"They are planning an end to the Great Separation," Gullkin said, and he shrugged and set off across the stage again.

"A return to the days of traps and torture and imprisonment. Please, those of you old enough to remember, take a moment to explain to the younger ones what the humans used to do to those Fels who refused to share their magic with them."

Gullkin put his hands on his hips and allowed the crowd a few moments. Some began to mutter old stories. Gullkin nodded gently.

"Are they pretty stories? Happy memories of our lives shared with humans? No. I think not." He set off across the stage toward me again. "Thousands and thousands of Fels were trapped and killed for their secrets in the way beavers are trapped for their fur."

The truth of Gullkin's words spread through both

parts of the crowd. Some of the crowd began to glare at me.

"And now the humans are coming *here,* to our last sanctuary. Just as I always knew they would." He nodded his head with exaggerated certainty.

"Oh yes, my intuition predicted this. I predicted that the humans would someday come here to enslave us. That is why I forbade the teaching of the Fellish arts to my beloved citizens. If a beaver has no fur, there is no point trapping it. If a Fel knows no magic, there is no reason to torture him."

The wisdom of Gullkin's words was reflected in a gentle hubbub. I could see that the mob was swaying toward him.

"Only I and my trusted warriors have the knowledge the humans are after," Gullkin said. "We have taken it upon ourselves to be the protectors of the Fellish arts, and if the humans come, then it is we who will fight and die . . . on your behalf."

The hubbub turned into a ripple of applause. The gull warriors who before had been standing guard over the crowd now stood erect like guardians. Gullkin once again pointed directly at me.

"The humans have sent two advance scouts under the ice. This human boy is one of them. This boy would bring mob rule and torture in his wake. Now, who here wants to see him executed, and who would have him set free to destroy our world?"

Before the crowd could consider this, Gullkin pointed at me and proclaimed, "This boy claims to be a descendant of the great king Will Wolfkin. That is his proud boast."

Suddenly Helva Gullkin puffed out his chest and shrieked. A huge wall of wind hit the crowd, blowing hats from heads and smoke from pipes. Children began to scream in terror. The crowd collectively took a step back. Gullkin twisted his neck in his collar, and his yellow eyes flashed.

"That is the cry of a Fel of true royal blood," Gullkin said as the echo of his screech died away. "Now let us hear the voice of the human, to see if there is a family resemblance."

I could feel the eyes of the population burning into me.

"Go on, speak," Gullkin said. I felt my face reddening. My tongue was as still as when I was in my chair. The crowd began to murmur and some began to jeer.

"Human? Tell us in your own words why you have come here to our world," Gullkin insisted.

"I . . . I was . . ." My voice sounded like a feeble squeak. "I was brought here against my will," I said.

I could feel the disbelief among the crowd. I searched for a face that I recognized, but there was not a single one. Where *were* the Blue Volcanoes? Where were Doctor Felman and Arthur and Earl Hawkin? Where was Emma?

"Against your will?" Gullkin said. "So why were you arrested with a rebel sword in your hand, putting up a fight against the royal guard?"

I tried to speak but no words would come.

"The truth is, human, you are a liar," Gullkin said. "You are no descendant of Will Wolfkin. You are a spy come to steal our magic."

Gullkin suddenly pulled a whip from inside his armor. The whip had three lashes, and each one had a snake head at the tip. The snake heads all hissed and writhed in the air. He slashed at my throat, and I felt my skin burn as it began to bleed.

"Does that look like royal blood?" shrieked Gullkin. "Or the blood of a spy?"

When the whip struck me, I saw a few of the Thrulls step closer. It was as if they had felt the blow themselves. The gentle look on their faces gave me strength.

"Gullkin has divided you into . . . slaves . . . and . . . masters," I said. My voice had come from nowhere. "You should all have freedom to live your lives. . . ."

Gullkin roared with laughter. "Did you *hear* that voice? That pitiful squeak? Speak up, boy, we can't hear you."

I swallowed hard and tried to yell, but no sound would come. Some in the crowd on both sides began to laugh. Gullkin stepped up with a swagger.

"Why is it that a *human*, a creature of inventions, believes he has the right to proclaim himself better than any of you? Or all of you put together?"

The crowd roared again, a mixture of laughter and anger. I felt exactly the way I had felt when I was in my chair . . . a freak, an oddity . . . and it was then that something snapped inside my head. I was suddenly blinded by a memory so vivid, it came between my eyes and my vision. It took hold of me completely and played itself out on the faces of the crowd.

Once, when I was about six years old, Sister Mary had taken me for an outing. She'd been planning it for days. She packed a sandwich, rolled up blankets, bought an umbrella in case it rained. Then on the allotted morning, we set off on the great adventure. A one-mile walk to the local park. It was called Cherry Tree Woods.

It was a beautiful summer day. The large oaks and chestnut trees were in full leaf, and the grass pasture had been newly mowed, so the air was green with the smell of cut grass.

And it was magnificent.

I'd hardly been outside the convent in my life, but the park was an asylum of color and noise and dogs and children. Sister Mary ran behind my chair, pushing me as fast as her stick-thin legs could manage, and even though it's impossible, Sister Mary swore for years after that I smiled. We ran through the park and would have flown if we could.

However, our mad dash along the straight path by the tennis courts attracted the attention of some older children who were lazily pulling apart the den of some smaller children, just for horrible fun. I suppose these teenagers were bored, and when their boredom was interrupted by a nun and a poor little cripple in a chair, it was too much for them to resist.

They began to chase us. When Sister Mary realized, she stopped and slowed down to a walking pace, turning to face them. They gathered around my chair to pull stupid faces and make idiotic noises.

Sister Mary tried to shoo them away, but it was hopeless. One of the boys, the biggest and boldest and stupidest, decided to start tickling my face with his fingers and calling me "lickle baby." The others began to tug at my fingers and pull my socks off. They were socks Sister Mary had knitted for me. They threw them into the trees.

My fury would have filled the universe, but I couldn't move. Instead, my anger built up and built up like steam in a piston. Sister Mary had begun to cry, and inside I could feel this mighty feeling swelling. I could have twisted steel girders with it.

When anger this great is met with a body that can't express it, there are no human words for the pain. But then, as luck or fate would have it, I saw a dog.

It was a husky, a big one with serious teeth and a massive head. Its owner was throwing sticks for it, and it was fetching in snarls and clouds of dust. I could see the dog just over the shoulder of one of my tormentors, and I decided with the simple logic of a small child that I should put this impossible feeling of fury into the dog. I stared at the animal, silently *willed* my anger into the dog, and demanded that it get these boys away from me. But it was more than a wish or an order. It was . . . something else.

And suddenly the boys were scattering.

The dog was among them, snarling with exactly the same fury I was feeling. It grabbed the biggest boy by the arm and hauled him to the ground. It then knocked another boy off his feet and swirled in a tornado of anger to bite a hole in the jeans of another of the idiots. Their eyes were popping, and I was howling inside with joy and fury mixed. Soon they were running, Sister Mary was on her backside screaming, and the owner of the dog was struggling to fix its lead.

"I am *so* sorry," the dog owner said to Sister Mary as she got to her feet. "He's *never* done anything like that before." The owner seemed to think the dog had attacked me, but Sister Mary put him straight and suggested that maybe an angel had entered the dog and made it do God's work.

Only I knew it was no angel. It was me. Emma had been right. I *did* have a memory of shifting. Even if my physical body hadn't changed, I'd had experience of how it felt to be inside the body of another creature.

This entire memory of the incident in the park hit me

in half a second. For the first time since then, as I stood facing the laughing crowd, this time of Fels and Thrulls, I felt equally angry. I felt the same click in the head, the same shifting of a mighty boulder.

I began to stare into individual faces in the crowd. And as I did, I felt a scratching and itching in the palm of my right hand. I couldn't look at it because my arms were bound, but I could feel something snarling and biting in between my fingers, as if I were holding a tiny but ferocious wild creature.

Then, to my astonishment, near the front of the mob, the face of Doctor Felman suddenly appeared. He had fixed me with the most piercing stare, and even though the crowd was baying and yelling by now, I could hear his voice coming to me in a whisper, just as if he were right by my side in the cart.

"Use that moment from your memory," he was saying softly. "Use the mist inside the memory. You have done it before. Do it again. You *can* do it, Toby."

As luck would have it, at that moment a rotten lump of walrus meat hit me in the face, thrown by someone in the crowd. It was the final tug of the rope to haul me to the very summit of my anger. The meat stank and the blood dribbled, and because my hands were tied I couldn't get it off. I felt something snapping and twisting around the fingers of my right hand and knew my wolf was in a frenzy. The meat became the fingers of the boy tickling my face in Cherry

Tree Woods, and I snarled and spat and bit to remove it.

Then I was lost inside a white mist. It dissolved my bones and turned my flesh to vapor. For a second I was just a detached memory floating in a beautiful cloud of whiteness, and I knew the volcano within was about to erupt.

I noticed that my hands had become free from their bindings. I opened my mouth to yell at Gullkin, but instead from my mouth came a blood-chilling howl. It was long and deep, and it echoed across the city. Suddenly there was total silence. For a second everyone simply stared at me. I saw Gullkin's look of horror as he dropped his sword in shock.

And it wasn't until I landed on the cold cobbles and the crowd began to flee that I realized I was landing on four feet.

I had shifted. I was a wolf.

17

Suddenly, from nowhere, the Blue Volcanoes appeared with a mighty roar.

They stepped up from their hiding places on the rooftops and began to fire their arrows at the gull warriors below. They were all wearing tunics that bore the symbol of the unblinking blue eye. A huge silk flag with the same staring eye was unfurled, and it rolled down the side of a tall building that stood beside the market square.

The archers fired a volley after volley of arrows, and the warriors guarding the stage began to take cover or shift. The crowds of families began to scatter and disappear into doorways and alleys, leaving only the soldiers from both sides on the streets. Some of the Thrulls grabbed what weapons they were carrying and charged the stage. Some among the Fels resisted them. Meanwhile other Fels and Vela took sides with the Thrulls and the Blue Volcanoes.

Civil war broke out in Langjoskull right there and then, and the war had been started by the howl of a wolf. That wolf was me.

Gullkin's reserve force of warriors spilled into the market square. More Blue Volcanoes came swarming in to do battle. The fighting spread to the rooftops as gulls landed and shifted to deal with the bowmen.

Meanwhile, I was getting used to the most incredible new sensation. It was more than just feeling myself inside a new body. It was a liberation. It felt like those moments when I took my first steps out of my chair. Once I was just a mind. Then I put on the clothing of a human. Now I was trying on a different set of clothes.

Being a wolf was wild.

I stood up on hind legs and roared. I saw the horses that pulled Gullkin's carriage rearing up and panicking, while their masters tried to whip them into obedience. I jumped to the ground as one gull warrior after another ran to face me. I knocked them all down. A geyser erupted in the distance and a shower of warm water began to fall, making the cobblestones slippery. Fels and Thrulls, Blue Volcanoes and gull warriors skidded and slipped over as they fought.

Gullkin's warriors were forming a ragged line. Then I saw Gullkin himself towering over them, transformed into a glowering, shrieking gull from the waist up with the powerful legs of a warrior. He stretched his wings and hopped over his forward line to face me. He then coughed and choked for a moment before bringing up the most mighty shriek from the roots of his soul.

I felt the blast of his anger, but this time I responded with a cry of my own.

My wolf howl was strong and so loud and so long that I thought it might demolish buildings. Every ounce of anger and indignation I had ever felt was in that cry. Gullkin was rocked back on his feet.

I saw a big red tongue lolling from my mouth, and the sight of my own tongue scared me.

"What happened to me?" I tried to say out loud, but instead there was only a strangled growling noise deep in my throat. I wanted to sit down, but my body didn't work like that anymore.

Then I saw a huge squadron of gulls circling and landing in the streets to the right of the market square. A second later I saw Doctor Felman directing a bolt of blue lightning in the direction of the stage where Gullkin had made his address. The stage burst into flames, and the flames spread quickly.

My intuition told me to turn, and when I looked around,

I saw what at first I thought was my reflection but was in fact another large red wolf.

I knew it was Emma and she howled a greeting to me. With that, the battle was in full cry.

I saw a snow leopard bounding into the square and leaping toward the line of gull warriors. My intuition let me know it was Egil, and he caused panic among the enemy as he crashed through their shields.

When the numbers of gull warriors grew too great, the snow leopard suddenly changed into a raven that flew up into the air to do battle with descending gulls. Meanwhile the Blue Volcanoes and the gull warriors were fighting hand to hand around the millstone that would have been the last place I would have rested my head if I hadn't finally broken free.

With my wolf senses I could smell the lava and the falling water and the bodies of the Fels who had fallen. Then I saw something flashing in front of my eyes. It was Helva Gullkin's golden sword, and it was about to cut me in two.

"Pretender!" he shrieked. "You will die anyway."

I opened my huge jaws and took the blade of the sword into my mouth. I gritted my teeth with all my might, and felt the gold of Gullkin's blade cracking like ice. I shook my head, and the sword broke in two. Gullkin went for his dagger, but I leaped through the air and knocked him to the ground. I was about to go for his throat, but he rolled out of my reach.

Then we stood facing each other. He had drawn a golden dagger, and his beak began to snap and chatter in fury. Our eyes were locked. His glare challenged me to make my move. Then Emma leaped through the air, and I realized she had taken an arrow that had been heading directly for me while Gullkin was keeping me occupied.

Emma screeched in pain, and as she landed she shifted back into the form of Emma the girl. The arrow that had hit her in the foreleg was now protruding from her upper arm. I snarled with fury to see her hurt and saw Gullkin stepping toward her with the broken half of his sword raised.

I managed to pounce on him and knock him from his feet. Meanwhile Doctor Felman fired another bolt of power across the marketplace and cleared a space for me to grab Emma's tunic in my jaws and drag her to safety.

As the battle raged around us, I felt myself shifting back into a boy. With my anger turned to anxiety for Emma, my body changed itself back without my willing it.

"Emma, are you okay?" I whispered.

She gritted her teeth and nodded.

"We came to save you," she said softly. "We must never let each other down."

I could see that her wound was deep. A second later, Egil skidded to our side with a small brown bottle in the palm of his hand. He poured some liquid that smelled of pine needles onto Emma's wound and then yanked the arrow out. To my amazement she didn't cry out in pain, and the wound healed instantly and right before my eyes. Egil put the little bottle back into his pocket.

"Grandpa says you two have to get out of here *now,*" Egil said.

Emma raised herself from the ground, and I could see that there was now no pain from her wound at all.

"No, we stay and fight," she said, bumping her fists together hard.

"Grandpa says that you are too precious. Now that Toby is free, you must hide."

Egil turned and glanced across the market square. "Things are not going well here."

As if confirming what Egil had said, three Blue Volcanoes fell from the rooftops, and more gull warriors streamed into the market square beneath golden shields.

"Then you need us all the more," Emma said.

"No, Emma," Egil said urgently. "Without you we are just a rebel army. *With* you we are on the side of the ancient law. There is a safe place. In the land of the Sleepless Warriors. You must hide there and stay safe."

I was about to ask Egil who the Sleepless Warriors were when suddenly a shadow fell across all three of us. A second later, a giant hawk swooped down and grabbed Emma in its huge talons. I felt the beating of the hawk's mighty wings around my head and cried out, "Emma!"

The giant bird was already fifty feet in the air, and I could see Emma struggling in its claws. Egil grabbed my arm.

"It's okay, Toby—the hawk is Earl Hawkin. He's taking her to the safe place. And you must go too."

At that moment Gletta the Iceland pony galloped to my side from the edge of the square.

"Gletta knows where to go. When you reach a waterfall, dive in. The river will take you to where Emma is waiting."

Over Gletta's shoulder I saw the battle raging. The Blue Volcanoes now held only one-quarter of the square, and they were falling back. Doctor Felman was nowhere to be seen. The huge flag of the Blue Volcanoes was being torn down by gull warriors.

"You must go, Toby," Egil said. "The future of Langjoskull depends on you staying alive."

The moment I was on her back, Gletta began to gallop at impossible speed through the crowd of Blue Volcanoes who were now being crushed together by the advancing gull warriors. I was a better rider now than when I first rode this horse, but the mad race made me hug Gletta's neck with both arms.

We were soon out of the square and into a side street where wounded Blue Volcanoes were being treated. I briefly glimpsed Professor Elkkin moving from soldier to soldier, pouring liquid onto wounds from the same sort of bottle that Egil had used on Emma.

Gletta didn't speed up and didn't slow down. We left the city, and as we did the light began to fade. Soon the Blue Volcano itself loomed out of the mist to the east, and after that I rode in half darkness.

We must have traveled twenty miles before I heard a roaring sound in the distance and felt a spray of ice-cold water that woke me from a half sleep in the saddle. I felt a fine mist, then saw a waterfall, a hundred feet across, straight ahead of us. Gletta didn't slow down, and I thought she was going to run on into the abyss. At the last moment she stopped. I dismounted and the sight of the waterfall so close made my heart stop.

The noise from the falls was a constant sound, like a powerful turbine. I peeked over the edge and saw the plunge pool below, the rush of the water pulling me toward it. The river ran east from the falls in a raging torrent. I turned to Gletta, who was still standing at attention.

"What is this place?" I asked. Gletta simply blew steam into the air.

I looked over the edge again. It was a long, long way down. Now all I had to do was jump.

Forcing your body to do the one thing it really, really doesn't want to do is not easy. Bodies are smart. Bodies know how to stay alive. Bodies know you don't throw yourself into a billion gallons of rushing water and drop three hundred feet into an ice-cold cauldron of certain death.

I paced back and forth on the edge of the roaring engine of water, speaking out loud to myself. "Idiotic, idiotic, idiotic idea."

After a while I sat down on a rock and began to give myself a really serious talking-to. It was then that my palm began to itch. I looked down and saw that my clan sign had changed. In place of the howling wolf there was now a fatter, flatter creature with a stubby nose. When it began to move, I realized it was a seal. The seal opened its mouth and let out a silent cry.

"Oh, help me, Sister Mary—I think I have totally lost my mind," I said, "but here goes."

Without thinking another thought, I ran to the precipice and jumped. It took a while for my descent to meet the descent of the falling water, but when it did, the whole world became whiteness and the fizzing of bubbles. My stomach rolled with the speed of the fall, and I instinctively flapped my arms. Then I was spinning in darkness like a sock in a dryer, and I knew I was at the mercy of downward currents. I tried to use my arms to swim, but I didn't have any arms to use. I wanted to flap my feet, but when I tried, I could feel only tightness. My legs were joined together into a fat tail just as they had been when I came ashore for the first time on the coast of Iceland.

Then a ripple ran through my body, and I was free of the vortex. In the darkness, I headed for what I assumed was up. I broke the surface in a fast-flowing current and looked down at my body. For a moment I saw that I had a seal's tail where my legs should have been. It was almost as shocking as that first time, but this time I knew it was real and not my imagination.

The river was running through a dark land split by flowing seams of molten lava. Where the lava and the river met, the water hissed and steamed. The lava also raised the temperature of the water so it actually became quite pleasant. I was being dragged along swiftly, and the river turned me and spun me around.

As the current slowed down, I felt my legs separating from each other and I flapped my feet. I was splashing with two legs and realized I was human again. I let the river take me in its powerful current, and after a few minutes I realized something. This was *fun.*

My white-water pleasure-park ride lasted half an hour. I was taken through gorges and narrow passes where seams of gold glistened in the red light. I saw strange paintings on the walls of the gorges, and they reminded me of the paintings Sister Mary had once shown me from a cave in France. Once

I got snagged on some rocks and realized that the rocks were studded with diamonds. I tugged a diamond free, then plunged back into the river with a great whoop of joy.

Almost any journey is enjoyable if it is taking you to where you want to be, and I knew this river was taking me to Emma.

Finally I was slowing down and the river was growing fat. I reached slack water, and there in the middle of the sluggish river was a white island, covered in the strangest bones I had ever seen.

My intuition told me that Emma was close, so I climbed out of the water.

I could tell the bones didn't belong to any creature I knew. I picked up one that looked like a leg bone, and it crumbled between my fingers like soft chalk. There were hip bones and rib bones that looked almost human, but I guessed they would have to belong to someone twenty feet tall. I was shivering with cold after being submerged in the warm water for so long. I looked around and saw two giant black holes in the cliff above my head. They looked like soulless eyes staring down at me. Then I heard a pebble falling down the cliff face and landing with a splash in the water before me.

Someone was sending me a signal.

I climbed up the bank. Another pebble fell from above, and I saw that it had come from one of the two caves. There were steps cut into the rock, and I began to climb. The rock was loose and treacherous, but after a long struggle I made it to the mouth of the cave. Suddenly a shadow came hurtling out of the darkness and flew toward me.

It was only as I stumbled back that I realized the shadow was Emma, and she was hugging me with all her might.

"Emma!" I yelled, and she grinned and shushed me at the same time. She grabbed my hand and pulled me into the darkness of the cave.

I said some silly things and she said some silly things, and we couldn't stop laughing for a long time. Emma had a lava fire and a teapot warming and lots of dried meat hanging from hooks driven into the cave wall.

When we stopped dancing and saying silly things, the darkness seemed to take offense at our happiness and slowly seeped into our bones. Emma poured me some horrible Fel tea that I drank just because it was warm, and I dried my clothes by the heat of the lava. I banged my head on an overhanging rock, and Emma giggled.

"This is some beautiful palace for a prince and princess, isn't it?" she said with a laugh, but for some reason it made us both instantly sad. The darkness of the cave took its opportunity to overwhelm us.

"How long have you been here?" I asked.

"A few hours," she said. "Earl Hawkin set up the fire and left us some food to eat."

"Did they tell you how long they expect us to stay here?" I asked, and she tried to look hopeful.

"Just until it is safe to return," she said. "Or until the Swearing of the Oaths."

"What sort of food is there?" I asked.

"Dried puffin," she said softly. "And dried berries."

We huddled closer to the lava fire. Emma looked up at me and smiled.

"You did it," she said. "You shifted."

I tried not to look too proud of myself.

"Yes. Twice," I said. "I just swam down a river as a seal."

"Easy when you get the hang of it," Emma said.

There was a note of sadness in her voice, and I could tell some part of her was still unsure that what we were doing was right. I took hold of her hand.

"How did it feel to be a wolf?" I asked, and we began to paint the walls of the cave with our memories from the battle we had just fought and from the transformations we had undergone. We were so engrossed in our storytelling, I hardly noticed that from time to time a wind blew from the darkness, and with it came a smell I hadn't smelled since the first day I came under the ice.

It was the smell of fresh air.

18

When I pushed her on it, I discovered that Emma felt the same way as I did about how it felt to shift.

Magnificent was the word she used for the feeling of losing one's shape and taking on another. I compared it to the feeling I had when I first walked after so many years in a chair. Sudden freedom, a fizz of possibilities, a realization that boring old solid things weren't really solid at all.

"The *mist,*" Emma said, impersonating Egil in a ludicrous way, "is the bits of imagination between everything that isn't."

We laughed, but now we both almost understood what Egil had taught us. I chewed some dried puffin and discovered it tasted exactly how you would imagine dried puffin to taste. Horrible. The smell of fresh air came and went, and I stepped toward the darkness in the throat of the cave to check it out.

"Before he left, Earl Hawkin told me that there are creatures living in these caves," Emma said with a shudder.

"What creatures?"

"Sleepless Warriors," she said. "This is their land. We're not really supposed to be here. There is a treaty between them and the Fels agreeing that they leave each other alone. But Earl Hawkin said if we were quiet, we would be okay."

"Did he tell you what they look like?" I asked.

She nodded but seemed reluctant to share her knowledge.

"Emma, I can read your mind anyway, so you might as well just tell me."

Emma stared into the fire. "He said they are tall. Thirty feet sometimes. They have only one eye, here in the middle of their face. It never closes. That's why they are called Sleepless Warriors. They carry swords made from burning lava, and . . ."

I returned to the warmth of the fire, not daring to look into the darkness that framed us.

". . . Earl Hawkin told me they can crunch you in half in their mouths," she said quietly.

"That was very helpful of him," I said.

"He just wanted to be sure we didn't go exploring."

In the nervous silence, I took some deep breaths. The smell of fresh air was now unmistakable, and I thought I could also smell the ocean.

"Emma," I said, "did Egil tell you how far this cave is from the roof of the glacier?"

"No," she replied.

"We have traveled a long way east," I said. "Perhaps we are close to the edge."

"Perhaps."

We glanced at each other. Then, over Emma's shoulder, in the cold light at the mouth of the cave, I saw the sweep of a mighty wing.

I was on my feet and Emma joined me. I reached for my sword, but of course all my weapons had been taken from me. Emma still had her golden pebble, but without my own weapon it was just a pebble. She had lost her shawl when she shifted. We were now pretty much defenseless.

We heard a loud and mournful cry that echoed in the darkness of the cave. It seemed to be filled with sadness, even though I could tell it was the cry of a bird.

A shadow swept across the mouth of the cave again, and I stepped forward to confront whatever monster was out there. Emma came to my side and we held hands. The clan signs in our palms touched, and there was a crackle of energy between us even though we had no weapons.

We stepped out of the shadows and looked up to see the giant hawk that had carried Emma away swooping toward us with its beak open. Its long yellow talons were outstretched, and each of its claws was the size of a small sword. The hawk gave another cry as it dived.

The hawk shifted as it landed. I saw the familiar tweed suit and green hat of Earl Hawkin. His clothes were torn and bloody from several cuts on his face and arms. He staggered a little and rested on a boulder for support. We ran to him, and he wiped some blood from his face with his hat.

"I must brush up on my landing technique," he said hoarsely.

We led him inside the cave, and I used some water that was dripping through the roof to clean his wounds. Emma fixed up a comfortable seat out of firewood and rocks, and he gradually gathered the breath to speak.

"Children, I'm afraid I bring very grim news from the battle," he said, and tossed his bloody hat onto the ground. His eyes looked dead inside his head, and his mouth was quivering with emotion as he tried to speak plainly. "I think I would not be putting it too boldly to say all is lost."

Earl Hawkin peered into our eyes, and I imagine he read the hope that still was inside our hearts. It almost choked his words, but he forced himself to speak. "Doctor Felman and Egil have been taken."

"Taken where?" Emma asked. This time Earl Hawkin

didn't dare to look her in the eye. "I mean they have both been . . . killed," he said.

Emma and I froze. Earl Hawkin nodded, and I saw a tear rolling down his face.

"Gullkin filled the city with his warriors. There was nowhere to hide. His Keepers of the Arts used powerful magic. Doctor Felman and Egil were together when—"

Earl Hawkin looked up to the roof of the cave as if he could force his tears back by using gravity. "They died like warriors," he said softly. "Unlike myself. Who made his excuses and left."

There was a long silence. A breath of sea air blew the smoldering lava fire into high flame. Emma and I looked at each other. We both saw the end of a dream, but there was no waking up. I remembered Egil gulping down stolen reindeer meat. I thought of all the adventures I had had with Shipley on the moon. At the convent Sister Mary would have assumed that the scatty black cat had been run over. Perhaps in another universe it had.

Somehow I simply couldn't imagine Doctor Felman being dead. I thought of him as a page in a book that still existed even if you tore the paper up.

"What of Professor Elkkin?" Emma asked.

"I believe she is captured," Earl Hawkin said. "I wish I could give you two children something to cling to, but I have nothing. Not even myself. I am a useless coward."

Earl Hawkin clenched his fists, and I saw that his fingers turned to hawk talons just long enough to pierce the skin on his palms. Blood oozed into his hands, but he didn't appear to feel the pain.

"I am the last Keeper of the Arts who supports the cause, and I am of no practical use to anyone," he said softly. "The revolution is over."

I stared at the palm of my hand. The wolf in my hand was still.

"So what are we to do?" I said after a long silence. Earl Hawkin looked up and began to speak urgently. "You must save yourselves. You have another world to go back to. You must go there."

"But how?" I asked.

Earl Hawkin struggled to his feet and pointed into the darkness of the cave. "These caves lead to a tunnel that leads to an old canal that leads to an abandoned mine shaft that opens onto the surface."

I got to my feet. Emma still sat by the fire with her head bowed.

"We are very near to the edge of Langjoskull here," Earl Hawkin said. "The surface is only about two hundred feet above us. There are fissures and caves. As a wolf-kin, can you not smell the ocean?"

"I can," I said, and turned to Emma, who still had her head bowed.

"It is your only chance," Earl Hawkin said. "That is why I came here. To tell you to leave us forever. There's nothing more you can do here."

I stared toward the darkness at the back of the cave. It looked like a grim route to salvation. "What about the Sleepless Warriors?" I asked.

"I don't know," Earl Hawkin said, running his fingers through his hair. "They are terrible creatures, but they are slow. Perhaps you can shift. . . ."

I stepped over the fire toward Emma.

"Emma? What do you think?" I said. Emma was sitting totally motionless with her head still bowed. She didn't move for a long time.

"Emma?" I said more softly. "Did you hear what Earl Hawkin said? Do you think we can make it?"

Emma looked up, and I saw tears in her eyes even though her face had no expression.

"If you want to know what I think," she said, "I think . . . we *always* lose. Always, always. The bullies win even before the battle can begin. Always, always."

After a moment Earl Hawkin leaned forward and gently took her hand. "Oh, my dear child," he said, and pulled her to her feet. She tried to hide her face and he embraced her. I imagine the warmth of his body broke the ice inside her soul, and she began to sob.

"My poor, dear child," Earl Hawkin whispered. "Perhaps

in a thousand years we may get to fight this battle. But for now you must think only of yourself."

Emma lowered her head. I turned to Earl Hawkin. "If we make it to the ice, what then?"

Earl Hawkin shrugged. "You must shift into the form of a creature that will survive. But if you are going to shift, you must do it before you reach the surface. Once you are above the ice, you will only be able to shift back into human form. After that, you will never shift again. None of your powers will work once you leave. I'm afraid that to give you the ability to take your powers into the human world, we would have needed a much longer education. We had so little time."

"I'm not sure we know how to choose what we become," I said.

"You are beginners. For you the Jerlamar chooses," Earl Hawkin said. "If the Jerlamar is on your side, you might make it."

It seemed like a remote possibility. However, we didn't have any choice. One more question troubled me. "If our powers no longer work when we leave, will Emma fall sick again?"

Emma turned to face us.

"And will Toby be still again?" Emma asked.

Earl Hawkin smiled. "No. All Fel cures are permanent. See that as our gift to you for trying to help us."

"And failing," I said.

"I think we should leave quickly," Emma said. "I sense danger nearby."

"I sense it too," Earl Hawkin said, looking toward the mouth of the cave. "I will fly around. If I see any of Gullkin's warriors, I will do what I can to delay them."

Earl Hawkin put his bloody green hat on his head and tried hard to look fierce. I took his hand and then hugged him hard.

"Someday there will be a fair fight," I said, and he nodded his head.

"Give my regards to Stephen Hawking," he whispered. He looked at us both, and I imagine he read our minds for the last time.

"Emma, Toby, ask the Jerlamar to take you home where you belong."

When you simply want to stay alive, you just keep walking one step at a time.

After only a few hundred yards, we were confronted with a maze of dark tunnels. But the sea air was strong, and we were soon certain which way we should go to reach the surface.

We felt our way along the wall of our chosen tunnel for half a mile, our feet sometimes stepping in warm puddles with bubbles that tickled our ankles. There was a strong smell of rotten eggs that was occasionally cleared by the sweet scent of free air coming from somewhere high above and ahead of us.

Then we saw a glowing red light in the distance. We made our way toward it and found a lava flow that followed a hand-dug canal that ran in a dead straight line. There was a crude footpath beside this glowing canal. The fresh air was blowing straight down this tunnel. The lava gave light and warmth, and the going became a little easier. On the walls we saw cave paintings, and I assumed they were left by the Sleepless Warriors.

"We are walking uphill," I said. "I can feel the gradient. And look, the lava is flowing faster here. We must be getting near the surface."

"I'm not so sure," said Emma.

We came to a junction where the lava canal met another that ran across it like a crossroads. The fresh surface air seemed to be coming from the direction straight ahead, which meant we had to somehow get across the lava canal in front of us.

I searched the footpath for boulders and rolled them into a pile at Emma's feet.

"The lava is pretty sticky and these big boulders will take a while to melt," I said. "I'm going to throw them in and we can use them as stepping-stones."

Without waiting for a reply, I threw five boulders into the lava flow and heard them hiss.

"Jump," I said.

"Are you crazy?" said Emma.

"Now! Before they sink!"

Emma leaped onto the first boulder and skipped to the next and the next, and then she was across. However, by the time she had made it over to the other side, the first and then the second boulders had been consumed by the lava.

"It's okay—I'll get more boulders," I said.

Emma glanced into the red half-light behind her. "Hurry, Toby!"

I was about to collect more boulders when I saw movement in the darkness. Emma was staring straight at me and couldn't see what was happening behind her. I saw a trickle of lava flowing down the rock wall. Then the trickle became a wand of red light as cracks appeared in the wall, tracing the outline of a giant body. There was a flash of blue, and a rumble as rock was cleaved from rock.

Emma saw my look of horror and slowly turned around. As she did, the rock wall came to life. Two pillars of stone turned into legs; then an armored tunic made of carved rock appeared, and the swishing of red-hot lava sword left traces in the air.

High above Emma was a head, a face, and a single staring eye.

Emma screamed. The creature's limbs were made out of limestone, and its head was a boulder of granite shaped by erosion. Its bones must have been made of rock. That was why the bones on the island had crumbled between my fingers. The creature was studying Emma intently with its huge blue eye, which looked like a blue volcanic pool.

There was no time to fetch more boulders. I decided I would try to leap across the lava flow to reach her. I took a running jump at the lava flow and just managed to clear it.

As I landed on the other side, I heard noises from beneath the lava that sounded like bricks being rubbed together. I turned to see three more of the brutes emerging from under the molten flow of rock. They began to wade toward us as if the lava were cool water.

The entire cave began to shake as the monsters walked. Each footfall was an earthquake, and the monsters roared like exploding volcanoes. Emma and I ran hand in hand. When I turned I saw that the monsters were scooping up handfuls of hot lava and drinking it. Some of them were laughing, and the sound was like the hissing of a scalding geyser.

They were enjoying themselves. Emma and I were sport.

We followed the line of the canal, and the smell of fresh air was getting stronger all the time. The Sleepless Warriors were taking giant strides through the lava, easily keeping pace with us. Emma fell to the footpath and almost rolled into the burning lava stream. As I dragged her to her feet, I saw that directly ahead of us there was a circle of light.

Yellow light. Pure sunlight.

We reached the light ahead of our pursuers and stopped running. We both stared upward, breathless with wonder and exhaustion.

"The mine shaft," I said.

The shaft was at least two hundred feet high, and the sides were sheer. Sunlight poured down it, and we could smell the snow and the sea and wild winds above us. Freedom was up there, directly above our heads, but we could never reach it.

The Sleepless Warriors were thundering in pursuit, sending dust cascading down from the walls of the mine shaft and making hazy sunlit clouds. Emma and I looked into each other's eyes. My intuition told me she was feeling the same as me. If this was to be the end, at least we had lived through this adventure and found each other as family before we died. A shower of rocks fell around us like rain, and we prepared to be consumed.

I held out my hand and Emma held out hers. We were about to clasp our palms together when we both saw the same remarkable sight.

The clan signs on our palms had changed again. Instead of wolves, there were two swallows. Two beautiful blue and cream swallows!

I stared at Emma's hand and she stared at mine. On her palm the swallow was gliding easily through free air with golden sunlight behind it. On mine the swallow was flapping to change direction in a strong wind. As I stared, I realized I had seen these two birds before.

The two swallows were Look and Leave, my two little friends from Africa who arrived at the convent drainpipe every spring. I'm sure all swallows look the same, but I had stared at these two birds for so many hours that I had no doubt these were the same ones.

"Look and Leave," I said with wonder, and Emma looked up from her hand with astonishment.

"What did you say?"

"At the convent there were two swallows . . ."

". . . called Look and Leave," Emma said, completing my sentence.

"Yes!"

"I used to watch two swallows too," she said. "I called them Look and Leave as well."

We stared at each other.

"They had a nest . . . ," I said.

". . . outside my house," Emma said.

"They came every spring."

"Every autumn."

"From Africa."

"From England."

"And I always wanted to . . ."

". . . fly away . . . and be like them."

We clasped our hands together tightly. The Sleepless Warriors had formed a circle around us. They were closing in, and the heat from their burning lava swords was so hot that I thought my hair was about to burst into flames. Emma and I were still staring into each other's eyes.

"Two swallows," I said.

We both closed our eyes tight. I began to picture my two little friends as they cuddled and huddled inside the nest under the drainpipe. I saw their shining black eyes, the smart parting of their tail feathers, the carefree way they chirped in the morning. I also felt the burning heat from the lava swords around us.

I felt my body beginning to melt. I also saw a swallow emerging from the mist. The heat was now unbearable. I felt my bones turning to soft jelly and then hardening again into straws. My face became tight and then stiff around the nose. I felt an urgent need to flap my arms fast to get away from the unbearable heat.

I felt myself lifting slowly from the ground.

For a while I was aware only of the swift flow of air around my body and the sensation of flying. But to compensate there was the giddy feeling of vertigo and a tremendous exhilaration.

I dared to open my eyes and almost stopped flapping with shock. The Sleepless Warriors were now twenty feet below, waving their lava swords frantically. In the daylight from above I saw the tips of my wings. I had wings! Long blue wings!

Then I heard a chirruping noise and I sensed elated thoughts beside me. When I looked to my left, there was a beautiful blue and cream swallow gliding on the hot thermals that were coming from the swords of our enemies.

We were rising effortlessly up the mine shaft toward the free and wild air.

As we approached the surface, the draft of warm air from below was met by a huge whoosh of ice-cold air from above. I had never before experienced a sensation quite like it. The tingling of ice and sky ran through my whole body. A moment later we burst from the shaft and rose up to the open sky.

When I looked down, all I saw was an endless expanse of white.

PART THREE

Freedom

19

How can a tiny bird you could squeeze into a matchbox fly all the way from Europe to Africa?

It makes no rational sense, but it happens. Swallows, hundreds of thousands of them, fly to Africa in the autumn and fly all the way back to northern Europe in the spring. They also always manage to find the exact same spot where they built their nest the year before.

The moment we rose up from the mine shaft, most of my human thoughts were switched off. I knew south, I knew cold, and strangely, I still knew Emma. There was a strong cold wind at our tails that we rode like a train for part of the journey; then we swooped lower to pick up an easterly wind that was warmer than the southerly we'd been riding. It was like hopping off one train and onto another.

I saw a constellation of stars below me. Except these stars were yellow and red, and I realized these were the lights of a human town. Probably Carlisle, or maybe Barrow-in-Furness. It was harder to fly over land because the wind wasn't as strong, but it was warmer and there was more to see. We swept over Manchester and Birmingham as we moved south.

I squeaked until my heart almost burst. I wanted Emma to know we were flying over London and that one of those lights down there among a vast galaxy of lights was the light of my room in the convent.

My intuition told me that Emma was excited to see where I had lived before we met. We slowed our flight a little to bask in the warm air that was rising from that great city, even though the air smelled of sulfur and car fumes and horrible things burning. It was a beautiful sight and I was proud of it. I remembered a little song that Sister Mary used to sing, and I began to sing it inside my head.

Oh, Mary, this London's a wonderful sight
With people here working by day and by night
They don't sow potatoes, nor barley nor wheat,
But there's gangs of them digging for gold in the streets.
At least when I asked them that's what I was told
So I just took a hand at this diggin' for gold

But for all that I found there I might as well be
Where the Mountains of Mourne sweep down to the sea.

Sister Mary used to sing it so sweetly, and sometimes it would bring tears to her eyes. I don't know why. She told me she'd never even been to the Mountains of Mourne. And she certainly didn't come to London looking for gold. What *was* she looking for, I wonder?

I saw lots of ships that night as we crossed the Mediterranean. They were little screwed-up handfuls of light in the dark, and I realized that the sight of ships at sea made me lonely. The air was so warm now that I was beginning to crave water, and as if in answer, we hit a rainstorm.

The fun of flying through rain is hard to describe. Little icy tingles all over your body and beakfuls of cool fresh water on your tongue. I began to dodge and swoop through the raindrops just for fun, and Emma began to do the same. It was dawn on the second day and we should have been exhausted, but the rainstorm turned us both into children again. The bloodred sunrise was warmer and faster here, and I began to smell smoke somewhere in the distance.

Burning oil. Burning tires. Danger perhaps.

When the rainstorm stopped and the clouds around us

cleared, I looked down to see a different kind of ocean. This time it was an ocean of sand. A vast desert stretched away onto the horizon in every direction, and the air we were flying through was filled with grit. The grains of flying sand pelted my face, and I squeezed my eyes tightly shut.

I heard a deep rumbling sound above my head and thought it was thunder. However, when I looked up, I saw a vapor trail and a smartly painted fighter jet shooting across the clear blue sky. I thought the sight was magical, but Emma began to squeak in a quite alarming way. For her sake I was glad when the fighter jet had disappeared over the horizon, though the deep scolding of its engine lasted for a long time afterward.

When dawn came again, I was looking down on a flat expanse of savannah. Cowherds stood in circles around the bodies of cows that lay dead. Flocks of vultures feasted on the carcasses. No rivers. Villages of straw huts dotted the land here and there. Green camouflage trucks were the only vehicles on the dirt roads, and they kicked up clouds of red dust.

Emma stopped moving her wings and began to lose height. I followed her and we began to spiral downward toward the ground. The descent gave me vertigo, and at the exact moment when I began to descend, my ordinary powers of thought began to return. It was as if the sky were filled with instinct and the earth were radiating human thoughts.

We had arrived at our destination.

As I began to think more clearly, the power began to fade in my wings. I knew that soon I wouldn't be able to fly anymore, and I could see that Emma was experiencing the same thing. We had to time this perfectly; otherwise we would crash-land. I tried to hold off my human thoughts but it was no use, and my wings were transforming fast. We were both heading for the same branch of the same stunted thorn tree, and I had the horrible feeling that Emma and I were going to smash into each other.

Next I felt a horrible thud in my chest, and I was rolling over and over in bloodred sand. Changing from ocean to land had been unpleasant, but from air to land it was appalling. I was rolling in the dust, being pricked by spiny, nasty little plants, catching my knees and elbows on sharp rocks. But the pain of that was nothing compared to the sheer horror of not being in the beautiful free air anymore.

It felt as if time itself had stopped dead.

It took me a while to uncurl from the ball I had rolled into. I saw a snake with brown diamonds all down its back rearing up and spitting at me. I stumbled out of range and in doing so drove some pretty hefty spines farther into my legs and backside.

"Bloody ouch!" I shouted as I carefully got to my feet and began the undignified business of pulling thorns out of my bum. After a moment I saw Emma's dusty head rise up from a vicious-looking circle of thornbushes, and she grunted in pain too.

The sand was hot as frying pans, and there were sharp rocks all over the place. One of them had found its way inside my shirt.

"So here we are," I said as I pulled the rock out and examined it.

"Yes, here we are," Emma said, getting to her feet.

"Where are we exactly?"

Emma scanned the horizon.

"From the look of the mountains, I would say we are not far from my home village," she said. "Why didn't you stop off in London?"

I looked at her and smiled. "I was enjoying myself too much."

I tossed the rock from my shirt into the undergrowth. When it landed, there was a huge explosion. After the initial shock I stared in amazement. At first I thought perhaps the rock I had thrown had somehow exploded, but as the rain of rocks and pebbles turned into a cloud of dust, Emma explained it in two whispered words that sent a chill down my spine. "Land mines."

She peered all around with a look of professional interest. The dry, dusty wind moaned. I remembered how I had rolled and crashed through the undergrowth when I landed and wondered how close we had both come to blowing ourselves up. Emma was standing dead still, and I knew I had to do the same. She was studying the ground all around with her eyes narrowed.

"Could it have been just one?" I asked hopefully, but she shook her head.

"They plant lots together. We are in a minefield."

I took a deep breath. No matter how terrifying things had been under the ice, I had never felt as afraid as I did in that moment. This didn't feel like escape at all. This danger was real. But there didn't seem to be even a flicker of fear on Emma's face.

"So what do we do?" I asked, the wind blowing grit into my face.

"We use our heads," she said softly.

Emma began to busy herself with twigs and thorns and seemed to know what she was doing.

"Have you ever been stuck in a minefield before?" I asked.

"Twice."

"And how do you get out of them?"

"The traditional method."

"And what's that?"

She had broken a branch from a thorn tree and then

crouched down, lifting the nearest blade of grass with it. She examined the ground underneath, checking for wires.

"Sometimes here you move forward inch by inch," she said.

Our progress was maddeningly slow. We were moving at the rate of perhaps one yard every hour. Every species of fly known to man was trying to get into our faces. The thornbushes all around were making grabs for our flesh.

And we knew that at any moment, we could be blown into a hundred separate pieces.

Emma showed me what to do and what to look for, and I began to search for wires too. She explained that some very clever person in a laboratory somewhere had managed to develop a land mine that was sensitive to vibration. It had probably taken a long time and a lot of effort to invent something so clever.

What this meant was you didn't actually have to step on the land mine to set it off. All you had to do was walk near it. Emma said there were four boys and twenty girls in her village who had lost feet or legs to the land mines. More girls than boys were affected because it was the girls who usually went to fetch the water, and the soldiers usually planted the mines near water because that was where people tended to gather.

Human invention is far cleverer than any of the Fellish arts.

We'd moved about three yards when we heard a noise that meant nothing to me but evidently meant something horrible to Emma.

We heard a cow mooing.

The sound came from behind some thorn trees just three yards away. After the moo came the sound of vegetation being torn up. I heard the sound of a cow grinding leaves and branches in its mouth. Emma gasped and froze.

"I think it's just a cow," I said, and Emma turned to me.

"Just a cow," she repeated.

"Yes. So what? Cows can't hurt you."

At that moment the cow appeared from behind the bushes. It was chewing in a bored way with saliva dripping from its mouth. It was a big zebu cow, the color of bone and sand, with a giant hump and two long horns. Now that I saw the enormous size of the beast, I understood Emma's reaction. Cows don't know how to tiptoe.

"It will set them all off for sure," she said softly.

Emma straightened up, and we stared at each other.

"Or we can run," she said.

The cow mooed again, a curious cry of greeting that we didn't return.

"I vote . . . we run," I said.

We both nodded our heads firmly.

"Which direction?" I asked.

Emma shrugged. "Any direction is as good as any other."

I looked all around. The wind blew the red dust in our faces, and even though it is hard to believe, Emma and I smiled at each other across the lethal ground. To make the point that time was not on our side, the big zebu cow nonchalantly stepped forward to examine the soft green shoots beneath a thorn branch. It began to tug at the twigs and devour them without a care.

"That way," I said, pointing straight ahead, and Emma nodded.

"So let's go, Toby Walsgrove," she said. "And if this is the end . . ." She looked down at her feet.

"What?" I said.

"You know."

"Yeah. I know."

I took a deep breath, and we both began to run at full speed across a hot Sudanese minefield. This was some strange kind of freedom.

20

The sand didn't burn my feet. The thornbushes didn't hurt my flesh. The rocks didn't hurt either, and the sun wasn't hot. The flies didn't bother me; the wounds all healed.

Just for those few mad minutes everything was perfect.

We ran in a line as straight as an arrow, side by side. It was an insane race, both of us competing to be the one who died first. It was terrifying. But also magnificent.

These might be our last moments, the last time our shadows would fall across the earth, but we didn't care. All we had to do was run. We ran for long enough to get totally out of breath, then forced ourselves to run some more. I hit an incline, and the steepness of the climb began to slow me down. I could feel Emma's breath on my back, and I half turned. I saw her fall forward and land in a cloud of dust. I could tell Emma knew we were clear of the land mines, but it took us a long time to get the breath to speak.

We panted like animals under the burning sun.

"We made it," I said finally. "We bloody made it."

"You run like a goat," she replied.

"You *look* like a goat," I said.

Suddenly there was an explosion. The cow was in the air, upside down. Then there was another explosion and another explosion, triggered by the first, until the air was filled with red sand and thorn branches and bits of the cow that kept being lifted high into the air over and over again.

When the last of the land mines had exploded, the wind howled around us. Now that we'd escaped from the minefield, I felt that the hot dry desert didn't hold any more dangers. But Emma knew better.

"The explosions will bring soldiers," she said, and even before she'd finished speaking, we heard the distant roar of a car engine. Emma looked all around and pointed toward a thicket of prickly pear bushes mixed in with some kind of strange blue-gray cactus. As a hiding place it looked painful, but Emma was already scurrying toward it.

I followed her as she squeezed herself into a small gulley between the spiky bushes that was only just big enough for a large rabbit. After a moment we saw a jeep fly over the ridge several yards away and land with a thump on the soft sand. The engine was cut, and even though the jeep was only a two-seater, I saw there were seven people crammed inside it. They were seven of the most extraordinary human beings I had ever seen.

Emma whispered that they were Dinka warriors. Her own tribe was related to the Dinka, but when I asked if that meant they might help us, she said that in this place men of any kind always spelled danger, more even than lions or snakes.

Three of them wore military uniforms and carried machine guns. The rest wore an incredible assortment of clothes. Some wore replica soccer shirts from Arsenal and Chelsea; others wore pajamas or feather boas, and two of the warriors wore dresses. The sight was made even more bizarre by the fact that they were all over seven feet tall, as Dinka tribesmen almost always are, so the patterned dresses they wore only reached to their thighs. One of them wore a pink ladies' sun hat and appeared to be the leader. Another wore a quilted puffer jacket with a fur-lined hood.

"They look seriously weird," I whispered as the group of warriors began to descend the sand hill toward the scene of all the explosions.

"Sudanese People's Liberation Army," Emma said softly. "They hang around minefields waiting for animals to blow themselves up. They've come for the cow."

"Why are they dressed like that?" I asked.

"We wear clothes donated by rich countries. The men are so tall, the trousers we get don't fit. So they wear dresses. The feathers and stuff are just for fun. Everybody likes big hats because of the sun."

The warrior in the pink sun hat had spotted the detached leg of the cow lying in the sand and let off a volley of machine-gun bullets in celebration. The tall, thin warriors began to spring into the air and give out short gasps of joy. I suddenly thought they looked magnificent silhouetted against the sun, even the men in the patterned dresses.

"Did they plant the land mines?" I asked, but Emma shook her head.

"No. The government plants mines."

"So they're the good guys," I said, gesturing at the warriors. Emma shook her head.

"No. They're just bad guys who can't afford land mines. We should get out of here."

We waited until the warriors began gathering together firewood and bits of cow. Emma said they would probably stay there for a few days to feast and tell stories.

"At night they will scare each other with tales of shapeshifters watching them from the bushes," Emma said.

"How utterly ridiculous," I said with a smile.

We ran across the rock-strewn desert with its patches of thorns and cacti without once falling over. Emma and I found a rhythm and we ran side by side, our breaths matching our strides. Emma said her home village of Kapoeta was just a few miles away if we traveled in a straight line, but because of the Dinka warriors we had to make a detour. The journey would be around fifteen miles.

Just before sunset Emma led us into a dried-up riverbed. She said there was a spring there where we could get water. The "spring" turned out to be a small patch of mud where the sand was just a little darker than elsewhere. I thought Emma had got her geography wrong, but she sat down beside the wet sand and began to dig with her hands.

"Not much of a spring," I said.

"I'm sorry to disappoint you," she replied. "Sometimes here the name is bigger than the thing itself."

"Jerlamar . . . *erupt!*" I said loudly to the spring. I just wanted to make Emma laugh, but she didn't. Something told me she was trying not to think about Langjoskull. I thought about Egil and Doctor Felman for the first time since we'd left the glacier, and the loss didn't feel any less painful here in the desert.

Emma scraped some damp sand away and wiped her brow with her wrist. Soon there was a deep puddle of water at our fingertips.

"This spring was always sacred to our people because no

matter how bad the drought, there was always water here," she said.

The water was bloodred and thick with sand.

"Sometimes this is the only water we have," she said. "Just this. For a hundred people."

She stopped digging and became thoughtful, as if this fact, which she had lived with all her life, were suddenly new to her. She peered into the distance.

"Looks like strawberry jam," I said. "Do we drink it or eat it with a spoon?"

Emma smiled. "You must learn to suck like this," she said, and she cradled a tiny amount of water in her palm and began to suck at it from a quarter inch away.

"It is a technique. You leave the sand behind. Watch."

She made the most ill-mannered sucking noise, and I began to laugh. She laughed too and spat all her water out. After a while I got the hang of what I had to do and began to suck up some of the water. I still got a mouthful of sand as well, but at least there was enough water to swallow without choking.

"Is this water safe to drink?" I asked.

"No. But we drink it anyway."

She gazed at the distant mountains, where the sun was setting. The cool breeze was a great relief. I suggested we try to light a fire, but Emma said the smoke might be detected by roving gangs of soldiers. We were sitting slap bang in the middle of the front line, she said.

"So who is fighting who?" I asked.

"Everyone is fighting everyone," she said.

Neither of us had slept since we left Iceland, and we were both weary in our bones. But this was also the first real chance we'd had to talk since we came out from under the glacier. We were here in Africa because of instinct, because of the seasons and the moon and the migration patterns of swallows. We hadn't planned this and now here we were, seriously in the middle of nowhere, defenseless without our Fellish weapons or powers, and in a war zone too.

I splashed my face with some sandy water to wake myself up.

"Will there be anyone in your village who can help us?" I asked softly. In an African sunset, it is almost impossible to speak loudly. Emma dug into the sand with a twig, and I could tell she didn't want to answer me directly.

"Don't you want to go to your own home?" she said. I didn't speak for a long time. The dry wind tugged at my hair.

"How would I even get home?"

"Fly, maybe," she said, and we both smiled.

"Go home to what?"

"Sister Mary?"

There was another long silence, and I felt an awkwardness

with Emma I had never felt when we were in Langjoskull. She read my mind.

"Under the ice we were the same. Here we are from different worlds," she said.

The wind was colder now. I wanted the conversation to return to Langjoskull.

"I wonder if Helva Gullkin knows yet that we've escaped."

Emma shrugged.

"I don't want to think about anything that happened to us," she said. "It is over now. I want to forget it."

"Forget it?!" I exclaimed. "How can we forget it?" I asked softly but with no less urgency. "We had a hundred adventures and we turned into wolves! And birds! And fought against one-eyed monsters made out of rocks! How could anyone forget that?"

"Our friends were all killed for fighting for a cause that had no chance," Emma said, and she peered at the muddy puddle. "So *that* world is just the same as this."

In all our time in Langjoskull I had never seen such despair in Emma's eyes.

"When you see my village, you will understand," she said.

She dropped her twig into the water hole for others to use.

"So you don't mind me coming to your village?" I said. Emma shrugged and got to her feet.

"I am just ashamed," she said quietly, and then set off walking. I waited a moment and then hurried to catch up with her.

The moon rose to light our way, and we were soon making good progress through the bush. Emma sang me some African songs and I sang her pop songs. Then suddenly we heard a roar in the sky above us. I looked up to see a little bubble of light shooting through the sky between us and the mountains. At first I thought it might be a shooting star, but then I realized it was the headlight of a jet. There was a brilliant white flash and two streaks of orange light that lit up the desert around us.

Emma dropped to the ground and I instinctively did the same.

A second later the desert was again lit up in bone-white light, like the flash just before a photo is taken. In that second I saw the outlines of stunted trees and the curve of a giant rounded boulder.

Then came the noise. It was beyond loud. It was not even sound, it was a tsunami of solid air. The only thing I could compare it to was the bellowing shriek of Helva Gullkin in the marketplace of Langjoskull.

The force of the explosions shook the earth with such violence that Emma and I were thrown up into the air. The sand beneath us was now cold as ice. When I landed I took a while to get my breath, and my mouth was full of grit. We ran toward the giant boulder we'd seen in the flash of light.

"The cease-fire is obviously over," she said.

The light of the plane rose up in a graceful arc and took its place among the stars. Then it began to descend again, and a few seconds later the noise of its jet engines split the air around us.

"Hang on," Emma said, and this time I was prepared. I spread my arms around the boulder and hugged it with all my strength. Emma did the same on the other side of the boulder, and our fingertips touched on both sides. We waited for the next pair of air-to-ground missiles to hit the earth.

Whoosh, brilliant light, then *wham, wham.*

Even the boulder shifted a little in its ancient resting place, but Emma and I were spared the flight through the air by holding on to its enormous weight. After the noise of the jet disappeared, Emma let go of the boulder and stared up at the sky, like a soothsayer looking for signs in the heavens.

"He's coming again," she said softly, and we took up our positions around the giant lump of rock. This time as we waited, I heard people screaming in the darkness. Women and children. Their voices sounded soft and weak in the face of the mighty whump that we knew was coming. They were about half a mile away, right where the rockets were landing.

Whoosh, brilliant light, *wham, wham.*

"Who are those people?" I asked as the wailing got louder.

"Refugees heading for Kenya," Emma said. "Good target practice."

The light of the plane arced in the sky and swooped low over our heads. I heard the deafening roar of its engines and saw the red and green lights streaking at the tips of its wings as it screamed across the desert.

"It is over," she said in a low voice. "They have gone. We who are left must continue. We who survive must continue. . . ."

She spoke the words like a chant or a magic spell, as if saying it would make it true. Then we heard the sound of another engine, and we both turned. Two engines. Two more headlights were coming low and fast toward us.

"So there is more," Emma said in a gentle voice that sounded unconcerned. "So we must hold on again."

Before the rumble of the plane engines got too loud, I again heard the faint sounds of women and children in the darkness, but there were fewer of them this time. The rumble of the two planes' engines was deeper and darker than that of the jet, and I could feel Emma squeezing my hands hard. I could feel her terror coming up through my arms. She glanced up into the sky and sighed.

"Five-hundred-pound bombs," she said. "Nothing we can do."

Then instead of holding on to the boulder, she grabbed hold of me. She wrapped her arms around my body just as she had done with the boulder, and I did the same with her. The sickening deep rumble above our heads got louder, and then came a soft, soothing whistle that was in fact two whistles in harmony with each other.

"We may not survive this," she whispered.

We waited and waited as the whistling noise grew lower and lower in pitch and the five-hundred-pound bombs fell. There was a crack in the earth, a flash of light. . . . Then there was silence.

21

I woke with a headache that felt like an axe in my head, twenty yards from the boulder. It was morning and the sky was bruised all over with clouds of smoke. The air smelled of burning plastic. I managed to drag myself to my feet and staggered toward the boulder.

"Emma?" I cried. There was no answer, just the gentle moan of a wolf or jackal. I stopped dead and peered in the direction of the animal cry.

"Emma?" I said.

Then I heard her voice coming from behind me.

"Over here," she said, and I ran to her.

"Emma, are you all right?"

"I'm okay," she said, sitting up and blowing hard. "I

fell on my head. I'm okay."

She had a cut on her head, and I began to clean it with my sleeve.

"This is some insane place to call home," I said.

I saw that she had been crying, but she didn't want me to see. She got to her feet and began to dust herself off.

"Toby, perhaps you would do something with your hair," she said. "The people in my village are very particular."

We avoided the road because Emma said it wouldn't be a pretty sight after last night's bombing raid. Instead we followed a ditch that had once been used to stop tanks. In the smaller ditches on either side of it there was burned-out military trash, cars, trucks, cannons, gear. Emma named every piece of wrecked military equipment and pronounced loudly the make, model, and deadly potential of it.

Then the thornbushes became more sparse, and we joined a bigger road that was rutted with the tire marks of heavy vehicles. On the near horizon I saw smoke rising, and after another mile we came to a crumbling ruin of a house with a single white wall, bleached in the sun. On the wall was some writing.

"Free Kapoeta . . . Sudanese People's Liberation Army." And beneath it were the words "Something comes from corruption it breaks quick."

Emma stopped and shaded her eyes.

"This is the entrance to my village." She walked to the

ditch at the side of the road and picked up two long sticks that appeared to have been left there for visitors. She handed one to me.

"If a stray dog comes, you hit it on the nose."

We began to walk into town. The sun was at its hottest, and tiny tornadoes danced in the sand. A few little dogs sniffed the air around us, but I guessed the smart ones had learned not to come too close to visitors with sticks. After a while we came to a line of shanties that looked like rotten teeth in a sore mouth. Every wall of every shack and shanty was studded with bullet holes, and the ground all around was cratered.

"Don't step away from the path," Emma said; "lots of mines."

I remembered what Emma's flower had told me about Emma's brother. I glanced at her and she spoke without looking at me. "It's okay—I don't blame myself for what happened to my brother anymore," she said. "I blame the whole world."

There was a blank disinterest in Emma's voice, and I realized that her mood fitted this place perfectly. There were no feelings of any sort here. The people we saw were mostly women and children. The children played in the dirt, and the women were busy tending cooking fires or washing lines of rags. No one greeted us and no one smiled. I asked Emma why no one seemed to recognize her, and she said in her village people came and went, always passing through in search of water or food.

"It looks like all the people I knew are gone," Emma said. "My mother must have left to look for food. So now I am a stranger everywhere."

We stopped when we reached a low veranda with a corrugated roof and a hanging basket that had some strange herb growing in it. The house leaned sideways on wooden poles, like a drunken man frozen in the act of falling over. It looked like a sort of funny house, the kind someone would draw in a cartoon and give a funny voice. The windows were all gone, and the wall at the back had a huge hole blown in it where sand was gathering in drifts. On the floor inside, in the darkness, there were some food tins and some toys and a pair of women's shoes.

Under the roof of the house, beside the hanging basket, I saw a small swallow's nest, made from mud and spit. I guessed that this was where Look and Leave spent their winters. I was about to comment on it, but something about Emma's silence stopped me. She peered into the darkness of the house for a long time, leaning heavily on her stick. I realized that this was what was left of her house and her family.

"Can we just stand here a moment?"

Emma stood dead still with her back to me. I sat down on steel fragments that appeared to be taken from an anti-aircraft gun that had been half buried to be used as seats.

The heat and the flies became one element, a kind of itching drone. I could stand it only because Emma could stand it. She was still for a long time.

"Emma?" I said, and she turned to me. I saw a look of fury on her face that I knew was directed at herself.

"I was given a chance to change things. . . ." Emma turned to survey the wreckage of her village. "I could have taken the gold from Langjoskull. Cups, plates, knives, spoons. I didn't appreciate the opportunity I had. I could have built schools, wells, paid doctors. I see it. Now that I'm here, I can see it clearly."

She stared back down the road where we had walked. "Now I have to live with the dream of what might have been as well as the reality. That is not fair."

I knew I had no words that would be any use. There was a feeling in the soil here that nothing different would ever happen. The whole village was stuck in a chair, staring out through a window at the rest of the world.

"Look," Emma said at last.

She pointed down the road, and I could see a woman walking toward us. She was carrying two heavy buckets. Emma shaded her eyes.

"Who is that?" I asked.

"It might as well be me," Emma said. "In ten years' time, or fifteen or twenty. Or my daughter. Or my granddaughter."

Emma sat down, and I could see that she was fighting tears.

"Nothing goes on forever," I said, and put my hand on her arm.

Emma spoke to the ground. "Could you live in this place? Could you walk three miles every day just to fetch water that isn't even fit to drink? Could you walk among land mines?"

Emma clenched her fists and then took a deep breath. Without looking we found each other's hands, and our fingers intertwined. We squeezed so tightly it hurt. Not so long ago, just to feel this sensation would have meant everything to me.

Then I noticed a little swallow with green eyes landing on the nest under the roof of Emma's house.

A few moments later, to our absolute astonishment, the green-eyed swallow had hopped down from the roof and shifted into the shape of a Fel. Egil Catkin was now lying in the sand with his arms outstretched, groaning with exhaustion.

"What a bloody flight." He grunted. Emma and I both leaped to our feet at the same time.

"Egil! You're *alive*!" I yelled, astounded to see his skinny frame and wild hair emerging from the exquisite neatness of the swallow.

"Well, of course I am alive, Tobes," he said, propping himself up on one elbow. "But only barely after that bloody journey. Three times I was chased by falcons. They don't even *eat* swallows—they just do it for fun!"

He got to his feet and dusted himself off. Emma had her hand over her mouth as she stared at him.

"Hello, Miss Emma, how are you?" he said with a smile. "Do I look a fright?"

"But you're dead," she said through her fingers. Egil rubbed some dust in his hair, like a bird taking a dust bath.

"Dead! What are you talking about?" he said.

"Earl Hawkin told us," I said. "He said you and Doctor Felman were killed. The Blue Volcanoes were defeated."

"How could Earl Hawkin have told you anything?" Egil asked, stretching his arms like wings. "He said when he got to the cave, you had already gone."

"We spoke to him," I said.

"I think you must have been dreaming," Egil said. "Anyway, he's in Gullkin's prison now."

"We can't both have dreamed it at the same time," Emma said.

A small whirlwind blew up around Emma's feet.

"You know, Emma, you are creating the most enormous air knots," Egil said. "Are you confused?"

"Yes," Emma and I said in unison.

"Well, please don't be," Egil replied. "I am alive, and so is

Doctor Felman, and so is Professor Elkkin. Just barely, but we *are* alive."

"So why did he lie?" I asked.

"Earl Hawkin is not the most worldly of Fels," Egil said. "He must have been confused. He took a blow to the head during the battle, I understand."

"The battle we lost," Emma said.

"The battle we sort of drew," Egil said. "We lost a lot of soldiers, but some of us escaped."

I stepped closer to Emma and took her hand.

"The remaining Blue Volcanoes are in the hills," Egil said. "Waiting."

"Waiting for what?" asked Emma.

Egil stepped around me and sat down on an upturned antitank shell next to Emma.

"Actually, you know, I don't think Grandpa will ever die. I think he'll just turn into a piece of furniture or something."

"Egil! Waiting for *what?*" I said.

Egil took some deep breaths.

"I think I'm going to sneeze," he said, and sneezed. "I'm not used to the dust, you see."

"Egil, please," Emma said.

Egil sneezed again, but this time he held his nose and said, "Brythnold. The Blue Volcanoes and Grandpa and everyone else are all waiting for you to return. That's why I'm here."

At that moment the woman carrying the water buckets who had been making slow progress up the road walked past us. We all fell silent. Emma's eyes flickered as the woman's shadow fell across her. Egil stared at her with fascination.

"Is she not tired?" he asked with an arched eyebrow.

Suddenly, Emma flew at me and grabbed my arms. "Toby, we *must* return!" she yelled.

"Bravo, hear, hear," said Egil, getting to his feet.

I could see a fierce certainty in Emma's eyes. Egil was taking an interest in a gigantic dragonfly that was fluttering around him. I could feel Emma's fingernails digging into my skin and also feel the heat of her smile.

"Emma, there is still no guarantee that we will win the battle," I said quietly.

"We will win," she said, "and this time I will return here to this village with the whole shipment of gold that Doctor Felman promised. We will fix Langjoskull and I will fix my own world all in one. We are being given a second chance."

I could see that Egil was glancing at me from the corner of his eye, only pretending to be following the flight of the dragonfly.

"You can't back out now, Tobes," Egil said. "Everyone is depending on you."

A dry wind blew. Egil snatched the dragonfly and put it in his mouth and began to chew. Emma and I stared at each other and I felt my intuition returning. Perhaps Egil's presence was switching it back on. I could feel her thoughts and she could feel mine. I knew she could sense my fear, but she didn't care because she was brave enough for both of us.

My intuition told me Emma was going to go back no matter what. Her intuition told her that if she went back, I would go back too because we were brother and sister.

Egil swallowed the dragonfly down.

"So come on, what are we waiting for?" Egil said.

Emma and I looked down at our palms, where we both saw swallows flying in front of a vivid blue sky. Emma turned to look into the darkness of her old house once more. Then she reached up to the hanging basket and broke off a branch from the strange herb. She sniffed it for a moment, and my intuition allowed me to see a thousand memories coming from the smell of the herb.

She dropped the herb to the ground. Then Emma, Egil, and I all linked hands and began to run as fast as we could down the dusty Sudanese road, pursued by half a dozen stray dogs.

I closed my eyes tight and felt myself taking to the air once more.

22

We flew directly north without stopping.

I flew the length of Europe without a single thought, and instead of thinking I breathed in my existence through the smells and tastes in the air. Once you are past the mainland of Scotland, the air takes on a uniform texture, and there are very few smells other than salt and ice and sometimes the stinging whiff of rotten seaweed.

When we arrived at the gates of Langjoskull, we circled round and round until some Fel hunters opened the gates. Then we swooped down from a rain cloud and dropped like stones into the secret darkness. The draft of cold air took us down the ice stairs, and we swept over the balcony where I had first looked out on the Fel city. When I looked down, I was shocked by what I saw.

Where before there had been a busy market and the hustle and bustle of commerce, now there was a kind of terrified sleepiness in the air. Smoke hung in heavy drapes across the rooftops. What light there was glowed red, and there was no music to be heard. Somewhere in the distance I could hear someone screaming. Troops of gull warriors marched down deserted streets. All the shutters were closed.

It felt almost as dead as Emma's village in Sudan.

After we left the city behind, we headed east. We flew past the Blue Volcano and continued on even beyond the land of the Sleepless Warriors. It felt as if we were flying to the end of the earth.

Soon we were flying down a small valley and out onto a plain of shale strewn with enormous boulders the size of four-story houses. In the middle of a circle of such boulders we found the Blue Volcano camp, and as we circled around it, some of our resolve began to drain away. Emma and I fell to earth heavily, and after we had shifted back we found ourselves leaning against a lump of granite in the middle of the circle of stones. Egil came to land beside us a little more elegantly. All three of us surveyed the desperate scene.

There were only maybe fifty warriors left, most of them huddled around lava fires. Others, the wounded and the sick, were lying under skin tents. Golden swords were pushed into the shale like crosses. A forge had been set up where weapons were being made, but other than that, the warriors seemed to be simply waiting.

"We have lost hope many times since you left," Egil said, stretching his aching arms. "This is all that remains."

It took a while for the first of the Blue Volcanoes to notice us. The smoke of the fires blew across and hid us from view for a while, but as it cleared intermittently, more and more of the warriors saw us.

"They have returned," said a soft and disbelieving voice through the smoke.

Then another voice repeated the same words, and then the words were repeated over and over again. First one, then three, then a dozen of the warriors pulled their swords from the shale and slowly lifted them above their heads. Their voices were hoarse at first, but then they came together to set up a powerful roar, which was answered by a rumble from the Blue Volcano itself.

"Long live the king!" they cried as one. "Long live the queen!"

Their voices were not as loud nor as numerous as the first time they had chanted in our honor, but the feeling was undiminished. Emma and I stepped forward one pace, and the warriors fell to their knees.

"I think they're pleased to see you," Egil said softly.

"Egil, take us to Doctor Felman," I said, and for the first time, I thought I almost *sounded* like a prince.

There was a place at the edge of the camp where two big boulders had fallen against each other and were leaning together for support. Under the cover of these two boulders we found Doctor Felman and Professor Elkkin, who also appeared to be leaning on each other for support.

Doctor Felman was brewing tea on a small lava fire while Professor Elkkin sharpened a knife on a whetstone. When Egil brought us into their presence, they hardly looked up.

"Ah, welcome back, children," Doctor Felman said calmly, as if we'd just been out for a stroll. "Would you like tea?"

Emma and I sat down by the fire, and Egil left us. Professor Elkkin poured two cups of tea. Doctor Felman was humming under his breath.

"Is that it?" I said.

"Is that what, dear?" Professor Elkkin said softly.

"We've just flown four thousand miles to risk our lives to fight your battle," I said, "and all you say is 'would you like tea'?"

It was only then that I saw the professor wipe a tear from her eye. She wafted the smoke, trying to blame it for the tear, and to my astonishment I saw that Doctor Felman had tears in his eyes too.

"We are both very old," Doctor Felman said after clearing his throat. "Old people don't get very excited about anything because we've seen everything, haven't we, Professor Elkkin?"

"Everything," Professor Elkkin said, wiping her other eye. "So since we are so old, you shouldn't expect too much . . . you know . . . emotional stuff. Not on the outside."

Emma and I smiled at each other.

"What about on the inside?" Emma said.

"On the inside," Professor Elkkin said, "I am not so very, very old."

Professor Elkkin couldn't help herself. She moved close to Emma and hugged her, and then she hugged me. I felt her tears on my cheek. Doctor Felman fussed with his teapot, keeping his eyes busy and invisible.

"But we are indeed . . . of course . . . very . . . pleased you finally decided . . . of your own free will . . . to . . ."

He fell silent too. I took his arm gently.

"We are doing this because it is right," I said.

Doctor Felman and Professor Elkkin both became extra busy very quickly and did everything they could to hide their faces from us. Emma and I suddenly found them both rather sweet, and I thought perhaps we had both just grown up a little bit.

"It looks like things have gone badly since we left," I said, and Doctor Felman was glad to get back to business.

"Gullkin has arrested or killed so many of us. But now that you have returned, we at least have the element of surprise. Gullkin doesn't know you are here. Tomorrow he expects to simply take the crown without a fight."

"*Tomorrow,*" Emma and I both said in amazement.

"Did Egil not tell you?" Doctor Felman said, stirring the leaves in his teapot, trying not to look concerned. "The Swearing of the Oaths is tomorrow. You have arrived back just in time."

He looked up quickly enough to catch my shocked expression. He then gave us a familiar look of cold steel.

"Tonight you will sleep and tomorrow you will fight," he said. "And the day after tomorrow we will all be free."

23

"O Fels and Thrulls and Vela of Langjoskull glacier!" echoed a voice across the frozen lake of the Blue Volcano. "We are gathered here to end the period of mourning for King Will Wolfkin. And witness . . . the Swearing of the Oaths!"

A great roar echoed across the crater. The inner slopes were covered with benches, and every bench was filled. Attendance at the ceremony was compulsory, and the entire population had walked or ridden in procession from the Fel city and surrounding areas to the slopes of the volcano. By special order of Helva Gullkin, the Fels and Thrulls had been forced to sit on opposite sides of the volcano, with the larger Thrulls crammed into the smaller section where the low sun made them shade their eyes. Armed gull warriors clattered their swords against their shields to keep order.

Above the crowd a gigantic golden bridge had been built in two sections that almost met in the middle. There was a gap of about two yards at the very apex of the arc. Above the bridge, sheets of thin gold leaf billowed in the chilly wind and caught the spring sunshine. Beneath these sheets, jets of water sprayed from the rim of the volcano and formed shimmering rainbows in the air.

The proclamation was being made by a tiny bull-chested Fel with Vellish features and a fearsomely loud voice. When he spoke, he sounded like a red deer rutting. The echo in the volcano was made louder by the thick sheet of ice that covered the blue lake. The drop from the bridge to the ice was two hundred feet.

Beyond the rim of the volcano, clouds of steam rose from the great herd of ponies that had been left standing outside, waiting at their carts and carriages for the ceremony to be completed. Under normal circumstances, it would all be over in a matter of minutes.

"Since the great Will Wolfkin died without a natural heir," the proclaimer announced, "the succession of the Wolfkin inheritance will be determined by . . ." He began to search his pockets for something and, as he did, began to lose his thread a little. "Determined by . . . that section of the parchment . . . that deals with unnatural succession. . . .

I had it a second ago. Ah. Here it is."

The proclaimer on the bridge produced a single roll of walrus skin that looked to have been smoked by age. There was silence as he leaned forward to untie a red ribbon. Then his spectacles slipped off his nose and dropped to the ice below. He cursed under his breath, then peered at the scroll for a long time and squinted. The solemnity of the occasion began to evaporate. A murmur of disbelief began to roll around the volcano.

"Ah, here! Look!" he said at last, his nose almost touching the parchment. "Here it clearly states . . ." He held the scroll up to the light and angled his head. "It clearly states that in the very situation in which we find ourselves, when the king dies with no living descendants, the power of the kingship shall go to the nearest living Fel relative of the king."

The proclaimer quickly cleared his throat and pulled at the hems of his golden tunic.

"And since King Will Wolfkin's closest relative is his cousin Helva Gullkin, I have great pleasure in announcing that the new king of Langjoskull, the inheritor of the seal and rings of Will Wolfkin, shall be . . . King . . . Helva Gullkin!"

Some in the crowd began to cheer. Others looked nervously at the gull warriors and applauded. Some remained silent. The Thrulls murmured to each other.

"The king is dead; long live the king!" the proclaimer said.

At that moment there was a great fluttering of white doves: A large wicker box had been pulled open on a drawstring and white doves released. The birds flew up in a beautiful white crowd through the rainbows and up toward the gold leaf. At the same time, a hundred trumpeters suddenly emerged at the far side of the golden bridge and began to blow a clarion call. A few moments later Helva Gullkin himself emerged through golden gates at the foot of the bridge, riding on a pure white horse. The horse began to prance up the slope of the golden bridge, with Gullkin waving his hand regally to acknowledge the cheering and applause that were being stirred up by the gull warriors.

Gullkin's horse snorted steam in the cold air.

"So then," said the bull-chested proclaimer, "with the succession decided, let us begin swearing the oaths of allegiance to Langjoskull."

"Wait!" came a mighty voice, and all heads turned toward the other side of the bridge. The golden structure swayed slightly in the swirling wind inside the crater. Doctor Felman made his way up the bridge and held on to a golden rail to steady himself.

"There is a challenge to the succession," Doctor Felman pronounced.

"A challenge?" the proclaimer said in a hoarse little voice

that had been hiding inside his big voice.

Doctor Felman reached into his blue robe and produced the handwritten parchment he had shown to Emma and me when we first arrived in Langjoskull. He quickly untied the red sinew bindings and unrolled it with both hands. His voice shook with anxiety and fatigue as he walked.

"I have in my hand a piece of parchment," he declared. "And the words upon it were written by King Will Wolfkin himself on the night that he died. And I was witness to it."

A buzz began to pass through the crowd. Gullkin's horse snorted more white steam into the air as if it understood what was taking place.

"In this last will and testament, King Will Wolfkin states clearly that he wishes to leave the throne of Langjoskull to the living descendants . . . *of his half-human offspring* . . . born on the Isle of the Sunset to the human woman Gwendoline McShaffrey."

"Mongrels!" Gullkin bellowed. "I am tired of talk of mongrels!" Gullkin began to strut his horse across the bridge and called out to the crowd. "King Will Wolfkin *has* no living descendants apart from the mongrel humans, with no powers and no knowledge of the arts, who fled back to their human world for fear of my wrath."

His white horse shied and bucked a little.

"And since they are not here, they cannot be counted as contenders!"

The proclaimer looked afraid and let the smaller parchment he had in his hand roll up naturally into a tight scroll.

Doctor Felman smiled. "You are mistaken, Helva Gullkin," he said. "The heirs to the will of Will Wolfkin did indeed flee . . . but now they have returned to Langjoskull!"

Doctor Felman waved his arm. From the crowd at the foot of the bridge stepped Emma and then I. We began the long walk up the arch of gold hand in hand, both dressed in blue robes with the unblinking blue eye woven into them. All our magical weapons had been retrieved by Professor Elkkin and returned to us. We both wore our reindeer-skin pouches inside our tunics. I had my fur coat and Emma had her shawl tied around her throat beneath her robe. Egil had made us victory crowns woven from myrtle leaves, and he assured us he'd spent the whole night getting them to look suitably victorious.

Even though I say it myself, I think we probably looked a bit magnificent.

"Fels of Langjoskull," Doctor Felman said as we arrived at his side, "the living descendants of our beloved king are here to claim their throne."

There was silence for a few seconds. Then, when the crowd realized we were really, really real—and really, really there—the biggest, most deafening roar I had ever heard echoed inside the giant crater. The cheering and bellowing went on for a long time, with the Thrulls to our left making the most noise and suffering the beatings of the gull warriors for their pains.

Helva Gullkin sat astride his horse and did not move a muscle. I imagined that the frantic activity was all on the inside. He watched our progress up the bridge with gull eyes.

The proclaimer began to shout. "I will need to examine this so-called will!"

Doctor Felman handed the parchment to him, and since he couldn't read it he began to study the seals with his fingertips. He ran his fingers over the red wax imprint of a wolf and glanced back at Helva Gullkin. He nodded gently.

"As the oldest Keeper of the Arts in Langjoskull," Doctor Felman said, "I declare that there is a lawful challenge to the succession and therefore, if the Jerlamar is to continue to bless us, the matter must be settled in the lawful way."

Doctor Felman paused for a moment. "It must be settled by *enchanted combat*."

The proclaimer knew what that meant. He turned and ran down the slope of the bridge to the safety of the crowd, which was now in total uproar. All of them—Fels, Vela, and Thrulls—were on their feet.

Gullkin didn't react with anger or astonishment. He just smiled and stroked the neck of his horse, which had lowered its head menacingly after he whispered in its ear. Gullkin had a sword and an axe and a helmet strapped to his walrus-skin saddle. I guessed he wasn't wearing his helmet because he believed he was only moments away from being given a golden crown.

He leaned forward on his saddle and whispered again to his horse. "I thought you'd got rid of them." The horse snorted. Then Gullkin spoke loudly enough for everyone to hear. "So I am to be challenged by the mongrel humans after all," he said.

Doctor Felman glanced at me and urged me silently to speak up.

"That's right, we challenge you!" I shouted, and my voice was deeper than it had ever been. This was one hell of a time for my voice to change. I could feel Emma breathing fast at my side.

"We are here to claim the throne," Emma declared, "and once victory is won, we will declare . . . a Fel parliament!"

Just the sound of the word *parliament* brought three-quarters of the crowd to its feet, and my next words were swallowed by a mighty outpouring. I had to shout at the top of my voice to continue. "A parliament that will put power into the hands of the Fels, Vela, and the ordinary Thrulls equally."

Now the uproar became dangerous, and I could see soldiers drawing their swords all around the perimeter. I didn't want Gullkin to use a riot as an excuse to abandon the ceremony. Doctor Felman saw the danger too, and he raised his hand to quiet the crowd.

"Be calm, be calm! The rule of law must be followed," he said.

The entire population was bearing witness. Gullkin was cornered, but that only made him more dangerous. He fixed Emma and me with an evil stare.

"Very well then, we will fight!" he cried. "But since there are two contenders on your side, it is only fair that there should also be two on my side."

Before Doctor Felman could respond, Gullkin jumped from his horse and pulled off the saddle. The horse reared up, then pawed at the gold beneath its hooves.

"And since my semidivine wife who would be queen is at the palace in bed with a bad foot," Helva Gullkin said, "I believe the law allows me to instead ask the most senior member of my future government to take her place."

The crowd began to laugh. I imagine no one knew that Gullkin's wife had a bad foot, or cared, but they found it funny. Doctor Felman looked suspiciously across the bridge as Gullkin unbuckled the bridle from his horse.

"Specifically," Helva Gullkin said, "I would like to be assisted in this combat by my prime minister."

Doctor Felman studied Gullkin for a moment, applying all his intuition.

"Gullkin, what prime minister are you talking about?"

he asked cautiously. "And since when did *you* employ ministers anyway? You have said yourself that you believe in the absolute power of the king."

"Nevertheless, the law states that the Swearing of the Oaths is a battle fought only between contenders for power," Gullkin snapped. "So if I elect someone to be prime minister, then he can fight alongside me. Is that not correct, Doctor Felman?"

The crowd was beginning to quieten. For the first time I heard the wind moaning through the structure of the bridge.

"So who is this poor unfortunate prime minister?" Doctor Felman asked, trying to sound assured.

Gullkin smiled and gestured at his horse. "Behold. My horse. I choose to elect my horse as my loyal prime minister."

A murmur of confusion ran around the volcano. The population knew Gullkin well enough to be afraid of his cunning.

"What game is this?" Doctor Felman called out.

Helva Gullkin turned to Doctor Felman with a deadly stare. Then he waved his arm, and the white horse began to shift. Its long white legs turned into Fel legs; its horse face contracted quickly to turn into a very familiar face with a graying beard and a twirled mustache. Within a second, the transformation was complete.

Gullkin's white horse had disappeared and been replaced by Earl Hawkin.

"Fels of Langjoskull!" Helva Gullkin pronounced. "Behold my deputy and your new prime minister."

Emma and I stepped back. Doctor Felman's eyes burned as he stared across the bridge. All at once many things became clear. Earl Hawkin had been a traitor in our midst all along. That was why he had lied to us in the cave. I remembered the moment when he was teaching us to listen to the voices in the trees. When I heard the words "I will betray you," I was being warned about Earl Hawkin, not about Emma.

"Earl Hawkin . . . a traitor?" Doctor Felman said softly.

Earl Hawkin stretched his legs and rotated his shoulders to get himself comfortable inside his body. He looked like a very peculiar boxer preparing for a bout. I turned to Emma.

Doctor Felman only barely managed to control his anger and stepped forward toward the gap at the top of the bridge.

"What reward will you get for this, Earl Hawkin?" he hissed.

Hawkin replied in his absentminded academic tone. "I have no interest whatsoever in practical things. I just want . . . order, you know? And Helva is my blood relative, and of course"—Earl Hawkin adjusted his green hat on his head and peered across the divide at Emma and me—"blood is thicker than water."

The noise from the crowd began to swell again, and Doctor Felman withdrew to stand between Emma and me. "This is very serious," he whispered. "Earl Hawkin is among the best practitioners of the arts I have ever known. You will have to be better than your best. He has many creatures at his disposal."

Doctor Felman glared once more across the bridge, then turned to us and put his hands on our shoulders. "But children, you have the Jerlamar on your side," he said. "You must trust it, and yourselves, to choose wisely."

While Doctor Felman was still speaking, the crowd suddenly gasped. When I looked back to where Earl Hawkin had been standing, there was now a gigantic white bear. It was the color of the sweet warm snow Earl Hawkin had made in his laboratory.

"You wanted a battle!" Gullkin cried. "So let battle commence!"

Before we knew what was happening, the bear leaped across the gap in the bridge and swiped Emma to the ground. Doctor Felman was knocked to one side and rolled back down the arch of the bridge. There was nothing more he could now do. I had already grabbed my sword and thrashed at the bear, but it used its massive paw to hurl me against the bridge support. A lightning flash flew from the tip of

Gullkin's sword, and he used the power of it to leap across the gap in the bridge with his axe raised high. I saw the axe head glint in the sun and was momentarily blinded.

Emma had disappeared into the bear's embrace, and it looked as though I was about to have my head parted from my body with an enchanted axe. It seemed that the battle was going to be over before it had even begun.

I raised my sword to deflect the blow from the axe. I kicked Gullkin backward and he stumbled, using his sword for support and making it bend like a bow. I then grabbed the golden dagger from my reindeer-skin pouch and dived under the bear's legs. Emma was waiting with her hand outstretched, and when our golden weapons touched there was a huge charge of power that sent the bear sprawling. Sparks from the thunderbolt stayed alight all the way down to the ice below.

Emma suddenly shifted into the shape of a wolf and leaped forward at the bear, pushing it from the bridge. It fell toward the ice with a roar. Gullkin and I struck and parried for a few moments, and I realized the slope of the bridge was making me give ground. Then I felt a searing pain in the back of my neck and felt a fluttering on my back. I half turned to see a giant bird pecking at the flesh of my neck.

Earl Hawkin had shifted into the shape of his kin creature, a hawk, and now it was going to have my throat.

I swiped at it, but it clung on, and Gullkin took the

opportunity to stab at me with his sword. He found a piece of flesh that wasn't protected by my coat and drew first blood. Then he was seized from behind by a mighty red wolf, and I felt my own wolf snarling in the palm of my hand.

I shifted easily into my kin creature. We snapped Gullkin against a golden girder, but he stretched out his arms and a giant herring gull flapped out from between our closing jaws. Earl Hawkin was now a lion galloping toward me. Gullkin watched as I slipped backward and my head hit the bridge with a crunch.

The lion was upon me, but Emma was at the lion's throat. Gullkin himself was shuffling his sword into a two-handed grip to drive it home into my exposed chest. In the confusion I saw Gullkin's elegantly shod foot. I reached for it from my position and I pulled with all my might. Gullkin lost his balance, his leather belt caught on a nail, and he dangled over the edge of the bridge.

At the same time, I drove my sword into the belly of the lion and it roared. Within half a second my opponent rose up in the shape of a huge vulture that had blood dripping from a wound under its wing. I now had Gullkin hanging from my hand high above solid ice. A moment later, though, he shifted and I had a seagull in my hand. It began to peck at me until I had to let go.

Emma and I were side by side and heard a warning cry from the crowd, but it was too late. The vulture smashed into us and sent us both toppling off the bridge toward the ice.

I looked down at my palm and saw my wolf tattoo transforming into the shape of a swallow. Emma's was clearly doing the same, and soon we had both shifted into swallows. I looked down to see a gull and a falcon coming toward us with their beaks open. The gull angled its wings and flew directly for me. I knew I had to shift again. I headed for the ice and found myself human again, skidding across the ice like a hockey puck, fighting off the falcon with my fists. Emma skidded to a halt at my side. The falcon was gone.

"Are you all right, Emma?" I said.

"Fine. Apart from the tigers," Emma said.

"What tigers?"

Gullkin and Earl Hawkin were galloping across the ice toward us in the shape of two white tigers. I used my sword to deflect their charge and we drew more blood, which dripped onto the ice and froze instantly.

When the tigers doubled back, we met them as two wolves who snarled them into a stalemate. The crowd was baying all around us as we and the tigers walked in tight circles around each other, bleeding, panting for breath, looking for a moment of weakness.

I could feel my power increasing. Great waves of it rose up from the Jerlamar flowing beneath the volcano. The feeling made me bold.

Then I had an idea. I wasn't sure if I was accomplished enough to carry it out, but I remembered Doctor Felman urging me to trust in myself. I leaped into the air and took flight as a swallow, but a few seconds later I landed on the ice behind the tigers as myself, with my sword in my hand. The tigers had no time to turn, and I struck a powerful blow at the neck of the nearest one of them. The sword hit its target, and the tiger roared and fell to the ice. When the second tiger came for me, I flew out of its grasp as a swallow again and landed as myself next to Emma.

The crowd was on its feet, cheering and applauding my deft move. The wounded tiger was losing blood fast, and as it did, it began to shift back to its natural form. I wondered which of them I had hit and after a few moments saw the ungainly figure of Earl Hawkin lying unconscious on the ice. Even though he was still alive, I believed I had put him out of the game.

The remaining tiger charged in a fury, and we parted at the last instant so that it passed between us. The tiger slid a long way on the ice and took the howls and the jeers of the crowd. Emma and I shifted back into our own forms to face him. Together we were sure we could defeat him.

"One down, one to go," I said.

Then I heard a slithering and a hissing behind my back. I turned just in time to see a large adder, bleeding but alive, coiling, then striking at Emma's leg. I pulled my sword and to my amazement, the movement of the snake slowed down just as the blackflies had once slowed down.

I guessed that the power I was giving to my sword was now almost as powerful as the power Doctor Felman had once given to it.

The magical effect didn't last long. The snake's head was moving toward Emma's flesh at some speed, even in slow motion, and the strike was already halfway through. I aimed a blow at it with my sword, praying I could cut off its attack. My sword hit the snake at the same time that the snake bit Emma. In slow motion I saw that I had cut off its head, but not before it had sunk its fangs into her flesh. The severed head spun round and round in the air slowly. Everything seemed to freeze for a moment. Then time resumed and the crowd was roaring and Emma was crying out in pain.

I kicked the writhing, headless body of the snake away, and Emma suddenly fell backward into my arms.

"What happened?" she whispered.

Before I could answer, the crowd roared a warning and the surviving tiger leaped at me across the ice. I struck it with my sword, but it was still snarling as it skidded to a halt and prepared to charge again. I knelt at Emma's side.

Emma gasped for air. "I feel weak," she said. "I feel poison."

When I looked up to see where the tiger was, I saw Helva Gullkin standing with his fists on his hips and his legs wide apart. He was staring at us with a smile on his face. "Is your sister sick, mongrel boy?"

I tried to get Emma onto her feet, but already she was so drowsy that she could hardly stand. She slipped down onto the ice again.

"Can't shift," Emma breathed; "the mist is gone. Too weak."

I started to kneel beside her, but suddenly I was knocked from my feet by the charge of a bull that tossed me into the air. I flew across the ice on my knees and came to a halt twenty yards away.

By then Gullkin had shifted back to his own form and was standing over Emma with his sword raised, ready to strike the final blow.

The crowd fell silent. I managed to stand up. Gullkin grabbed Emma and put his golden sword to her throat.

"So, human mongrel," Helva Gullkin yelled, "do you wish to continue with this battle? Because if you do, the girl dies."

He moved the sword closer to Emma's throat. I stared across the ice and with my intuition felt Emma's desperation. No clouds of white breath rose from the crowd because no one was breathing. I could feel my own heart beating.

"Give me your answer," Gullkin barked. "I will give you the girl if you will give me the crown."

Then I heard a voice in my head. It was the calm voice

of Doctor Felman. I turned and looked into the crowd and found his face easily. Egil was by his side with his eyes closed, and Professor Elkkin was behind them. Doctor Felman was staring directly at me and speaking to me with his intuition on behalf of all my teachers. "Trust the strength of the bond between you," he said.

The crowd was again in a frenzy, baying for me to fight. But I knew I could not let Emma die. I dropped my sword onto the ice and the crowd groaned as one.

"The crown is yours," I said. "Now let her go."

I could see Blue Volcanoes clambering over seats to get near the exit. They would fight on regardless, I guessed. Gullkin didn't loosen his grip on Emma.

"Give me your sword and your coat and your other little trinkets."

I hesitated, and Gullkin once again pulled his sword tight against Emma's throat. I unbuckled my sword and kicked it across the ice. My coat and my reindeer-skin pouch followed. Gullkin smiled, and I knew he wasn't finished with me yet. The crowd was falling silent again.

"Now come here, mongrel," Gullkin said. "That is an order from your king."

I hesitated.

"Toby, don't trust him!" Emma cried, but I knew I had no choice. I began to walk across the ice and finally stood before Helva Gullkin.

"Now kneel," he said.

I stared into Emma's eyes. Our thoughts took some time to find each other in the mad panic of fear and anger.

"Kneel before your king!" Gullkin roared, and he turned to address the crowd. "I won this battle fair and square. So I order this *subject* to kneel before me."

Slowly I fell to my knees without taking my eyes off Emma. Our intuition was working now, and we both knew we had to do something fast.

"And now," Gullkin said softly, "I will take your miserable mongrel head for my trophy room."

He drew back his sword and the crowd gasped. I heard Doctor Felman's words from long ago. We are like a dormant volcano . . . someday we will erupt. *Whoosh.*

"*Whoosh,*" said Gullkin's sword as it cut the air and came down toward my neck.

The thought hit Emma and me at the same time. As Gullkin's sword flew through the air to end my life, Emma and I called out in unison.

"Jerlamar . . . *erupt!*"

Even before our voices echoed, a huge crack appeared in the ice and shot across the length of the crater. I was thrown onto my back and Helva Gullkin fell too. Emma fell from his grip.

A hundred more cracks appeared in the ice, and jets of steam began to shoot up from them. I flew across the ice to grab Emma and dragged her clear of Gullkin's thrashing sword. The ice cracked in a circle around us, and suddenly we were alone on an island of floating ice ten feet across. Gullkin charged at us in the form of a bull, but the ice gave way beneath him and he splashed into the freezing water.

He shifted almost immediately into the form of a giant walrus and heaved himself onto our island of ice. The weight of him almost capsized us, but before he could shift again I drove my sword into the thick leathery skin of the creature's neck. I felt the skin giving way to blubber with a loud pop, and I heard a human cry.

A second later, the walrus began to shift back into the form of Helva Gullkin, who now seemed mortally wounded. He made one last attempt to use his sword, but his blood was already freezing on the ice. I used my foot to shove him into the water. But as he slipped from the ice, he grabbed my ankle and clutched it with a mighty death grip. When he plunged into the ice-cold water, he took me with him.

His golden armor and golden sword and buckles made him sink fast, and his hand didn't loosen its grip. We sank into the infinite blueness of the volcano as I kicked and struggled to free my leg. I saw Gullkin's hair floating wildly in the water, which grew darker with his blood. And below I saw a terrifying sight.

A thousand feet down in the very roots of the volcano, molten lava was rising in a giant bubble. I could already feel the heat of the eruption in the water around me, and there was a fizz of bubbles, hot as embers, rising past my face. It looked as if the entire earth had melted and was about to blow out through the volcano.

I looked at my palm and saw my tattoo changing into a seal. I was almost out of breath and the shift seemed to take an age, but finally my tail slipped from between Gullkin's fingers and I was free.

I swam to the surface as fast as I could.

I arrived at the island of ice where Emma was huddling inside the fur coat. Human again, I managed to haul myself up onto it, and Emma and I hugged each other.

"Emma, the poison!"

"It's okay. Egil brought me a flower that contains an antidote," she said. She picked the remains of a small purple flower from the ice. A hummingbird buzzed around her head, and from the strange tufts of feathers sprouting from its head I knew it was Egil.

Emma smiled weakly. "Toby, I think we won."

"Yes," I said with an exhausted breath, "I actually think we did."

The crowd whooped and roared. A huge army of Thrulls had broken through the lines of gull soldiers, who were one by one turning back into gulls and flying away. The Thrulls began to cry out, "Freedom! Freedom!!"

I rowed the small island of ice with my hands toward the edge of the lake, where Doctor Felman was waiting for us. He took both our hands and smiled.

"The Jerlamar welcomes your victory," he said. "Yes indeed, the Jerlamar welcomes . . ." Doctor Felman raised his eyes to the heavens and blinked quickly to push back the tears of joy.

"Come, children, you are wet and cold. I will get you some hot tea or something."

I dared to grab hold of Doctor Felman and gave him a huge hug.

"No tea, Doctor," I said with a smile. "I can't stand the stuff."

Then suddenly I was lifted from my feet by six giant hands. The next thing I knew, I was on the shoulders of the crowd, Fel, Thrull, and Vela. And across the sea of heads and waving arms I saw Emma, who was on the shoulders of another dozen Thrulls. We both struggled free of the clutches of our subjects and walked across the crowd toward each other, using the big bony heads of the Thrulls and the golden helmets of policemen as stepping-stones.

And when we met, we held each other tight.

Over Emma's shoulder I saw a shock of wild black hair and a pair of remarkable green eyes staring up at me. Egil was waving his big bony arms wildly, trying to get my attention. "Tobiest of Tobys!" he shouted.

"Egil, can't you see I'm busy?" I replied.

Egil cupped his hands around his mouth, then whispered. Even though the crowds were yelling and chanting and fireworks were exploding, I heard his words as if he were whispering in my ear in a silent room. "Sister Mary wants you back," he said softly. "Sister Mary needs you. Sister Mary wants you back. Sister Mary needs you." The whisper turned into a chant that turned into a hiss. "Sister Mary wants you back. Sister Mary needs you. . . . Sister Mary wants you back."

Epilogue

I was woken up by the feeling of a rough tongue licking my face.

The whispering, chanting voice turned into the whoosh of cars on a wet road and the sound of water dripping. When I opened my eyes, I saw the drainpipe through the convent window. It was a rainy day, and water was dripping everywhere.

There was a cat on my lap, but it wasn't Shipley. It was a white cat with a black tip to its tail. The cat stared at me and mewed.

My body was lifeless, as it always had been. My head was held in place by the metal brace. My arms were curled like herons' necks. I could smell bacon and cabbage.

The new cat jumped off my lap, presumably to search for mice. Before I had time to even blink, a swallow landed on the drainpipe and stared down at me through the window.

If the swallow had landed even a second later than it did, I would have had time to feel a great wave of despair at waking up in my chair. But the swallow used its intuition to speak to me the moment it landed and saved me from that awful feeling.

"Toby, it's me, Emma," the swallow said to my mind. "I have to go to Africa because it is the end of summer. But I will return in the spring, and we will return to Langjoskull to collect our rewards."

With my mind I told Emma I would be waiting for her right here. I told her to be careful, and I think I managed to tell her that I was really happy to have a sister in this world. She said it was the same for her too. Then she hopped off the nest and flew away.

I looked down at my body, and it looked like an object someone had left lying around or an oddly shaped piece of furniture. That's all a body is, really. It's a comfortable chair for your mind to sit in. And when I looked at my palm, I saw something shining.

It was a tiny golden dagger, with a handle spun from spiderwebs.

I wanted to clutch the dagger tight to prove it was real, but of course I couldn't. But it was enough to know that it was there. Then the door opened, and Sister Mary came in with a towel and a bowl of warm water. When she plopped herself down in the chair beside me, I blinked at her and she dropped the bowl in shock.

She got to her feet and stared right into my eyes. I would have smiled if I could have, but had to make do with just blinking quickly. Sister Mary put her hands to her face and gasped. "He's back!" she cried, clattering the upturned bowl with her foot. "His eyes are open at last! He's back!"

She stared at me one more time before hurrying toward the door.

"Mother Superior! Everyone!! Toby Walsgrove is back in the land of the living!!"

STEVEN KNIGHT is an Oscar-nominated screenwriter. *The Last Words of Will Wolfkin* is his first book for children. He lives in England with his family.

To find out more about the world of the Fel, visit www.willwolfkin.com.